DISTURBED

JOSEPH J. SWOPE

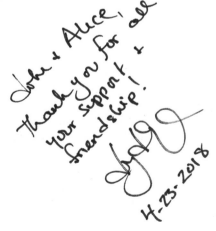

Black Rose Writing | Texas

The final approval for this literary material is granted by the author.

First printing

This is a work of fiction. Names, characters, businesses, places, events and incidents
are either the products of the author's imagination or used in a fictitious manner.
Any resemblance to actual persons, living or dead, or actual events is purely
coincidental.

ISBN: 978-1-68433-056-0
PUBLISHED BY BLACK ROSE WRITING
www.blackrosewriting.com

Printed in the United States of America
Suggested Retail Price (SRP) $19.95

Disturbed is printed in Plantagenet Cherokee

Dedicated to my children – Chandra, Shane, Savanna, Marissa, Logan and Lucas – who are my biggest fans and my constant inspiration.

DISTURBED

PROLOGUE
1830S THROUGH THE 1870S

For more than a century, King Coal reigned supreme in Northeast Pennsylvania. With the discovery of anthracite coal in the Appalachian Mountains of the region, a lucrative coal-based economy flourished. Wealthy coal barons built towns and lined their pockets on the backs of hard-working miners, who risked their lives toiling in dangerous conditions for little pay. Many died from accidents and coal-related illness, such as Black Lung Disease. The mining camps were grim, desolate places where many workers and their families lived pitifully. Worse, when a miner was unable to continue employment, he was cast aside and his family evicted and left homeless.

Enter the Molly Maguires.

The economic boom of the Coal Region came to full fruition after Frederick W. Geisenheimer invented a process for smelting iron with anthracite coal. That innovation helped create an enormous market for coal in Pennsylvania and across the rapidly-industrializing country. With the parallel development of the railroad system to economically transport this much-desired energy source, coal production in the United States rose more than eight-fold from 1840 to 1860. At its height, more than eight million tons of coal were mined each year.

At the same time, a famine engulfed much of Ireland, sending more than two million Irish families to the United States. Tens of thousands settled in the coal country of Northeast Pennsylvania. Irish immigrants brought with them a spirit of rebellion and a penchant for forming secretive groups and societies, such as the Whiteboys and the Ribbonmen. Molly Maguire was a semi-mythical figure who protected Irish tenant farmers from English landlords. She was supposedly a widow in the early 1840s, who led worker unrest in Ireland. When miners began to rebel against working conditions in the United States, they originally were known as the "Sons of Molly Maguire," a name that was eventually shortened.

In the coal mines, the Irish immigrants were the subject of ethnic discrimination and occupied the lowest rung of the mining hierarchy. The Welsh and the British immigrants were assigned the skilled work, leaving the Irish to haul the coal to the surface and sort out the slag. This work was difficult and dangerous. The pay was exceedingly low, with coal miners earning less than two dollars per day. Hundreds of workers died in mine-related accidents, as safety measures were an afterthought. Nearly a quarter of the workforce were children as young as seven years old. Since the pit bosses were also typically British or Welsh, ethnic slurs that characterized the Irish as drunken, lazy and superstitious were frequent.

Many workers, including the Irish, were paid in "bobtail check," or mine scrip, which could only be redeemed at the stores run by the mining companies. Workers paid above-market prices to shop in these stores and rent company homes. Most lived in squalid, poverty-stricken conditions. Often, their pay did not cover their expenses for food and rent, and they quickly fell into debt with the mining companies – a debt they could rarely, if ever, repay.

The Molly Maguires became active in the 1860s and remained so through most of the 1870s. They advocated for better working conditions for Irish laborers and were seen by the coal barons as a clear threat to form a unionized workforce. Many historians believe the leaders of the coal industry were terrified of that possibility and were willing to stop that threat at any cost. This fear was exacerbated by the loss of many able-bodied workers who volunteered to fight in the Civil War, significantly diminishing the available workforce.

The Molly Maguires allegedly infiltrated local chapters of the fraternal organization, The Ancient Order of Hibernians. The Order was founded in the United States in 1836 to protect the Catholic Church from anti-Catholic forces and assist Irish immigrants. But at the height of the Molly Maguires' power, the Order was suspected of being a hotbed of their activity. The Hibernians were eventually accused of aiding "the terrorist activities of the Molly Maguires."

As the dispute between the mine owners and the Molly Maguires heightened, events became increasingly more violent.

Wildcat strikes began hitting Schuylkill County – located in the heart of coal country – in 1862. Without a ready supply of replacement workers, coal companies could ill afford such actions and were committed to quash the burgeoning labor movement at all costs. The state militia was called in to help subdue the strike, leading to rioting and conflicts between workers and the militia.

The aftermath of such actions was deadly. From 1864 through 1866, sixteen mine managers and other bosses were killed in the Coal Region. Most had been involved in some type of labor dispute. The violence became so serious that the Commonwealth of Pennsylvania passed legislation allowing mining companies to form their own private police forces, emboldening them with broad powers to enforce the law, make arrests, and hold court proceedings – in other words, giving the coal companies the power of judge, jury and executioner.

On June 14, 1862, during a celebration to recruit more volunteers to fight for the Union in the Civil War, Frank Langdon had a public argument with a young miner named John Kehoe, the continuation of a dispute that had gone on for some time. Langdon was an unpopular "ticket boss" often accused by miners of "shortweighting," them, thus depriving them of wages. Later that night, Langdon was beaten to death by "persons unknown." It wasn't until more than a decade later that Kehoe, by then the supposed "King of the Mollies" and known as "Black Jack" Kehoe, was arrested for Langdon's murder.

Alexander Rea was a mining superintendent for the Locust Mountain Coal and Iron Company. Rea also founded the town of Centralia, which later would meet its own tragic fate. In 1868, Rea was travelling one evening from the nearby town of Mount Carmel to

Centralia. Only his horse returned home. A search party found his body the next day. Rea had been shot and beaten to death along the road.

Soon thereafter, police extracted a confession from a jailed Molly Maguire that implicated four others in a plot to rob and kill Rea. The accuser had sustained a bullet wound during his apprehension and died shortly after his confession. The four named suspects were acquitted at their subsequent trial. It wasn't until eight years later that Pinkerton detectives convinced an illiterate homeless rapist who had been expelled by the Molly Maguires to testify that he and eight others had planned the robbery in which Rea was killed. Manus Coll, also known as Kelly the Bum, received whiskey, cigars, clothing, a thousand dollars and a pardon for the robbery sentence for which he was serving. The Molly Maguires were convicted, despite 25 witnesses, included a former state senator, who testified Coll could not be trusted.

In 1869, the Avondale Mine disaster claimed the lives of more than 100 workers and two rescuers in Plymouth, Pennsylvania, just west of Wilkes-Barre. The wooden lining of the mine shaft caught fire and ignited the coal breaker built directly overhead. The shaft was the only entrance and exit to the mine, and the blaze trapped and suffocated the miners.

In 1871, Morgan Powell, an assistant superintendent of the Lehigh & Wilkes-Barre Coal Co., was shot in the chest and killed as he stepped out of a general store in Summit Hill. John "Yellow Jack" Donahue and Thomas Fisher were both convicted and later hanged for the murder. Donahue insisted he never knew Powell and had no reason to want him dead. Fisher also made a dramatic statement of his innocence just before his hanging. Many observers at the time believed Powell was more likely killed by the husband of a woman with whom he was having an affair.

Nevertheless, the coal barons responded to the increasing wave of violence by bringing in the Pinkerton National Detective Agency as their private police force. James McParland arrived in Port Clinton to launch an undercover operation to infiltrate the Molly Maguires and the Ancient Order of Hibernians. He worked under the alias "James

McKenna."

But as McParland worked undercover gathering evidence, the conflict continued and tensions grew more pronounced.

In December 1874, spurred on by a wage reduction imposed by the coal companies, about 10,000 miners began what was to become known as "The Long Strike," which was only broken when the state militia again intervened seven months later on orders by the Governor.

William "Bully Bill" Thomas, a Civil War veteran who consistently feuded with a number of Irishman, was shot and left for dead in 1875. According to McParland, the attack was ordered by Black Jack Kehoe. Thomas survived the attack.

Violence continued to escalate. A Tamaqua police officer was shot and killed as he extinguished a street light. A justice of the peace and a bartender were murdered shortly thereafter, and two more mine managers were killed in the ensuing months.

The violence was not all one-sided. Early in the morning of December 10, 1875, in a small town called Wiggans Patch, outside of Mahanoy City, a group of armed and masked intruders burst into the home of three men believed to be involved in the murder of a mining superintendent and a Welsh miner. The assailants killed one of the suspects, Charles O'Donnell, as well as Ellen McAllister, the pregnant wife of suspect Charles McAllister. McAllister himself was wounded but survived the attack. In addition, McAllister's mother-in-law was pistol-whipped. Ellen McAllister's sister was married to Black Jack Kehoe. The attackers were thought to be irate residents trained by a captain in the Coal & Iron Police, and documents unearthed in recent years suggest the execution was funded by the coal companies and planned with the assistance of the Pinkerton Detective Agency. No one was ever arrested or prosecuted for the crime.

By 1876, McParland's undercover work began to bring the desired results. Michael J. Doyle was the first Molly Maguire to be prosecuted. He was convicted of the first-degree murder of attorney James Jones. Shortly thereafter, warrants were issued for 17 more members of the Molly Maguires.

On August 12, 1876, a jury returned guilty verdicts against all nine defendants in the case of *Commonwealth v. Kehoe and Others*, which focused on the attempted murder of Bully Bill Thomas. Five months later, Kehoe was convicted of the murder of Frank Langdon. A month later, three more Molly Maguires were tried and found guilty for the murder of Alexander Rea.

On June 21, 1877, known by some as "Black Thursday," ten Molly Maguires were hanged. Four hangings – including those of Doyle and Donahue – occurred in Mauch Chunk, where it was dubbed "The Day of the Rope." Six more hangings took place in Pottsville. Over the next two years, nine more Molly Maguires, including Black Jack Kehoe, were "hanged by the neck until dead."

While the reign of violence and terror ended with the executions that occurred from 1877 through 1879, it was rumored the Molly Maguires remained active, especially in the borough of Centralia, until well into the 20th Century.

A local legend also told of how the first Catholic priest to live in Centralia cursed the town after being assaulted by three members of the Molly Maguires in 1869. A day would come, declared Father Daniel McDermott, when St. Ignatius Roman Catholic Church would be the only structure remaining in Centralia. One day, the angry priest continued, the town would be erased from the face of the earth

In 1889, Franklin Gowen, an attorney and former president of the Reading Railroad and Coal Company who had hired the Pinkerton Detective Agency and personally prosecuted a number of the Molly Maguires, was found dead of a bullet wound inside his hotel room in Washington, D.C. The door was locked from the inside. Did Gowen commit suicide in an act of madness? Or had – as some have suggested – the ghosts of the Molly Maguires finally exacted their long-sought revenge?

In 1979, then Pennsylvania Governor Milton Shapp granted a posthumous pardon to Black Jack Kehoe following an investigation by the Pennsylvania Board of Pardons. Shapp called the Molly Maguires "martyrs to labor" and heroes who fought for fair treatment of workers.

In 2005, the Pennsylvania House of Representatives unanimously passed a resolution proclaiming that police and judges involved in the arrest, prosecution and execution of the Molly Maguires were connected to mining companies; that witnesses were intimidated into committing perjury; and "to say due process and constitutional rights lacked in the trial would be an understatement."

A number of historians have suggested that at least some of the violence of the era was planned and executed by the coal barons themselves as a way of discrediting the Molly Maguires. Opinion to this day remains divided: were the Molly Maguires early champions of the working class, or ruthless thugs who embarked on an unbridled spree of terror, mayhem, and murder? That debate is likely to continue well into the future.

Meanwhile, though the anthracite industry is much diminished from its height, in many ways, Big Coal still defines the culture and history of Northeast Pennsylvania. And according to many, the ghosts of the Molly Maguires still wander the highways and byways of the region to this day.

CHAPTER 2
JULY 1987

Sarah Frost sat down on the rocking chair in her living room and picked up her well-worn Bible. She was 43, pregnant with her first child. After years of being unable to conceive, she did so after her and her husband, Robert, had given up all hope of having children.

The Lord has His own plan, Sarah thought, *in His own time.*

Sarah considered her pregnancy a gift from God. And as such, she began to read the Bible fervently, reciting it aloud each evening to her and her unborn child. She was now in her third trimester, and she was sure he – yes, the baby was a boy – could hear her.

"Let's see what we'll read today," Sarah said, opening the Bible at random. She didn't believe that, of course. She was sure God directed her hand to the page He needed to reveal to her a deeper truth.

"Here we go, the Book of Jonah," she said. "From the Old Testament."

She started reading softly and fervently, rubbing her belly lovingly as she did so.

The word of the Lord came to Jonah the son of Amittai saying, "Arise, go to Nineveh the great city and cry against it, for their wickedness has come up before Me."

But Jonah rose up to flee to Tarshish from the presence of the Lord. So he went down to Joppa, found a ship which was going to Tarshish, paid the fare and went down into it to go with them to Tarshish from the presence of the Lord.

The Lord hurled a great wind on the sea and there was a great storm on the sea so that the ship was about to break up. Then the sailors became afraid and every man cried to his god, and they threw the cargo which was in the ship into the sea to lighten it for them. But Jonah had gone below into the hold of the ship, lain down and fallen sound asleep. So the captain approached him and said, "How is it that you are sleeping? Get up, call on your god. Perhaps your god will be concerned about us so that we will not perish."

Each man said to his mate, "Come, let us cast lots so we may learn on whose account this calamity has struck us." So they cast lots and the lot fell on Jonah. Then they said to him, "Tell us, now! On whose account has this calamity struck us? What is your occupation? And where do you come from? What is your country? From what people are you?"

He said to them, "I am a Hebrew, and I fear the Lord God of heaven who made the sea and the dry land."

Then the men became extremely frightened and they said to him, "How could you do this?" For the men knew that he was fleeing from the presence of the Lord, because he had told them. So they said to him, "What should we do to you that the sea may become calm for us?"—for the sea was becoming increasingly stormy.

He said to them, "Pick me up and throw me into the sea. Then the sea will become calm for you, for I know that on account of me this great storm has come upon you."

However, the men rowed desperately to return to land but they could not, for the sea was becoming even stormier against them. Then they called on the Lord and said, "We earnestly pray, O Lord, do not let us perish on account of this man's life and do not put innocent blood on us; for You, O Lord, have done as You have pleased."

So they picked up Jonah, threw him into the sea, and the sea stopped its raging. Then the men feared the Lord greatly, and they offered a sacrifice to the Lord and made vows.

And the Lord appointed a great fish to swallow Jonah, and Jonah was in the stomach of the fish three days and three nights.

Then Jonah prayed to the Lord his God from the stomach of the fish, and he said,

"I called out of my distress to the Lord,
And He answered me.
I cried for help from the depth of Sheol;
You heard my voice.
  "For You had cast me into the deep,
Into the heart of the seas,
And the current engulfed me.
All Your breakers and billows passed over me.
  "So I said, 'I have been expelled from Your sight.
Nevertheless I will look again toward Your holy temple.'
"Water encompassed me to the point of death.
The great deep engulfed me,
Weeds were wrapped around my head.
"I descended to the roots of the mountains.
The earth with its bars was around me forever,
But You have brought up my life from the pit, O Lord my God.
  "While I was fainting away,
I remembered the Lord,
And my prayer came to You,
Into Your holy temple.
"Those who regard vain idols
Forsake their faithfulness,
But I will sacrifice to You
With the voice of thanksgiving.
That which I have vowed I will pay.
Salvation is from the Lord."

  Then the Lord commanded the fish, and it vomited Jonah up onto
the dry land.

Sarah felt a warm glow at the end of the verses. She could tell her child was particularly attentive and content. Suddenly, inspiration struck her.

That's why God led me to this passage, she thought.

"Robert," she said, as her husband came into the room. "I think we should name our son Jonah."

"Jonah," he repeated. "That's quite biblical."

He looked down at the book on his wife's lap.

"Of course it is," he said. "Jonah is a fine name. Jonah Frost has a nice ring to it."

"What do you think?" Sarah persisted.

Her husband pondered the idea for moment more. Then, he smiled at his wife.

"Jonah it is," he finally said. "Let's hope life doesn't swallow him the same way the whale did his namesake."

"Oh Robert," Sarah said, stroking her husband's hand softly. "You're quite silly. But thank you. I love you."

"I love you, too, my dear," he said. "Why don't you get some rest? You look a bit tired."

Sarah agreed and sat back in the chair, closing her eyes. Sleep would arrive soon.

CHAPTER 3
NOVEMBER 2006

"Mr. Peterson, you're going to have to return to your room," Alexandra Rodriguez, registered nurse, said to the elderly man walking down the hall with his hospital gown wide open in the back.

"I'm not sure who you are speaking to, ma'am," the patient responded. "My name is Abraham Lincoln. I have an urgent need to travel to Gettysburg as soon as possible. Can you please call my carriage?"

Alexandra, better known as Alex, contained her smirk as best she could.

"I'm afraid that trip is going to have to wait," Alex said. "Let's get you back to your bed."

"But I have a speech to give," the patient objected. "I worked on it all last night. We're in the middle of a war, don't you know? This is no time to lay in bed! The nation is depending on me."

"We'll talk about that tomorrow," Alex acknowledged, "when you're feeling more yourself."

"When I'm feeling myself?" the patient continued to protest. "Just who do you think you are speaking to? I am the 16th President of the United States."

"Well, Mr. President," Alex responded, "we're still going to have to get you back to your room."

The nurse gently helped the white-haired man back where he belonged. Mr. Peterson, aka Abraham Lincoln, wasn't pleased, but finally acquiesced.

Pleasant Valley Hospital and Medical Center was a mid-sized

regional hospital serving Central Pennsylvania. Its emergency department was busy day and night, but psychiatric patients drew special attention. Few of the medical staff – more accustomed to dealing with lacerations, fractures and other physical trauma – preferred dealing with the unruly and cluttered minds of the mentally ill, whose symptoms were both confounding and unpredictable. Alex was one of the rare nurses who felt comfortable in this section of the department, thanks in part to a two-year stint in the psychiatric ward before transferring to emergency. Alex had a rare gift in dealing with these patients, one she had retained even though she had opted to move to a side of nursing with more hands-on medical practice.

But even her considerable skills were challenged on this day.

Earlier that morning, a 350-pound woman had run down the hall wearing nothing but black mesh panties. When the 130-pound nurse recognized the mismatch, Alex promptly called security for help. The officer arrived less than a minute later without warning of the situation.

"Oh my God!" the security officer cringed when he assessed the problem. "It's 7:15 in the morning. Couldn't you have least bought me coffee first?"

Alex laughed.

"No time for coffee," she said. "She's all yours."

"Oh no," the officer responded. "You're helping with this one."

Together, Alex and the security officer finally wrestled the patient back into her bed. When the patient continued to be uncooperative, the nurse was forced to use restraints to make future escapes unlikely. Alex then returned to the nurse's station to work on the endless required documentation. Shortly thereafter, an elderly woman shuffled up to her and leaned menacingly over the counter.

"The devil shoved his cock all the way down your throat," the woman screamed, her face contorting in a mask of demonic terror, "and you liked it."

"OK, Mrs. Ellison," Alex said calmly. "Let's get you back to your room."

When the nurse returned, the other nurse in the section looked over at her.

"Did you like it?" she asked, a sly smile crossing her face.

"Didn't sound like I had much choice."

Suddenly, the emergency department loudspeaker roared through the halls.

"Ambulance coming in," the nurse supervisor announced. "Psych patient said to be extremely disturbed."

"Oh great," she muttered underneath her breath. "Another one. Is it a full moon?"

The ambulance pulled into the bay two minutes later, with a police cruiser on its tail. The crew pulled the stretcher out of the back of the medical vehicle. As they did, two officers departed their patrol car and stayed warily nearby.

The patient's hands were handcuffed to the stretcher, his feet shackled. He shook his head in agitation, and occasionally tested his restraints, to no avail. Periodically, he would scream angrily and unintelligibly.

The ambulance workers wheeled the patient into the emergency department, past the "normal" patient rooms toward the back of the building. The rooms in the psych unit were sparse: no cords, no computers, no medical equipment, nothing that would allow the disturbed patient to harm himself or others. The paint was a neutral something – gray, beige, off-white – depending on the viewer. By the time the patient had reached his designated room, he was somewhat calmer, apparently resigned to his fate – for the moment. Alex knew a situation like this was potentially volatile and could change in an instant.

"Nineteen-year-old male," the paramedic said to Alex outside the patient's room. "Police received a 9-1-1 call at his parent's home, where he had become violent and incoherent. Injured his mother. Father said he has a history of mental illness."

"Do we know his med history?" she asked.

"Father either didn't know or was too distraught to remember," the paramedic answered. "Patient hasn't been living at home. The mom was in pretty bad shape. I didn't get much information."

"Where's the mom?" the nurse queried.

"She came in on a separate ambulance a little while ago," the paramedic answered. "I don't know her condition."

"OK," Alex said. "I'll check her status later."

Nurse Alex walked into Jonah's room. The patient was surrounded by two police officers and the ambulance staff outside of the paramedic.

"Hello," she said, "My name is Alexandra. I'm going to be your nurse tonight. Do you know your name?"

Alex never gave psychiatric patients her last name for safety reasons. Even her hospital identification only revealed her first. She studied her patient carefully.

Sweat drenched the patient's forehead. He appeared to think hard. Then, with concentration, he finally looked up.

"Jonah," he finally stammered.

"Do you have a last name?"

"Yes."

The nurse frowned at Jonah, who forced a smirk.

"Frost."

"Jonah Frost," Alex repeated. "Jonah, are you calm enough that we can take you out of these restraints?"

Jonah thought for a moment. The ambulance personnel and police officers looked at the nurse doubtfully. The patient worked visibly to calm down.

"Yes, I'm OK," he finally answered.

Alex looked at Jonah earnestly.

"I'm going to let you out of your restraints," she said, "but you're going to have stay calm or you're going right back into them. You understand? Security guards and police officers are all around you. It will do you no good to start acting up."

Jonah nodded blankly, but seemed to look past the nurse. He finally focused enough to spot the beefy men surrounding him.

Carefully, the restraints were removed. Over the next few minutes, the ambulance crew and police left the hospital, turning Jonah over to the care of the emergency department. The police noted they would likely return after they completed their investigation. Hospital security stayed nearby, alert and ready to pounce.

"We're going to have you change into a hospital gown," Alex said to Jonah, and as she explained this, hospital security came back into the room. "We need you to take off your clothes and give them to us. We're going to put them into this bag and keep them safe for you."

Alex quickly perused Jonah's attire. His plaid button-down shirt was torn and flecked with blood. His jeans were dirty and ripped. His shoes were dark and stained.

"I'm going to leave the room," the nurse said. "You can give your clothes to the guard."

As Alex turned toward the door, she made eye contact with the guards.

"We're going to need to keep these clothes as possible evidence," she said softly. The guards nodded.

A few minutes later, the door opened and Alex re-entered the room. At the same time, the security guards left. One of them took the bag of clothing and ran it through the metal detector before tagging the bag with identification. He placed the bag in a locked compartment to be processed later. The other guard stayed close to Jonah's room, relatively inconspicuous but never losing his view of the nurse or her patient.

Back in the room, Alex was still negotiating her way around Jonah's confused mind.

"Security is going to check to make sure you're not hiding anything dangerous," she explained to him. "They're just going to run the wand across your body."

The guard who had tagged Jonah's clothing had returned to the area and now re-entered the room. He approached Jonah with an electronic wand. Jonah jumped back, confused and suspicious. The guard paused, assessing whether the patient was becoming a renewed threat.

"He's not going to hurt you," Alex assured him. Jonah looked at the nurse doubtfully, but finally nodded his assent.

The guard ran the wand up and down the front and back of Jonah's body then between his legs, working carefully in an effort not to aggravate him. The scan was clear. The guard then subtly double-checked the entire room, making sure nothing was available for Jonah to hurt himself or others. He nodded to the nurse, and began heading toward the door.

"I'll be right outside if you need me," he told Alex.

The nurse then began her standard assessment. Her previous work with psych patients and her uncanny ability to relate to them had gained the awe and respect of other nurses. An assessment of a mentally ill patient, something that may have flummoxed another nurse, came naturally to Alex.

"Do you think you could give me a urine sample?" she asked.

Jonah looked at her blankly.

"Really?" he finally asked.

"Really," Alex said matter-of-factly.

Jonah paused for a long moment, then finally nodded his head affirmatively. He took the container from the nurse, walked into the rest room and emerged a few minutes later.

"Happy?" he asked as he handed the jar back to the nurse.

Alex labeled the sample as Jonah sat back down on the bed.

"Are you having any thoughts about harming yourself?" Alex asked.

"No," Jonah said, looking past Alex into the corner of the room. "But she wants me to."

"Who's she?" Alex asked, turning her head and seeing no one behind her.

"Don't you see her?" Jonah asked, slightly more agitated. "She's right there, crouching in the corner of the room. An old woman."

Alex again did a quick glance over her shoulder and saw nothing but walls behind her.

Hallucinations, she thought. *Check.*

"Are you having any thoughts about harming others?" the nurse persisted.

"No, but I already hurt my mother," Jonah said. "And she's telling me I shouldn't trust you."

He suddenly looked past the nurse with an agitated expression on his face.

"Shut the fuck up!" Jonah screamed. "She's talking. I'm trying to listen to her."

Alex paused and waited for Jonah to fix his attention on her again.

Command auditory hallucinations, she noted.

She glanced toward the door to the room. *I may need security after all*, she thought. She was happy to see one the guards at the door, watching the scene carefully.

"Do you take any medications?" Alex asked.

"I don't know." Jonah answered dismissively.

"Have you taken any medications recently?" Alex persisted.

No answer. Jonah remained silent, his body rocking back and forth. Alex started to worry that her patient was beginning to circle the psychiatric drain.

"All right," Alex said. "We'll get to that later. Dr. Gordon is on duty tonight. I'm going to talk to him and he'll be in to see you shortly."

"What are you going to tell him?" Jonah asked.

"I'm just to go over what we talked about," Alex assured him. "I'm going to have someone stay with you until the doctor comes in, just in case you need anything."

Alex glanced outside the room and motioned a personal care assistant to come in.

"Jonah," the nurse said. "This is Carole. She'll be right here."

Somewhere deep in his addled mind, Jonah knew Carole wasn't there to be his personal valet. He was on a one-to-one observation. He remembered the scenario from past hospital stays. He couldn't be trusted to be left alone. Jonah and Carole eyed each other carefully, Jonah laying down on the bed, Carole on the chair just a few steps away. Jonah again saw the old lady crouching in the corner of the room, glowing unnaturally while wriggling her crooked finger at him.

"She's with them," the old woman cackled. "She's going to kill you when you're not looking."

"Shut up!" Jonah growled. "She's not going to hurt me. Don't try that shit on me again."

Occasionally, Jonah would hear the sounds of other voices wafting through his brain – some unintelligible, all created in the deep recesses of his diseased mind – blotting out the comings and goings of the hospital around him. Finally, trying to expel his own demons, he stared at the ceiling in an almost coma-like trance. Carole kept a silent vigil.

Sometime later, Dr. Everett Gordon, the psychiatrist on duty, stepped into Jonah's room, Alex following behind him. Dr. Gordon was a distinguished looking man in his late 50s, with a full head of gray hair and a goatee. He read Jonah's chart through his Oakley-framed prescription glasses.

"Mr. Frost," Dr. Gordon said. "I see we've seen you before."

Jonah glared into space.

"I don't remember you," he finally said. "You must not be very memorable."

The doctor ignored the insult.

"How are you feeling?" he continued. "Any better?"

Silence once again.

"She thinks you're an asshole," Jonah finally said, again looking into the corner of the room. "She said you've always been an asshole."

"Does she?" Dr. Gordon said, glancing toward the wall where Jonah's eyes were focused. "Well, I'm not speaking to her. I'm talking to you."

Jonah's body tightened. Whatever semblance of calm he had gathered since his time in the hospital imperceptibly began to unravel.

"We're going to give you some Zyprexa to help you gather your thoughts," Dr. Gordon said. "I would also recommend that you be admitted and see what we can do to help you."

The figure of the old woman suddenly appeared directly in front of Jonah's face.

"He's the devil," she hissed. "Can't you see? He's the one sent here to kill you. He'll 'admit' you and no one will ever see you again."

A few tense seconds passed. Suddenly, Jonah gave into the voices in his mind. He coiled upward and off the bed, flailing about and screaming, jolting the psychiatrist across the room.

"Bullshit," the young man screamed. "You're trying to kill me. I won't let you hurt me. I'm not taking any of your fucking pills."

Jonah postured threateningly to those in the room.

"Mr. Frost," Alex said in a firm voice. "If you don't calm down, we're going to have to restrain you again."

"See," the old woman whispered in his ear, "you'll never get out of this room alive."

The patient paused for a moment, then jumped violently forward, swinging his arms wildly. The hospital staff in the room took several steps backward to avoid the blows.

"Code Orange," the nurse said urgently into her Vocera.

Nearly instantly, the two burly security officers ran into the room and approached the patient. Alex and Carole joined the guards in trying to restrain Jonah, with mixed results. Dr. Gordon, seemingly stunned by the sudden outburst and Jonah's initial push, backed off until he hit the wall behind him. The security officers received the brunt of Jonah's attack as they tried to shield the medical staff while fighting off the out-of-control patient.

Less than a minute later, two more security officers dashed into the room, providing more of an advantage against the adrenaline-fueled Jonah. A male nurse followed just behind them. People suffering from mental illness can display incredible amounts of strength during a violent episode, and Jonah was giving the hospital staff all they could handle. Despite being outnumbered seven-to-one, Jonah kicked, bit and punched, landing more than several blows. No one was leaving this skirmish without a souvenir.

"Goddammit, knock this shit off," one guard growled as Jonah landed a kick in the shins.

"*Hijo de puta,*" Alex swore. "Let's get him into four-point restraints."

The combined group of security and medical staff wrestled Jonah back onto the bed. Two people held down each of Jonah's arms and two others held down each of his legs as they fought to place him in restraints. Jonah thrashed, yelled and spit at whoever he could.

"Leave me the fuck alone!" he screamed. "I won't let you kill me!"

"No one is trying to hurt you," Alex said. "We're trying to help you."

"Bullshit," the old woman cried.

"Bullshit," Jonah screamed.

The staff fighting Jonah did a careful dance, some holding him down while others cuffing his arms and legs.

"That burns, goddammit!" Jonah cried. "I'll kill you! I'll have her kill you!"

"No one is going to kill anyone, Mr. Frost," the nurse finally said, more commandingly. "You need to calm down now before you hurt yourself."

Dr. Gordon had stood in the background, avoiding the conflict for the most part. But the psychiatrist finally decided to act.

"HAC him," he ordered.

Alex nodded in agreement.

Finally, she thought with a tinge of frustration.

"You have him?" Alex asked the guards and rest of the staff, pushing her words out between heaving breaths.

"We got him," the closest guard to her affirmed. Despite the restraints, the staff continued to hold down Jonah as he flailed to and fro attempting to free himself.

The nurse stepped back and left the room to retrieve the necessary medication.

"HAC?" a younger nurse who had just arrived on the scene asked.

"Haldol, Ativan and Cogentin," Alex said. "Two shots. You can mix the Haldol and Ativan. The Cogentin has to be injected separately. You can help with this."

HAC is a typical drug combination for a psychiatric patient who is out of control. Haldol is an antipsychotic used to treat schizophrenia, acute psychosis and aggression. Ativan is a benzodiazepine medication used to treat anxiety disorders, trouble sleeping, seizures and active aggression. Cogentin is an anticholinergic drug used to reduce the side effects of antipsychotic treatment. It's a potent combination.

Alex and the second nurse came into the room with two filled syringes. Typically, the patient would be given a choice to take medication orally or through injection, but Jonah was out of control and the situation too dire. He was in no condition to be given alternatives.

"Hold him as still as you can," Alex instructed the staff still trying to control Jonah. "Especially the legs."

Alex moved to one side of Jonah and the second nurse positioned herself on the other. The rest of those in the room shifted in a well-practiced maneuver, so that two people held each leg firmly, one at the hip and the other below the knee.

The nurses wedged between them, looking for a spot at the outer top part of the thigh to give intramuscular injections. They identified their spots and jabbed down with the syringes into each side, pushing down the plungers nearly simultaneously.

"Oww," Jonah cried. "Son of a bitch!"

"They're doing it," the old woman howled inside Jonah's head. "They're killing you. Don't let them!"

Jonah continued to battle with new life. The injections didn't end the struggle immediately.

Unlike the movies, antipsychotic drugs do not work instantly. Typically, they take a half-hour or more to achieve full effect. So Jonah didn't suddenly fall limp or become more compliant. The scuffle was unremitting and Jonah was temporarily even more disconcerted, fighting anew against both his restraints and those in the room.

It took over five minutes until Jonah was more controlled. He still shook the bed, quaking from head to toe, swearing and cursing at whoever came near. But the medications were slowly beginning to take effect, and as the minutes passed, Jonah and his demons had to expend more effort to unleash their vindictiveness. It would take some time, but even the madness would temporarily succumb to the powerful combination of drugs streaking through his system.

Slowly, the hospital staff moved outside of the patient's room and stood for a moment together in the hallway in various states of exhaustion. Medical and security staffs were both drenched in sweat, leaning against the wall breathing heavily.

"Thanks, guys," Alex said.

The closest guard smiled.

"It was fun," he said. "Let's not do it again anytime soon."

Dr. Gordon came down the hall, surveyed the crew from head to toe, and turned to the nurse.

"Let's get a mental health delegate down here to petition a 302," he told her. "Danger to himself and others. Involuntary commitment."

The psychiatrist headed down the hall, paused and looked back. "And clean yourselves up," he admonished. "It looks like you were in a cage match."

Dr. Gordon gave the subtlest of smirks, and walked away.

Alex nodded. "I think that patient is right about one thing," she said, watching the doctor walk down the hall. "He is an asshole."

The nurse headed toward her station, where another nurse offered her help.

"I need to call crisis services," Alex said. "Can you find out where there's a bed in a mental health facility. We have an intake."

CHAPTER 4
SUMMER 2017

The young couple's wedding was planned for the fall, and they excitedly embarked on the search for their first home. This was the third property on their list, an older home on a quiet street in a small town in Northeast Pennsylvania. The property was not too far from their jobs or their families, but out of the way enough to relax and enjoy themselves as newlyweds. It looked like the perfect starter.

They pulled up in front of the "For Sale" sign and met the realtor, an attractive middle-aged woman in a blue business suit named Susan. They shook hands and discussed the outside of the property for a few minutes. It was a brick and stucco home with a small yard and a smaller porch built sometime in the early 1900s. The home showed some wear, but appeared to be structurally sound without need of major repairs.

The realtor and the couple then opened the front door and walked into the house. At first, the prospective buyers looked around the downstairs and were reasonably impressed. The house could use a good cleaning, but the original walnut wood work that decorated the stairways and door frames was intact and in good shape. Some of the wallpaper on the plaster walls was outdated, but there was no real damage. A hard wood floor in the dining room could use some tender loving care and a good polish, but offered promise. The kitchen appliances were functional, but could be modernized. The house even boasted a bedroom on the first floor.

Upstairs was more of the same. Outdated wallpaper. A few stains here and there. A lion's claw tub that was a conversation piece if not exactly up-to-date plumbing. A fixer-upper to be sure, but nothing the couple couldn't tackle with some modest investment and sweat equity.

The three returned downstairs and started to have a more serious discussion about the home. However, as the conversation progressed, both the realtor and the young house hunters felt a general unease. Inexplicably, the building seemed to come alive around them.

Suddenly, walls shook, doors creaked, and what sounded like an angry voice gurgled up from the depths and permeated the house.

"What in the world was that?" the young bride-to-be asked in shock.

"Did we just have an earthquake?" the prospective groom echoed.

"I have no idea," Susan answered. "I'm not aware of any earthquake activity in this area."

"Maybe it's a mine collapse," the young man suggested. "This is coal country, you know."

"I don't think so...," the realtor said tentatively.

But as Susan uttered the words, whatever was occurring became more ominous. The light in the house was blotted out by darkness. A foul odor permeated the air. The three occupants felt hands touching them, poking at their backs. The distinct angry words of an angry woman boomed off the walls.

None of the neighbors happened to be home that day. Thus, no one in town heard the odd noises coming from that house, nor the otherworldly glow emanating from the windows. The only three people who heard the ominous words, "Get out of my house! And don't come back if you want to live!" were those inside the home on the tour.

They didn't need to be told twice.

The young couple were the first to flee the structure, looking back in sheer terror. Susan was more reluctant, wondering if this was some elaborate trick by a competitor.

Who knows what they can do with computers these days? she thought.

She stood defiantly at the front door challenging whoever or whatever was standing against her, until a powerful gust blasted her from the front porch onto the lawn beyond. As she watched, the front door slammed shut.

"You are not wanted here," the voice boomed angrily. "Leave and never return!"

Susan pulled herself up and saw her potential buyers running toward the car.

"Wait!" she said desperately. "I'm sure there's some logical explanation."

The couple didn't bother to respond. By now, they were climbing into their seats and the future groom was revving the engine and shifting into drive.

"I have other properties," Susan said weakly. "I know they'll be more inviting than this one."

She watched the couple pull away without looking back. She leaned over, picked up her purse, and glanced back at the home one last time. For just a moment, she thought she saw a demon-like figure glaring back at her through the window. She rushed down the sidewalk and jumped into her car. She pulled out of town, never to return again.

"Not worth the commission," she said to herself as she sped down the highway.

CHAPTER 5
SUMMER 2018

"So how do you feel you're doing?" Dr. Janice Sheffield said to her patient, assessing him as she spoke.

Jonah squirmed in his seat. Now 31, with a flop of unruly dark hair, contacts or glasses depending on his mood, and disheveled but clean attire, he had become accustomed to his regular appointments with his psychiatrist. They sat in her office, brightly painted with framed photographs of famous landscapes. Tastefully decorated, but impersonal. No family photos could be found. Jonah could see Dr. Sheffield's jet black hair, her forty-something face, and her impeccably tailored conservative gray dress, but that was all she would reveal.

The psychiatrist burrows into your soul, Jonah thought, *but hides her own from view. I'm the only glass house in the room.*

"I'm doing much better," Jonah finally answered. "I'm not having hallucinations anymore and I'm not hearing the voices in my head – at least, not usually."

He forced a quick smile.

"I'm joking, of course," he added.

Dr. Sheffield jotted down a note in her omnipresent binder.

"So you feel your medication is helping?" she asked.

"They take some getting used to," Jonah acknowledged. "But I'm taking them regularly. You never quite feel the same on meds, but I'm accepting that as the new normal."

"I know they have some effects," Dr. Sheffield affirmed. "But it's important you stay on them."

Jonah nodded affirmatively.

"I don't have much choice," he said matter-of-factly. "I've seen myself without them. I know the consequences."

"I'm going to keep them the same for now," the doctor said. "But we'll continue to evaluate them as we go. You have to be completely honest with me for me to judge their effectiveness."

"I know," Jonah said. "No matter what meds I take, I'll always be crazy if I go off them."

Jonah thought about his litany of diagnoses and medications.

Schizoaffective disorder. A combination disorder where the patient displays symptoms of paranoid schizophrenia, combined with symptoms of mood disorders, such as mania or depression. Unlike other mental disorders, schizoaffective disorder is neither well understood nor well defined, because it presents as a blend of mental health conditions – with the mix often unique to each individual. Treatment is difficult, involving a mad mix of mental health medications.

Risperdal. An antipsychotic drug used to treat schizophrenia and bipolar disorder.

Lithium. A drug to treat bipolar mania.

Abilify. An antipsychotic drug used to treat schizophrenia, bipolar disorder and manic-depression.

Jonah had been on various drug cocktails since his teenage years, ever since he began seeing figures, hearing voices and acting out violently. His family's crashed SUV and his mother's broken arm, concussion, and lacerations were just two examples of what was originally considered "bad behavior" and eventually was diagnosed as mental illness. Jonah spent years in and out of hospitals, psychiatric facilities, and group homes until he was finally stabilized – for now. Mental illness remains notoriously difficult to treat, in great part because patients resist continued use of their medications. Even Jonah knew he could return into the darkness at any time.

"I know you don't need me to tell you this again," Dr. Sheffield continued. "but I need to emphasize this. You need to stay on your medications. They take time to be fully effective. If you're having side effects, you need to call me and we'll manage your medications appropriately. Don't try to change things yourself."

Jonah nodded. He knew that speech by heart.

"Got it, doc," he said. "Set up a routine and stick to it."

Dr. Sheffield smiled, then shifted topics. "Are you still going through with your plan to move into a place by yourself?"

Jonah's father had recently passed away, just a few months after the death of his mother. Though he and his parents had made amends after the violent incident more than a decade ago, Jonah remained distant. His parents never quite learned to trust him again, and Jonah found his old home unwelcoming and uncomfortable. Nevertheless, Jonah was their only child. Perhaps as a posthumous olive branch, Jonah received a modest inheritance and with that, he had decided to buy his own home for the first time in his life.

"I put a down payment on the place just the other day," Jonah said, suddenly perking up. "I really need to live alone. Roommates drive me crazy. There's too much noise in apartments. Kids running on the floors above you, neighbors blasting their TVs, husbands and wives fighting drunkenly. I need some place just for me. I need to be a solitary man."

"Aren't you a little young for Neil Diamond?" Dr. Sheffield smiled.

Jonah smirked. Dr. Sheffield couldn't tell at first if he knew the reference to the singer's hit song or not, but Jonah had a deep knowledge of American pop music.

"Not usually my type," Jonah admitted. "I'm more of a classic rock fan myself."

The doctor nodded, showing the slightest hint of a smile.

"I just want to make sure you believe this is a wise choice," the doctor pressed.

"It's hard for me to get along while I live with others," Jonah said somewhat defensively. "They freak if I act the least bit peculiar. They're always on edge. I've had people call 9-1-1 on me for no good reason. Then it's a day convincing police officers and doctors that I'm not having a psychotic break. I've had my share of unnecessary trips to the hospital escorted by law enforcement. They're never pleasant."

Dr. Sheffield jotted down another thought.

"I understand," she agreed verbally, though her tone expressed some doubt. "In some ways, I think this is a definite step forward. Let's just keep an eye on how you do and make sure there's no unexpected ramifications."

"Isn't that why I come here?" Jonah smiled. "For you to keep an eye on me?"

"Point taken."

Seriously, I'll be fine. This is exactly what I need."

Dr. Sheffield wrote down several notes in her patient journal once again. "I'm sure you'll do well, as long as you continue your medication as prescribed and call me if you sense the slightest difficulty," she acknowledged. "You know in the past change has sometimes been difficult."

"This is a change I've decided to make," Jonah asserted. "It's not one forced on me. I am finally deciding to move forward with my life and take responsibility."

"OK, then," Dr. Sheffield concluded. "I think we're making real progress. Let's see you again in three weeks."

Jonah stood up. "I'm pretty sure that's how you end every session."

CHAPTER 6

Jonah bought a home in the out-of-the-way town of Clayburn on an out-of-the-way street with a definite purpose in mind – it had been left behind by the lightning fast pace of the modern world. He was ready for the quiet regularity of life in a small town.

Clayburn was located in Northeast Pennsylvania, sometimes called NEPA by local residents and business organizations. The Schuylkill County borough thrived when coal was king, but had fallen on hard times in recent years. While the name of this municipality was Clayburn, it could have been called by the names any number of the hundreds of small Coal Region towns that had suffered the same fate.

As the coal industry withered, jobs were lost, towns were abandoned, and houses fell into disrepair. Clayburn had been losing population for decades as loyal residents aged and finally passed away, with no one to take their place. Many of the town's youth had left in search of more secure employment and brighter futures – a scenario that repeated itself across many other municipalities in the region. Jonah was attracted to the town for exactly the same reason most people had abandoned it. No one would run him over on the way to the next task or opportunity. Clayburn was a quiet and peaceful respite from the high-speed world.

Indeed, nothing much moved quickly in Clayburn. Someone died, a funeral was held three or four days later, and most of the town attended. For many, that served as the social event of the week. At the reception following the funeral – and there was always a reception following the funeral, usually involving a significant amount of food – attendees looked around to determine whose service was likely to be next. Many a bet were won or lost by grieving guests over a bountiful luncheon.

Few residents were in a terrible hurry. People ambled to their car, truck or SUV to travel to the grocery store or the drug store, and took their time doing so. Since many of the remaining residents were retired and unemployment was high even among those who weren't, there wasn't many other places to go. Shopping provided both needed commodities and plentiful conversation. Residents hit the Walmart several miles out-of-town several times a week and usually stopped at a local restaurant's early-bird special.

Nothing to do, Jonah said to himself, *and all day to do it.*

It didn't take long for Jonah to notice that, for some reason, no one called their mode of transportation a car or a truck in this part of the state. They were all "vehicles."

"I'm dropping off my vehicle at the garage today for an oil change," he'd overheard a patron at the convenience store, or "I'm not sure that is going to fit in my vehicle" as a customer surveyed a box in the appliance store.

Good from the stroller to the hearse, Jonah thought. *You never had to change the name of your transportation.* These were practical folks, if nothing else.

The house that Jonah purchased was a three-story brick and stucco Victorian built in the early 20th Century. As were most houses in the area, the first two floors were finished, topped with an unfinished attic. The house was likely built at a time when homes couldn't go up fast enough as miners flocked to the area to support the energy that drove the Industrial Revolution. Even today, with the coal industry a mere shadow of its once omnipotent self, the memories of that era were everywhere: scarred hillsides where strip-mining took place, locations marked by the locations of mines (getting into town, Jonah had to crest the "Number 9" hill), processing plants, rail cars, and the ever-present threat of a cave-in of an old mine that could swallow a car (or a "vehicle," Jonah chuckled) or even a house. Jonah learned quickly there was a reason that coal miners never dug under local churches: they didn't want to risk the wrath of God as His place of worship toppled into a collapsed mine.

But Jonah was unconcerned about the potential perils of abandoned mines as he began to settle into his new residence.

"Home, sweet home," Jonah whistled as he walked up the uneven sidewalk toward his front door. He carried with him a couple of suitcases of clothes. He stepped onto the front porch, then opened the door and walked into his living room, setting down his load on the floor. The few pieces of furniture he owned had been hauled to the house by a moving company the day before. There would be several empty rooms in a house much too big for one person.

Jonah found that his inheritance went a long way in this leftover town, and available real estate was incredibly cheap. This house could use some updating and minor repairs, but it was structurally sound (assuming no coal mine ran underneath it) and didn't need any immediate work.

The house sat near the end of a block on the outskirts of town. It was bordered by the base of a tree-covered hill on one side and several grassy lots on the other. At one time, the Victorian was one of eight row-homes that dotted the south side of the street, with a matching eight on the north side. But a fire in the 1940s had taken down two homes, and years of disrepair claimed four more. Only 10 of the original structures still stood, and it appeared at least one or two of them were, for all intents and purposes, abandoned.

Everything about the home's surroundings spoke to a more glorious past. The macadam road was cracked and in disrepair, but Jonah noted that few of the borough roads had been re-paved in this century. The sidewalk in front of the house was pitted with seams and crumbling on the edges. The concrete had lifted around the electric pole that fed power to Jonah's home at 225 Easley Avenue. At least the pole seemed sturdy, if a number of decades old.

Jonah returned to his six-year-old Chevrolet Malibu to retrieve the last of his possessions. The car was parked directly in front of the house, with little competition for spaces. Jonah spotted only three other cars on the block. Jonah thought about buying a new car with his newly subsidized bank account, but reconsidered. There was nothing wrong with the Malibu, and outside of his regular appointments with Dr. Sheffield, he didn't have a whole lot of places to go. He had found from years battling his demons that the more he travelled into unfamiliar places, the more likely he would need to fight inner battles. He didn't need any unnecessary distractions or temptations.

Keep life simple, he told himself. He looked up and down the street.

"Some avenue," Jonah whispered to himself as he glanced at the street sign and the condition of the roadway. He grabbed the last of his boxes and sauntered into his house.

As Jonah entered the home once again, he saw three of the cartons he had carried in earlier and set against his living room wall had toppled over.

"What the hell?" he said to himself. "I guess I have to be a little more careful. Damn floors are probably uneven. Maybe there is a coal mine under the house after all."

Jonah brought the rest of his possessions into the house without incident. His belongings were as his sparse as his furniture, and the moving company certainly did not have a difficult job the day before. A bed with a dresser and nightstand. A small kitchen table and two chairs. A desk and chair. A sofa, end table, and TV stand. And while Jonah was relatively frugal with his purchases, he actually had splurged and bought a larger Smart TV, figuring that the town had either cable or Internet – and preferably both.

"Guess I should have checked first," he said, smiling.

There were no churches in close vicinity to his house, since Jonah had learned too late from the locals the admonition of buying your house near your place of worship.

"That's all right," Jonah muttered to himself. "If I lived too near a church, one of us would catch on fire, and it probably wouldn't be the church."

He took his time unpacking. Jonah opened one box and found a medium-sized ornately engraved walnut box. It looked vaguely Middle Eastern, but Jonah couldn't say for sure. It was closed by a small metal latch, which Jonah flicked open as he lifted it and placed it on the kitchen table. The inside was lined in red cushioned fabric.

The contents of the box may not have seemed particularly special to an outside observer, but they were Jonah's most valued possessions. A family photo of Jonah and his parents when he was about six – when innocence was still a way of life and before the nightmares of mental illness fully enveloped him. A lock of hair from his first haircut. An 1883 Carson City Morgan silver dollar, passed down from his great-grandfather signifying his ancestor's birth date. A small ledger from his father that he referred to as his "Doomsday Book," which provided information on life insurance, bank accounts, funeral arrangements and more, a resource Jonah had found invaluable when arranging for his parents' affairs, and a lasting reminder of his father's meticulous nature. Perhaps most importantly, a hand-written note from his mother. It said simply: "Jonah, I forgive you. It wasn't your fault. I will always love you. Mom." At the time he received it, he was in no condition to appreciate the sentiment. But as Jonah had gained better control over his demons, the note took on more importance. And finally, at the bottom of the box, the well-read copy of the *New American Bible* that his mother had read to him each day she carried him and after his birth, complete with hand-written notes indicating her favorite passages – and those she perceived Jonah responded to most positively while still in her womb. The passage containing the story of Jonah and the whale, the story that inspired his name, was dog-eared on the corner.

"I'm sorry I wasn't a better son," Jonah said softly, a tear in his eye.

Jonah closed the box, latched it, and placed it carefully in his nightstand. He would look at it every night to remind him that no matter what had happened in the past and what would happen in the future, there was always hope and forgiveness. Jonah knew that would be one of the keys to keep him sane and sober.

Jonah walked into the kitchen and opened his refrigerator. It was powered on, but was cooling an empty space.

"Ah shit," he said. "Forgot food. I guess I have to find a grocery store."

Jonah grabbed his car keys and walked out to his car. Across the street he saw a man that looked to be in his early 20s walking with an older woman. A dog of indeterminate breed was on a leash held by the woman. The dog barked twice, until the woman leaned over and threatened to swat her pet. After quieting down the dog, she looked over and stared at the newcomer as he opened the doors to his Malibu.

"Hello," Jonah said, "I just moved in and I need some groceries. Is there a store nearby?"

The young man looked up and tried to make eye contact. He opened his mouth to say something, but then stopped and looked awkwardly away. The woman patted her companion reassuringly on the back, then looked over to Jonah.

"Hello, young man," she finally said. "We live right across the street from you on the corner. I'm Helen Paskiel, and this is my son, Oliver. If there's anything you need, you just stop over anytime."

"Nice to meet you," Jonah acknowledged.

"It's good to finally have someone in that house," Helen said. "It's been empty for quite some time. It's always gratifying to have a good neighbor. Lord knows enough of them have died off in recent years."

"Thanks," Jonah said.

I think, he added to himself.

"I'm looking forward to getting settled in," he said to his neighbor.

Helen looked at Jonah, then put her hand to her head as she remembered Jonah's original question.

"Oh, silly me," she cackled. "You asked about the grocery store. Turn left at the stop sign and then go up to Broad Street and make another left. There's a Boyer's about three blocks down on the right hand side. Not the biggest store, but then again, this isn't the biggest town!"

Jonah smiled and thanked her. The young man glanced over at Jonah momentarily and gave a halting and tentative wave, then looked away again. Jonah waved back, hopped into his car and drove off.

"This is certainly going to be an interesting place," he said softly.

CHAPTER 7

The next day, Jonah spent most of the morning unpacking boxes and arranging shelves. In between, he did a little cleaning, but like most young men his age, whatever effort he made to the task was haphazard at best. Finally, he tired of the chores and felt the need to explore.

A good excuse for a break, he thought.

"I need to find out where the hell I am," he said to himself. "Time to check out what's around here – if anything."

He put away a few last items, then grabbed his car keys and headed out the front door.

He climbed into his Malibu and decided to start by quickly exploring Clayburn and its immediate vicinity then moving further outward. He found the post office after a couple of wrong turns, but had more success with the local CVS pharmacy. He figured out that a sandwich shop on 3rd Street named Pete's looked like a prime spot for hoagies and cheese steaks. He found Grandma's Kitchen, a 24-hour-diner a few miles down the highway, that claimed to make an excellent breakfast. He noticed there were no shortage of places to buy cigarettes if he ever took up smoking. And after a bit of searching, he found the Walmart next to a bowling alley and a Chinese restaurant. Once he discovered the nearest McDonald's further down the highway, he decided it was time to expand his horizons.

"Road trip," he proclaimed, and turned the volume on his radio full blast. He coincidentally found Bruce Springsteen's "Born to Run" blaring from his speakers.

In the day we sweat it out on the streets of a runaway American dream
At night we ride through the mansions of glory in suicide machines
Sprung from cages out on highway nine,
Chrome wheeled, fuel injected, and steppin' out over the line
H-Oh, Baby this town rips the bones from your back
It's a death trap, it's a suicide rap
We gotta get out while we're young
'Cause tramps like us, baby we were born to run...

Jonah bobbed and weaved out of local traffic and roared toward the closest route to the open road. A few older residents watching nearby wondered why youngsters were in such a hurry racing their vehicles down the road like that. Fortunately for Jonah, no local police were on patrol in the vicinity that day.

Jonah soon learned that the landscape of Northeast Pennsylvania was a study in contrasts. Miles of tree-lined hills and mountains created picturesque postcard scenery. He could imagine the spectacular view when the foliage began to change in the fall. The winding, twisting back roads cut through rock and skirted the hillsides on their path from one old coal town to the next.

But just as you began the enjoy the natural beauty, a scar of an abandoned surface mine came into view. Those mines produced plentiful coal in their day, but now sat empty and forlorn, the land around it hopelessly violated. A struggling pine tree or two thrust defiantly through the coal dust surface, but for the most part, the growth failed to cover the previous abuse. There was little to be done to remedy it. Hopefully, time and entropy would erase the evidence.

Beyond the mines themselves, rusting hulks of decaying coal plants and relics of mining equipment dotted the landscape. Conversely, power lines of every shape and size crisscrossed the mountains, both up and down and along the top. Even windmills could be found perched along the hilltops. With its genesis in coal-fired electricity generation – which dominated Pennsylvania's electric production until recent years – the Northeast had accumulated a significant amount of energy company infrastructure that powered the

44

nearby population centers.

For every small town that offered charm and elegance or a hint of modernity, there were three others – suffering from decades of economic losses – filled with any number of rundown homes, closed churches and businesses, and pothole-filled streets. There were pockets of an economic renaissance here and there across the region, but for the great majority of old coal towns, hope of a comeback still remained an unattainable and distant dream.

Two major interstate highways cut the Northeast into quadrants. Interstate 81 ran north and south, heading up past Wilkes-Barre and Scranton through New England and stopping at the U.S. – Canadian border. Southbound, I-81 skirted the northern edges of Harrisburg, the state Capital, then wound itself through Maryland, West Virginia, and Virginia before ending in Tennessee. Interstate 80 ran west to east, intersecting I-81 north of Hazleton. I-80 is a transcontinental highway that runs from downtown San Francisco to Teaneck, New Jersey, in the New York City Metropolitan Area. One way to look at it is you can reach almost any destination in the United States from the I-80/I-81 intersection, something that did not escape the attention of corporate retailers. The Northeast Extension of the Pennsylvania Turnpike also runs nearby, providing easy access to nearly every major metropolitan area throughout the Commonwealth. Much of whatever economic resurrection had occurred in the region came in the form of distribution centers, warehouses and manufacturers who needed relatively close proximity to markets such as New York, Boston, Philadelphia, Baltimore, Washington, D.C., Pittsburgh and Cleveland.

Jonah had lunch at a restaurant called the Top of the 80's because he liked the name. In truth, Top of the 80s is really at the intersection of I-81 and Route 93, several miles south of I-80, but north of Hazleton.

Close enough, Jonah said to himself. *I'm hungry.*

The restaurant offered a magnificent view of the valley below. Jonah sat at a table near the window, glanced at the menu briefly, and greeted the waitress when she came by.

"I'll have a Chicken Caesar Salad and a Coke," he said pleasantly.

He ate peacefully, paid with cash, provided a healthy tip, and was soon on his way again. Jonah eschewed the big interstates and instead took a circuitous route through the small towns and back roads of the Northeast. He was fascinated by the shops he saw along the way. Not the big box stores you could find anywhere, but the mom-and-pop stores that still survived. He saw smoke shops and pizza parlors, hardware and craft shops, stores that sold homemade pierogies, restaurants and sandwich joints, and bars. He actually lost count of the bars.

"I guess it's true," he finally said to himself. "The church is on one corner, the bar is on the other. Actually, where there's not a church, the bar is on both corners."

Jonah travelled north, through Wilkes-Barre and Scranton. He didn't find the invisible wall most locals swore existed between the two cities, but did didn't dismiss the possibility out of hand.

Probably a gate between the two somewhere on 81, he decided.

He headed south again toward the Poconos, admiring the now snow-free ski slopes and the tourist traps that accompanied them. He decided against stopping in at Kalahari, the fancy, new-fangled indoor water park that operated year-round.

Didn't bring my swim suit, he thought.

On the way back home, Jonah discovered Eckley Miners' Village, a restored miners' town in Weatherly, outside of Hazleton. Now a state-operated museum, the village gained fame when it served as the film location for the 1970 film, *The Molly Maguires*. From there, Jonah found the Pioneer Coal Mine, open for tours in Ashland; and finally Leiby's Ice Cream House and Restaurant, located outside of Tamaqua and well known locally for both its ice cream and elaborate pie and cake dessert menu.

"I'm going to have to eat there one day," Jonah said as he drove by.

By the time he returned to Clayburn, he had seen firsthand the dichotomy of the Northeast. The old and the new clashed at every turn. The region had not quite completed its divorce from its King Coal history, but it was slowly – more slowly in some areas than others – embracing a new economy and a different future. The land showed the deep wounds of the past, but was giving way to whatever lay ahead as it inevitably emerged. Old, decaying towns with broken roads clashed with new construction. The world would move forward. Some of these towns would adapt. Others? Jonah wasn't so sure. Somehow, it didn't seem completely fair, but nothing ever was.

Jonah eventually pulled his Malibu back into the streets of Clayburn.

"I guess no one unpacked the rest of the boxes for me," he said ruefully as he pulled back onto Easley Avenue.

He looked across the street. Oliver watched carefully out his bedroom window, his dog standing on the window sill by his side. Jonah waved. Oliver hesitatingly waved back. He made eye contact for no more than a second or two, then turned away.

CHAPTER 8

Over the next several days, Jonah continued to work to get his new house in order. He had enough furniture for a rudimentary living room, dining room and kitchen, as well as a bedroom. Jonah's house was one of the few in town with a bedroom on the first floor, most likely renovated at some point by a past owner. In one of the rooms upstairs, he set up his desk and a chair, which made for a sparse but workable office. The other two bedrooms were empty and became the storage area for boxes and things that Jonah would get to later. If ever.

Jonah wasn't much of a cook, so he used meal times to test the cuisine of the various diners, sandwich shops and restaurants he spotted on his expedition. He discovered that food was one area where Northeast Pennsylvania excelled. Portions were ample, and the meals delicious, if not particularly healthy. Smoked meat, butter and cream-filled potatoes and pasta of every sort, as well as rich desserts, seemed to dominate every meal.

I have to learn to cook better, Jonah thought, *or I'm going to end up being 400 pounds. I need to remember to buy a couple of cookbooks.*

After dinner, Jonah would return to his humble new home and continue his work, putting up a picture and unwrapping silverware. He set up a comfortable living room, laying out his couch, end-table and TV in what he considered its ideal formation after several rejected iterations. He had an old but classic-looking lamp and a clock for the table, which he plugged both in, screwed in an LED bulb into the lamp and set the time on the clock.

Every so often, Jonah noticed any number of odd occurrences in the house. His lone family photo – a framed 8-by-10 – ended up face down on his bedroom dresser despite his certainty that he placed it firmly in its place. He'd would set down a screwdriver or other tool only to have it disappear, later to show up in another part of the house. Several small tools and other items completely vanished, never to return, even though Jonah was positive of their location. More than once, some utensil or household item he was sure he had put in a drawer ended up back on the counter. His emptied boxes had an annoying habit of toppling over.

"What the fuck?" Jonah muttered as he piled them back up for the third time. "This is ridiculous."

Jonah would pick up the boxes, walk away, and not give them another thought.

Every so often, Jonah would spot Oliver standing on the sidewalk across the street staring intently at his house. The observer didn't look dangerous or threatening, but Jonah found the attention unsettling. Finally, one day later in the afternoon, as he began to relax on his sofa to watch a bit of TV, Jonah spotted Oliver again and decided to try engage him. He jumped up and moved quickly out the front door.

"Hey," Jonah shouted, "Oliver! Can I talk to you?"

The young man shuffled nervously, then quickly turned and started walking down the street back toward his house at a brisk pace.

"Hey," Jonah said, "hold up!"

Jonah started to jog toward the young man, and though his prey looked back nervously, he didn't pick up his pace any further. Just a short way down the block, Jonah caught up with him.

"Buddy, slow up," Jonah said. "Talk to me for a minute."

Jonah reached out to touch Oliver's shoulder, but Oliver saw Jonah's hand out of the corner of his eye and flinched. Jonah instinctively pulled away and came to a stop.

Oliver took another step or two, then halted and turned slowly toward Jonah, but didn't make eye contact. Jonah patiently looked over Oliver, this time with a bit more scrutiny. He was generally unremarkable: average height and weight, with his own mop of unruly and poorly combed brown hair and wire-framed glasses that needed a good cleaning. Despite the summer heat, he wore an Army-Navy jacket a size too big and a bit frazzled over a T-shirt and faded jeans.

"I'm Oliver," the man said softly, his gaze firmly on the ground to the side of Jonah.

"Nice to see you again, Oliver," Jonah said. "We met the other day. I'm Jonah."

"Hi," Oliver said flatly. "I know your name."

A perplexed look flashed over Jonah's face for a moment, but he let it pass.

"Can I ask you a question?" Jonah asked. "Why are you always watching me outside my window?"

Oliver shrugged, making brief eye contact before turning away again.

"Just wondering about you and why you're moving here," he said. "Most people I know are moving out."

Jonah chuckled. "I do always seem to swim against the tide."

"You swim?" Oliver asked.

Jonah stopped and studied Oliver as he formulated a sharp retort, but he could quickly see Oliver was perfectly serious.

"A little," he answered. "Anyway, you live across the street from me?"

Oliver pointed at the house on the corner at the intersection of Easley Avenue and First Street. "Right there," he said. "With my mom."

"So we're neighbors," Jonah said. "Well, look, I could use some help getting the house in order. So if you want to come over and help out, you don't have to stand on the sidewalk. You can come in."

Oliver flashed an uneasy smile that quickly disappeared.

"OK," he said. "I'd like that. I'll have to ask Mom if it's all right."

"You do what you have to do, buddy," Jonah said. "Maybe I'll see you tomorrow?"

"All right," Oliver said, turned and started walking toward his house. He stopped suddenly and swung back toward Jonah. "What time tomorrow?"

Jonah thought for a second. "Not before 10."

"A.M.?"

Jonah was incredulous for a moment, but held back making a snide remark.

"Yes," he answered. "A.M."

"OK," Oliver said. "Ten A.M. I'll see you then."

Oliver then turned again and headed back to his house.

"And I thought I was fuckin' crazy," Jonah said and walked back down the block. "Nice kid, though."

•   •   •

The next day, Jonah was cleaning up the kitchen when he heard a knock on the door. When he answered, Oliver stood timidly on his front porch.

"It's 10 o'clock," he said. "Mom said it was fine."

Jonah glanced at the clock. Sure enough, the digits said 10:00 on the dot.

"All right then," Jonah answered. "Glad to see you're on time."

Jonah smiled, but Oliver's facial expression remained inscrutable.

"I'm always on time," Oliver said. "Why wouldn't I be?"

Jonah had no response. Instead, he simply waved Oliver to enter.

"Come on in," Jonah said. "I was planning on working in the basement today. It's kind of filthy. I could use the help cleaning it up."

"All right," Oliver agreed.

Oliver walked in and looked tentatively around the house. He moved about with only great care, as if the surroundings somehow intimidated him.

"This was where Miss Donahue lived," he finally said without affect. "She was very old. She died."

"So I've heard," Jonah said. "Did you ever visit her?'

"No, she wasn't very nice," Oliver answered, then again examined the house closely, a tinge of unease in his appearance. "There's something still not nice about this house."

"What do you mean?" Jonah asked. "I'm doing the best I can. You have to give me some time to clean the place up!"

"No, it's not you," his new friend continued, in a tone seemingly indifferent to Jonah's consternation. "It's her. There's still something about her that's here. It's very disturbing. She was always very mean to me and to everyone else."

"Well," Jonah finally concluded. "If she's here, she's probably in the basement. So the faster we clean it out, the faster we'll get rid of her."

"All right," Oliver agreed, and headed down the steps. Jonah paused for a second and considered what Oliver had said, then followed him into the cellar.

The two worked for several hours, sweeping the floor and walls, hauling out trash, and washing off decades of dirt. There was some ramshackle wooden shelving hung on the old stone walls that would need repair or replacement. Thankfully, the floor was concrete, though poured in a patchwork quilt pattern that indicated it had been done in piecemeal fashion over time.

"Guess she couldn't afford a contractor," Jonah mused, looking over the obviously do-it-yourself work. "It's almost even."

Still, Jonah felt vaguely uncomfortable about the concrete work and basement in general, though he couldn't say why. The feeling grew as they worked, but Jonah tried to ignore it as best he could.

Oliver wasn't actually much help – though he was better at carrying trash out than actually cleaning – but he was welcome company.

"Tell me about yourself," Jonah said. "Why are you still living here?"

Oliver considered Jonah for a second, seemingly reluctant to be completely open.

"Where else would I be?" Oliver asked.

"Anywhere but here," Jonah said. "There's a whole world out there that's a lot more exciting than Clayburn. You don't have to be stuck here with your mother."

Oliver scrunched up his face deep in thought. Finally, he resolved himself to tell whatever he was thinking.

"I'm autistic," he finally said, but turned away as he spoke.

"Oh yeah?" Jonah asked lazily. "What's that mean?"

"Actually, I have what they used to call Asperger's Syndrome,"

Oliver explained. "I have trouble making friends. I don't...," the young man paused, searching for words, "do well with people. It's hard for me to shake hands, or look at people, or not sound rude or inappropriate. I do my best, but I don't always succeed."

Oliver abruptly stopped. Jonah studied him for a moment recognizing his nervousness, then smiled broadly.

"That's cool," he finally said. "You don't seem that rude to me. And I promise not to shake your hand."

"OK."

Jonah stopped what he was doing and looked more closely at Oliver. Now that he actually paid attention to his young neighbor and gave it some thought, it was clear that Oliver landed somewhere on the autistic spectrum. Jonah wasn't an expert on autism by any means, but he had met a number of people on the spectrum in his mental health travels.

"Listen, don't worry about it," Jonah said reassuringly. "You're not the only one who's different. I'm not normal either, whatever normal is supposed to be. I have what they call schizoaffective disorder."

"What's that?" Oliver asked.

Jonah thought about the long explanation and decided to go the simple route.

"It means I'm nuts."

"OK," Oliver said, only the slightest tint of uncertainty in his voice.

"But don't worry," Jonah assured his guest. "I'm not dangerous. I'm on my meds."

"I didn't think you were dangerous," Oliver answered. "You don't seem the type."

"You don't know me very well," Jonah said knowingly.

"I don't think you would hurt me," Oliver said.

Jonah scrutinized his new friend carefully once more.

"No," he agreed, "I wouldn't."

At that moment, the two men heard a loud crash upstairs. They glanced at each other, and Jonah bounded up the stairs leaving Oliver far behind. When Oliver finally caught up, he found Jonah staring incredulously in the kitchen. All the pots and pans that Jonah had recently put away had decided to fly out of the cabinets by themselves and now lay scattered across the floor.

"What the hell?" Jonah growled.

"It must be the ghosts," Oliver said without additional elaboration.

The owner of the home whirled around and stared at Oliver incredulously.

"Ghosts?" Jonah asked demandingly. "What ghosts?"

Oliver turned away from Jonah's uncomfortable glare.

"Oliver," Jonah said, this time less sternly. "What ghosts?"

"Didn't they tell you when you bought the place?" Oliver asked matter-of-factly. "This house is haunted."

CHAPTER 9

Haunted? Jonah thought to himself. *No, that never came up during settlement.*

Jonah continued to consider Oliver's statement, trying to decide what to make of his claim. His mind spun in any number of directions. It took him a few seconds to remember that most people on the spectrum tended to be very direct in their statements. Hyperbole was rarely a strong suit. It was unlikely Oliver was making this up or being sarcastic. True or not, Oliver clearly believed it. Jonah took a couple of deep breaths.

"What the hell do you mean exactly by haunted?" Jonah finally pressed his new friend.

"Oh, I don't know for sure," Oliver said. "But I've heard stories. And, I've seen some very odd things through my window."

Well, he certainly has studied the house, Jonah thought.

"What odd things have you seen or heard?" Jonah continued. He was careful to be very specific in his request and not sound too anxious. He didn't want Oliver to shut down.

"Well," Oliver continued, "when the realtor was showing the house, some people ran out because they heard noises and saw things flying across the room. Or at least that's what I heard."

"What about you?" Jonah asked. "Have you ever seen anything?"

Oliver hesitated.

"Every so often, I see someone looking out the window," Oliver admitted. "Sometimes it looks like old Miss Donahue. But of course, she's dead."

"So I've heard," Jonah said with the slightest bit of sarcasm. "But

I'm starting to wonder."

"Other times, it looks more like children in the window," Oliver said. "But Miss Donahue never had any children."

"And if she did," Jonah added, "they wouldn't be children anymore."

"Good point," Oliver admitted. "I didn't think of that."

Jonah studied Oliver once more. Oliver looked uncomfortable but forthright. Jonah decided his young friend was really incapable of either lying or fictionalizing. He felt the familiar tingle in his neck, like a thousand voices trying to break into his brain, but he shook his head violently, fighting off the unseen intruders.

You can handle this, Jonah said to himself. *I will not give in. Not today. My demons will not win today.*

"It's funny," Jonah said. "The realtor didn't mention anything like that to me. But I guess that's not something you tell a prospective buyer."

Oliver peered at Jonah curiously.

"I don't understand why someone wouldn't be honest," Oliver said.

"Trust me," Jonah answered. "Happens all the time. There's only so much truth a sales person can handle."

"Did anything happen when you looked at the house?" Oliver asked.

"Not a thing," Jonah answered. "The place couldn't have seemed more normal."

"Hmm," Oliver thought for a moment, then offered his own hypothesis. "Maybe she wanted you."

"She?" Jonah asked loudly. "Who the hell is she? Old Lady Donahue?"

"She did live in this house her entire life," Oliver said, his eyes surveying skittishly around the small home. "She died last year when she was 84. Some people around here said she never wanted to leave, so maybe she's still here."

Jonah scanned the downstairs himself, then started picking up the pots and pans and returning them to their shelves.

"Some old bat isn't going to scare me away," he said defiantly. "Especially one who's dead. And if she wants to scare me, she better do a hell of a lot better than throwing some cooking utensils around."

Oliver thought he heard a soft growl, but Jonah didn't appear to notice.

"OK," Oliver said. "But Miss Donahue wasn't a bat. At least I don't think so. She was an old woman. I never saw her turn into a bat. Maybe she did after dark – I don't know that for sure. I usually don't stay up that late."

Jonah inspected Jonah with a disbelieving look for a second, then broke into a broad smile. "Figurative language isn't your strong point, is it my friend?"

"I guess not," Oliver said. "What do you mean?'

Jonah patted Oliver on the back and the two went about their work. In a few minutes, the kitchen was cleaned up and Jonah and Oliver went about other chores around the house. Jonah tried to stay as literal as possible in hopes of keeping the conversation moving forward and the explanations at a minimum.

•   •   •

After that incident, life seemed to return to normal to 225 Easley Avenue. Jonah continued getting his new house in order, cleaning rooms, re-painting where needed, and even framing out a small garden. For now, he left the wallpaper alone – replacing that seemed an effort for another time. Jonah set up his medications precisely and set an alarm on his phone so he took them on schedule faithfully. By now, he knew his daily pill regimen was the only thing keeping him from falling into the abyss of madness.

The one continuing odd occurrence was the behavior of the small clock he set up on the living room table. Each morning, Jonah walked into the room, only to find the clock flashing, stuck at 3:33 a.m. He would reset it every day, only to have the same thing happen the next.

"Some electronic glitch," Jonah concluded. "I'm going to have a get a new one."

Meanwhile, Oliver came over daily and, rather quickly, Jonah and Oliver formed a unique but close bond. Oliver's mother stopped over a few times, seemingly to put a stamp of approval on her son's new friend. She made small talk, looked around the house, and eyed Jonah up and down like she was judging prized cattle. When she arrived one day with a fresh baked apple pie, Jonah knew he had passed whatever test to which he had been subjected.

"Thank you, Mrs. Paskiel," Jonah said. "Come on in."

"You can call me Helen," the plump mid-50-something woman with grey-streaked red hair said.

"I don't know," Jonah said. "No matter how I try, I think you're going to be Mrs. Paskiel to me."

Oliver's mother chuckled.

"That's up to you," she said. "You know what they say. Call me whatever you want, just don't call me late for dinner."

Jonah smiled. *No,* he thought, *she likely doesn't miss too many meals.* Outwardly, he just nodded.

Changing the subject, Mrs. Paskiel looked over at her son, who was busy unpacking another box.

"You don't know what a joy it is for Oliver to find a friend," she said. "It's...," she paused momentarily, "difficult for him to make connections with people."

"I understand," Jonah said. "Maybe you have to be a little different to understand someone who's a little different."

"That may be the case," Mrs. Paskiel acknowledged. "If that's so, then I'll count Oliver lucky for finding you. It hasn't been easy raising him alone, and he could use another male in his life. I'm really the only constant he's had up until now."

"What happened to his father?" Jonah asked, immediately regretting the question when he realized the mine field into which he may have strayed and the hurt feelings he may have dredged to the surface.

But Helen just sighed, seemingly unoffended.

"Mr. Paskiel couldn't accept Oliver," she said. "He was a man's man, you know. Always wanted his son to be the high school quarterback. He couldn't abide by the fact his son was different than the others. He blamed me."

Mrs. Paskiel paused as if re-living a bad memory.

"He left when Oliver was five," she said. "I never saw him again. I have no idea where he is or what happened to him. Oliver doesn't remember him at all, or if does, doesn't mention him."

"I'm sorry," Jonah answered awkwardly.

"Not your fault," the woman said, suddenly more pleasantly as if she had cast the bad memory aside. "He's the dumb son of a bitch who missed his son growing up. Oliver is special in his own way, and if that didn't suit Mr. Paskiel, then he's the worse for it. I'm the lucky one who's had the pleasure of raising him."

Jonah looked at the middle-aged woman, slightly stunned by the profanity that he never would have guessed she was capable of uttering, but impressed with her inner strength and resolve.

"Oh, I shouldn't talk like that," Mrs. Paskiel said, admonishing herself. "I guess that has to be in my next Confession."

She glanced over at her son once more, and gave Jonah a quick smile.

"Oliver is a wonderful boy, even though he's not like everyone else," she said resolutely. "It's too bad Mr. Paskiel didn't recognize that."

"Fair enough," Jonah concluded. "I think he's pretty great myself."

Then it was time for Jonah to change topics, a difficult task when talking to the runaway train that was Mrs. Paskiel.

"Listen, while you're here," he asked, "what can you tell me about the Miss Donahue that used to live here?"

Helen looked at Jonah curiously, noting the concern on his face.

"Why do you ask?" she finally said. "I didn't know her that well. Kept to herself mainly."

"I don't know," Jonah answered. "Oliver told me some strange stories about what happened over here."

Mrs. Paskiel waved her hand dismissively and began to laugh.

"Oh, has that Oliver been telling ghost stories again?" she said. "Listen, some of the towns' folk know Oliver is a little gullible – he isn't so good at figuring out when someone's pulling his leg, you know. So they got him all riled up with stories of the old woman coming after him after she's dead. I admit old lady Donahue sure wasn't that pleasant when she was alive, no question about that. Oliver was scared to death of her, and I didn't find her all that agreeable myself. But I don't expect to see her flying about in a white sheet any time soon. Don't listen to all that. Just some people having fun at my boy's expense. He doesn't mean any harm."

Jonah nodded, relieved at Mrs. Paskiel's dismissal of tales of hauntings and malevolent spirits.

"Well, now listen, you enjoy that pie," Helen concluded, eyeing Jonah up and down. "It looks like you could put a few pounds on that skinny frame of yours. You certainly need it more than I do!"

As the woman was leaving the house, she turned around one last time. "By the way, I hate to be so forward," a statement Jonah found ironic, though it apparently didn't seem so to Mrs. Paskiel, "but are you looking for a job?"

Jonah laughed. "I have been thinking of getting some work somewhere," he admitted. "But you know, with my background, it's not easy to get hired."

Helen waved her arm cavalierly. Jonah noticed Mrs. Paskiel talked with her hands nearly as flamboyantly as she did with her mouth. He made a note to himself never to stand too closely when his neighbor was on an extended monologue, or else risk being accidentally slapped.

"No one cares about that stuff around here," she said, "as long as you don't stir up trouble now. Oliver works part-time up at Mr. Kershaw's shop. I hear the owner is looking for someone. If he can work with Oliver, he can certainly work with you. I'll put in a good word for you. You show up tomorrow morning first thing, and I'll make sure he's ready for you."

With that, Mrs. Paskiel left the house and sauntered across the street to her own. Jonah noted she didn't wait for his assent to serve as his employment agent. In her own way, she served as the mayor of Easley Avenue. Jonah was glad she had taken a liking to him. He got the feeling life would be much more difficult otherwise.

That night, Jonah took his Malibu and explored the streets of Clayburn a little more closely, seeing that he would have to find the location of his job interview.

If I'm going to work here, he thought, *I better pay a little more attention.*

It was a small town, perhaps 10 blocks long and six blocks wide, climbing the side of one of the low peaks of the Appalachians. The state "highway" – a two-lane road that didn't impress Jonah as much of a highway – cut through the valley between the town and an abandoned strip mine on the other side. Some of the homes in the town leaned crazily to one side or another.

"Coal mine underneath," Jonah said to himself. He learned quickly.

Jonah spotted a half-dozen churches, at least four of which were abandoned. Any number of small businesses were closed and innumerable homes were empty. Clayburn was fighting off death, and not well. The "downtown" of Clayburn consisted a second-run movie theater, a doctor's office, a small grocerette, a sandwich shop and, after Jonah finally spotted it, Kershaw's. As best as Jonah could tell, Kershaw's was a little bit of everything – part tool and implement dealer, part general store, part lawn and garden shop. The store had survived by being just enough of everything to everyone to eke out a business. One oversized parking space outside the store was designated for deliveries only. The storefront windows were packed with products both old and new, some of which had apparently been unmoved for many years while others looked as though they had just been stocked.

It seemed like a perfectly fine place to work.

When he returned home, he stopped by the Paskiel's house and told Helen he would be happy to drive Oliver to work the next day, seeing that he was going there for an interview anyway.

"Oh, isn't that nice of you," Mrs. Paskiel responded. "Such a fine boy you are. I'll make sure Oliver is ready!"

CHAPTER 10

The next morning, Jonah walked across the street and knocked on the Paskiel household door once again. Immediately, he saw their dog fly through the living room, barking madly at the entrance. It was a medium-sized black, brown and white dog, and despite its growl, didn't seem all that intimidating.

Right behind the dog came Mrs. Paskiel, still in her house coat, holding a spatula she was apparently using for some concoction she was baking in the kitchen. Now, however, it turned into a potential weapon – at least for the poor dog.

"Daffodil, shush," she said. "It's only Jonah. For goodness' sake."

She swatted the spatula fruitlessly several times at the dog, who easily avoided the blows.

"Oh my, come in, ignore her," Mrs. Paskiel said. "She makes a lot of noise, but she's harmless."

Jonah took a few steps into the living room, and Daffodil seemed to retreat. Jonah put his hand out. The dog carefully sniffed it a few times, then licked Jonah's hand.

"See that, she likes you already!" Mrs. Paskiel said. "She's a good judge of character."

"What kind is she?" Jonah asked.

"Oh, she's a Heinz 57," Oliver's mother said. "I got her from the pound a few years ago."

Mrs. Paskiel suddenly turned and looked toward the stairway leading upstairs.

"Now where is that boy?" she asked no one in particular. "Let me call him for you."

"That's OK," Jonah began to protest. "I'm a few minutes early..."

That failed to deter Mrs. Paskiel, who walked to the bottom of the steps, then summoned a voice whose volume near shook the foundation of the old house.

"Oliver!" she pronounced. "Are you coming? Jonah's here!"

"Coming!" Oliver said promptly. Seconds later, he ran down the steps.

"I don't know what takes you so long to get ready!" Mrs. Paskiel said, castigating her son softly. "You're just going to Kershaw's."

"Sorry," Oliver said, then turned toward Jonah. "I'm ready. It's only 8:17. I thought you were coming at 8:20."

"It's fine," Jonah assured his friend. "We have plenty of time."

Oliver walked quickly into the kitchen and picked up the lunch Mrs. Paskiel had made and tucked neatly into a brown paper bag. He came back to the living room, kissed his mother on the cheek and headed toward the door. As he and Jonah stepped out and headed down the steps, they heard Mrs. Paskiel from the doorway.

"Now you boys have a good day at work," she said. "Don't do anything I wouldn't do."

Jonah considered a response, then thought better of it. Instead, he waved goodbye and unlocked the car doors.

Oliver typically walked the four blocks to work, a task that had become an expected routine in his life. So it was unsurprising that he was overly timid as he prepared to climb into Jonah's car for the first time.

"Are you sure this will be all right?" he asked.

"Did you Mom say it was OK?" Jonah asked.

"Yes," Oliver said tentatively, "but..."

"OK then," Jonah interrupted. "Then as long as you don't jump out the car while I'm driving, we'll be fine."

Oliver glanced over at Jonah with a quizzical expression.

"Why would I jump out of the car while it was moving?' Oliver asked.

Jonah looked back at his passenger. "You wouldn't," he finally said.

"No," Oliver agreed. "I wouldn't want to get hurt. Jumping out of the car would be dangerous."

"Yes it would," Jonah finally agreed. "Let's both remember that. I won't jump out either. Now get in the car."

Oliver obeyed Jonah's command, and carefully buckled himself into the passenger seat. Jonah turned on the ignition, and pulled his Malibu off Easley Avenue. The drive to Kershaw's took less than five minutes, and only that long because the Clayburn Borough Council must have gotten a deal on stop signs by the dozen. There was a small employee parking lot behind the store, and Jonah parked next to the store's beat-up aging white pick-up truck held together with rust and duct tape. He followed Oliver into the shop, a ramshackle affair with old wooden shelves lined up wherever they would fit and supplies piled high. Inventory had been collecting since the first day the store opened and apparently did not have an expiration date.

At the counter stood Harvey Kershaw, a white-haired man looking all of his 78 years. Deep lines creased his face, and his body was lean and slightly bent from years of manual labor. Harvey looked over his thick glasses to get a better look at Jonah.

"So I hear you're looking for a job?" the old man said.

"Yes," Jonah acknowledged. "I just moved into town."

"So I hear," Harvey said. "Can you drive stick?"

Jonah wasn't quite ready for that question, so it took him a moment.

"It's been a while," he admitted. "But I drove a five-speed Mustang in my teens."

Harvey laughed so hard his slight frame rolled.

"Well, that old vehicle back there isn't any Mustang," he said. "But I need someone who can make deliveries with it. I'm getting too damn old."

"I can do that."

Harvey looked Jonah over.

"I only have four rules for my employees," he said. "First, show up for work. Second, do your job. Third, be courteous to our customers and your fellow workers. And fourth, don't steal."

"That sounds easy enough," Jonah said.

"You'd think so," Harvey said. "But I've had a lot of fellas couldn't follow them. The last guy had a particularly hard time following the fourth rule. Found out he always gave himself a tip on Fridays so he could go out drinking."

"I don't drink," Jonah said. "so you don't have to worry about that."

"Fair enough," Harvey said. "Helen Paskiel vouches for you, and if I don't listen to her, there will be hell to pay. I don't need her barking in my ear. Hard of hearing already from the Mrs. working it over for the past 50 years. So are you ready to start?"

Jonah paused. "Mr. Kershaw," he said. "Before you hire me, you should probably know about my past medical issues."

Harvey waved his arm dismissively. "I've already heard about them," he said. "Do you think old Helen can keep her mouth shut when she has some good gossip? She probably gave me a better rundown than your doctors could."

Oh great, Jonah thought, *the whole town must know by now.*

The old man came over and put his arm on Jonah's shoulder. "Listen," he said. "I gave Oliver a chance when no one else would, and I haven't regretted it one minute. And then there's my dear Katie..."

Harvey looked around. "Where the devil is she?" the old man asked no one in particular.

"I'm coming, I'm coming," a female voice said from the back room. "Don't you remember you sent me upstairs to get this case of towels?"

"Oh, that's right," Harvey said. "My memory is still good, just short."

Katie emerged and set the case down on the nearby counter. "Hi," she said, extending her hand. "I guess you've already figured out I'm Katie. You must be Jonah."

Jonah nodded. "Nice to meet you."

As he shook her hand, he noticed a slight quiver. Katie could have been anywhere from her late 20s to mid-30s, with shoulder length brown hair. She was pretty in a small town-sort of way, with little make-up except lipstick. But what Jonah noticed most was her eyes. They were big, blue eyes, but they had a sad, faraway look, as if she was gazing right past you while staring at you at the same time.

"I have MS," she said bluntly and unexpectedly.

Jonah stood dumbfounded, his mind not quite catching up to what he heard.

"What...," he said dumbly.

"Multiple sclerosis," Katie said matter-of-factly. "You'll find out soon enough, so I figured I might as well tell you right up front."

Jonah had to think for a minute. Multiple sclerosis – a disabling disease of the brain, spinal cord and central nervous system. In MS, the immune system attacks the protective sheath that covers nerve fibers and causes communication problems between the brain and the rest of the body. Much more prevalent in women and typically developing in one's 20s and beyond, symptoms include numbness and tingling, loss of balance, weakness in one or more limbs, and blurred or double vision. There is no cure for this progressive disease, though attacks can be mitigated somewhat by medication. Recent medical advances had helped those with MS live to near normal life spans. Jonah had learned about MS much as others in school and through online articles, but never really had met anyone with the disease.

"I'm sorry," Jonah said weakly.

"It's OK," Katie said. "It is what it is. Some days are a bitch, but there's not much I can do about it. I take my meds and hope for the best."

"Fair enough," Jonah said, then decided to be just as upfront as well. "If it makes any difference, I'm crazy."

"So I've heard," Katie said, looking at Jonah intensely. "You don't look crazy."

"Trust me, I am," Jonah said. "But you know how it is. I take my meds and hope for the best."

Jonah smiled. Katie smirked.

"Fair enough," she mimicked.

By now, Harvey and Oliver, who had been working in another part of the store, had heard enough.

"OK, enough of the chit chat," Harvey said. "Are you going to start working or not?"

"Does that mean I'm hired?"

"Unless you want to fill out an application form," Harvey said

66

sarcastically. "Not that I know if we have any."

"Well, in that case, I'm happy to accept your offer," Jonah laughed. "When do you want me to start?"

"Right now," Harvey answered. "I got a delivery that's got to get out to the old Stanton place off Route 93 by noon. We have to get the vehicle loaded up and out of here. It doesn't go as fast as it used it. Of course, neither do I."

So began Jonah's first job in any number of years. His bouts of hospitalization and his frequent lapses off his medication had made him an untrustworthy and undependable employee. Manic episodes following long bouts of near catatonic depression were hardly conducive to employment. A steady job was the least of his concerns. Only in the past year or two had Jonah achieved enough stability to even think about living an independent life. Still, on the rare occasion when he searched for work, he typically found potential employers skittish and even fearful about hiring someone with such a checkered past. Many times, Jonah believed it would be impossible for him to ever find a job. But in Clayburn, a town that most of civilization had passed by, he was given a clean slate and new opportunities. He was determined to make the best of it.

His first task, however, gave him fleeting doubts of the wisdom of accepting this position. Mr. Kershaw's "vehicle" offered a punishing ride, to say the least. Jonah was pretty sure whatever shocks the old truck had ever possessed had blown out years before. The steering wheel had enough play to cover a baseball field, and the clutch was a tricky affair that likely needed replacement many miles ago. Nor was the ride equipped with GPS, and Jonah's lack of knowledge of the area would likely send him on a circuitous route.

"Nothing to it," Harvey said. "You don't need any new-fangled GPS to find the place. You turn left at the big maple tree, then bear right at the big pothole in the road."

Harvey's directions proved to be just as imprecise as Jonah feared. As he drove into the country, Jonah quickly discovered just how unhelpful they were if you're weren't familiar with the landscape.

"This whole county is nothing but maple trees and potholes," he said. "With a bunch of pine trees and coal dust thrown in for good measure."

Nevertheless, Jonah eventually found his destination after spotting an especially big maple tree and a pothole that encompassed nearly the entire road. The "Old Stanton Place" turned out to now be owned by the Lockhart family, ever since Bill Stanton had passed away three years earlier. But it would likely be known as the Stanton place for a good deal more time until the Lockharts further established themselves in the area. The new owners had turned the tract into a fledgling horse farm. Jonah unloaded the supplies into the barn, wished the family well, and headed to Clayburn.

Remarkably, Jonah found his way back to Kershaw's, with only one or two wrong turns.

Nobody tells you how to get back, Jonah thought. *I hope they send out a search party if I fall into an old coal mine.*

He pulled into the lot at the store and turned off the truck, accompanied by a loud backfire and a puff of smoke.

"I have to get this son of a bitch tuned up whether the old man likes it or not," Jonah muttered.

Jonah stayed at the store that afternoon, learning what he could. He found that Mr. Kershaw had a surprisingly brisk business. Despite the odd lot of employees he had assembled, the shop ran amazingly efficiently. Between Oliver, Katie and the owner himself, they seemed to know where everything was located, even though there was no apparent order that Jonah could discern. The breadth of inventory was truly incredible. Kershaw's had been open for more than 50 years, and the store's contents had been collected – purchased would have been too precise a term – over those five decades plus. Jonah had some fits learning to use the decades-old cash register, but at least Mr. Kershaw had graduated to having a credit card machine sometime in the last few years.

Not going to even bring up Paypal, Jonah thought. *Or Apple Pay.*

Eventually a customer came in and walked down several aisles of the store, picking out a box of carpenter nails, a pack of AA batteries, several packs of light bulbs, and a can of Rustoleum spray paint.

"Why don't you take care of Clarence on your own," Mr. Kershaw said softly to Jonah.

The customer, a balding, gray-haired man, came up to the counter and laid down his merchandise, looking over his black-rimmed glasses at Jonah.

"You're new here," he said matter-of-factly.

"I am," Jonah answered. "My name is Jonah."

"I'm Clarence," he said, shaking Jonah's hand then glancing over at his boss. "Now let me give you some advice, son. You keep an eye on old Harvey over there. If he cheats his employees the way he cheats his customers, you'll probably be paying him to work here."

The customer paused.

"Ain'a, Harvey?" Clarence said loudly, guffawing as he looked over at Mr. Kershaw.

"Whatever you say, Clarence," Harvey answered. "Funny thing is, you keep coming back. You have for 40 years. So I've been cheating you for a very long time and you don't seem to mind."

Harvey and Clarence had a good laugh. Meanwhile, Jonah looked over at Katie.

"Ain'a?" he mouthed silently.

Katie waved at him dismissively and covered her mouth to hide her laugh.

Jonah rang Clarence up, collected the cash and dispensed appropriate change.

"I'll see you around, son," Clarence said. "Despite what everyone says, Harvey's not a bad guy."

Harvey waved goodbye to Clarence.

"Get the hell out of here before they start believing your crap," he said. "I'll see you later."

Clarence went out the front door and Harvey returned to the back. Jonah stared at Katie.

"Ain'a?" he asked. "What the heck is an ain'a?"

Katie laughed.

"You obviously aren't from around here," she said, smiling.

"Obviously not."

"You'll get used to it," Katie said. "It's a common expression up here. Heck, you'll likely end up using it yourself."

"I'm sure I won't," Jonah said.

"We'll see."

At the end of the day, the three employees cleaned and straightened up as best as the store allowed. Jonah took the broom to the floor, but there were only so many generations of dirt that could be collected in one attempt. Finally, the store was deemed "good enough" and the work day was over. Mr. Kershaw followed the three out, then locked the store behind him. Harvey lived right next to the store, as he had since the place opened.

"See you all tomorrow," the old man said, then turned to Jonah.

"You coming back?" he asked.

"Yes, sir," Jonah affirmed. "You can't get rid of me that easily."

Mr. Kershaw chuckled.

"That's what I've been telling Mrs. Kershaw ever since we got married," he said. "Doesn't stop her from trying."

Jonah watched as Mr. Kershaw climbed the steps to his house, then he and Oliver headed toward the car. Jonah turned toward Katie to say goodbye and recognized she was having a bad moment, moving haltingly and unevenly.

"Do you need a ride?" he asked.

"I just live a block and a half away," she objected mildly.

"Maybe, but it looks like you could use some help," Jonah said, moving toward his co-worker. "Oliver, can you help me get Katie to the car?"

"OK," Oliver said tentatively. In truth, Oliver wasn't much assistance. He was far too nervous to actually touch Katie, even by the arm, but he did manage to walk beside her as Jonah helped her along. She climbed in the front seat while Oliver settled in the back. Jonah drove the short distance carefully, and then assisted Katie into her apartment.

"Are you going to be OK?" Jonah asked, scanning Katie up and down with concern.

"Yes," Katie assured him. "I just need to lay down for a while. I over-did it today. Then when I walked outside, the sun hit me. Sometimes, I'm really sensitive to light."

Jonah watched her dubiously, but Katie assured him again she would be back to normal with some rest.

"Give me your cell phone," he said. When she did, he programmed his number into her phone.

"Call me if you need me," he said.

"I promise," Katie assured him. "I'm sure I'll feel better once I lay down for a bit. But if I need help, you'll be the first person I'll call."

Jonah nodded and turned to return to his car.

"Not," Katie added.

Jonah whirled around and caught a glimmer of a sly smile, despite her discomfort.

"Just kidding," she said, then disappeared into the apartment.

Jonah chuckled, then returned to his car and climbed back into his Malibu. Oliver assumed his place in the front seat once again.

"She didn't look so good," Jonah said as they pulled away.

"She has her good moments and her bad," Oliver said. "I think she likes you."

Jonah rolled his eyes.

"Shut up," he said.

"What did I say wrong?" Oliver asked.

Jonah looked at Oliver thoughtfully.

"Nothing," he finally said. "You didn't say anything wrong."

Jonah shifted the car into gear, and drove home. After he parked, said his goodbyes to Oliver and walked into the house, he noticed the cushions on his sofa had been stacked up one on top of the other.

"If you're really a ghost, you've got to do better than that," he yelled into the air. "That doesn't scare me."

Jonah looked over at the clock, which was flashing 3:33 a.m.

"Guess I didn't check it this morning" he said. "I have to see if Kershaw's has a clock in that store somewhere that actually works," he said.

CHAPTER 11

Jonah and Oliver stopped by Katie's apartment the next morning and were pleased to find she was feeling much better. Jonah offered Katie a ride to work, which she accepted. The three were readying the store for opening when Harvey came bolting through the front door. A look of mild agitation creased across his face.

"I have to take the Mrs. to the doctor this morning," Mr. Kershaw said. "Her arthritis is acting up again and she's as cranky as a constipated bear. I can't take much more of that. I'd have to start drinking before lunch time. You three take care of the store while I get Mrs. Kershaw and her joints calmed down. No one will be happy until then."

Before anyone could answer, Harvey was back out the door. A few minutes later, Jonah saw him and his wife drive by the store – in a late-model, dark Adriatic blue Cadillac XTS.

"What the hell?" Jonah said in surprise. "We have to drive that piece of junk out back and he's driving a luxury sedan?"

Katie and Oliver laughed.

"Why do you think he lets you do the deliveries?" Katie asked sarcastically. "Harvey drives in style. He can't stand to drive that truck either."

"That old man is pretty damn shrewd," Jonah concluded.

"Yes," Katie agreed, "but Mrs. Kershaw keeps him in line."

"That's obvious," Jonah agreed. "Her and her arthritic joints."

Either the wife's doctor's appointment was a near all-day affair, or one or the other decided they had additional chores – most likely Mrs. Kershaw – but the three employees didn't see Harvey again until near closing time. Business was steady but not nearly as busy as the day before, and Jonah, Katie and Oliver had more time to socialize.

"So let me get this straight," Jonah said, looking back and forth at Oliver and Katie. "You're autistic, you have MS, and I'm clinically crazy. Does the old man collect misfits or what?"

"I think he's on some kind of mission," Katie replied. "He likes to give chances to people who wouldn't get one anywhere else."

"He's had others like us?" Jonah asked.

"Not too many," Katie smiled. "And definitely none like you."

Jonah smirked.

"Of course not," he shot back. "I'm one of a kind."

"I know," Katie said. "A legend in your own mind. But anyway, Harvey has had a few others. Some didn't work out. Some did. Some moved on. Now it's us three."

"Harvey does have his quirks," Jonah said.

"I think he's just a nice man inside," Oliver added. "He just doesn't always like to show it."

"He does have a big heart," Jonah concluded, resting his arms on the antique sales counter. "And he's collected quite a crew here. We're a real freak show."

"Hey," Katie mockingly objected, "I think I represent that."

"That's not very nice," Oliver said straight-faced.

"It's not if someone else calls us that," Jonah explained. "But it's OK for us to call ourselves that in fun. We should be proud that we're different. It's like a badge of honor."

It took Oliver a minute or two to sort through that logic, and his facial contortions worked their way from confusion through satisfaction. For a moment, he was tempted to check his shirt for a badge of honor, then resisted. Finally, Oliver cracked a wide smile and flapped his arms. "All right then," he said. "The Freak Show it is."

The young man paused and pointed a finger upward, holding that pose through his thought. "I'm not sure Mom will like that title."

"Don't worry," Jonah said. "I'll explain it to her. She'll understand."

The three of them went about their business, continuing to serve customers as they stopped by to purchase a variety of items. Kershaw's clientele included men and women, from the retired doing household chores, to employees of nearby businesses doing maintenance, to a few teenagers working on cars or other projects. Noon came and went, and the afternoon waned. The temperature outside reached the high 80s with muggy humidity, and Harvey's combination of a rickety old window air conditioner and a fan proved to be inadequate for the job. Katie finally hooked up several additional fans to keep them as cool as possible. Jonah took the slowdown in business to root through some of Kershaw's inventory, eventually finding a couple of cookbooks and a replacement clock for the unreliable one sitting in his living room.

"How much are these?" he asked Katie.

"I'll put them on your tab," she answered. "Harvey will figure it out on payday. You cook?"

"Not well," Jonah admitted. "That's why I need to learn."

As the end of the day neared and the heat and humidity brought customer traffic to a halt, the mood inside the shop became more philosophical.

"So how does it feel to be autistic?" Jonah asked Oliver, suddenly turning serious.

The young man gave the question a good minute or two of thought, as he worked to find the words to express his real feelings. It was difficult for Oliver to talk about himself.

"I don't really know any different," Oliver said. "I've always been this way, so I don't know what it's like to not be autistic. Mom used to worry that I didn't have many friends, that I didn't get invited to parties, and that I spent a lot of time alone in my room. But I like it that way. It takes work to be near people. A lot of work. I'm very happy with who I am. I'm comfortable this way. I can't be anyone else but myself."

"Sometimes it takes work to be near people even if you're not autistic," Jonah observed. "Trust me, I know the feeling. You're not alone, my friend."

Oliver smiled shyly, like someone had just shared with him a secret. Then Jonah turned toward Katie.

"So what about you?" Jonah asked. "What's it like to be the girl at the party with MS?"

"I hate MS," the woman said. "I was only diagnosed three years ago. Up until then, I lived a normal life. You never get used to feeling shitty all the time."

Katie wiped a tear from her eye as a flood of emotion overcame her.

"I lost my boyfriend, I lost most of my friends. I can't do what normal people do," she continued. "I never know when I'm going to have an attack. Sometimes I go all night without sleeping. Sometimes I can't stand to be in the sun. It's a bitch, and it's only going to get worse. Eventually, it will kill me. I just don't know whether that will be sooner or later."

Jonah tried to think of something to say and came up empty. He felt true empathy for Katie, obviously in pain with no escape from her daily turmoil.

"I'm sorry," he finally uttered weakly.

Katie shrugged.

"Not your fault," she said. "You didn't give it to me."

The young woman then eyed Jonah more deliberately.

"So what about you, hotshot?" Katie asked. "Stroll in here like the big-city boy in a small town. What's it like to be mentally ill?"

Jonah considered that question for a long time. It was not the first time he pondered his fate. He looked around the store, but no answer was coming from Kershaw's eclectic collection of inventory. Finally, he spoke quietly.

"You know I'm named after the biblical figure Jonah," he said. "That's very appropriate. Having mental illness is like being caught in the belly of a whale. It's dark, you're disoriented, you're scared, and there's no way out. You hope and you pray, but nothing does any good. You don't know how you got there, and you don't know which way to go. Every direction you turn, it's darkness. You lose control and you lose your way. Eventually, the darkness becomes your new normal. This is the way things are supposed to be, you tell yourself. So you go deeper and deeper, losing all sense of reality. The things that aren't real become real to you. Those things that are real don't matter. You create your own reality, which has nothing to do with what's actually happening around you. The deeper you get, the crazier you become. And the more dangerous to yourself and those around you."

Jonah paused, searching for the next words and not coming up with any.

"How do you get back out?" Katie asked, absorbed by Jonah's description.

"Only by force," Jonah answered. "You can't get back out by yourself. You need help to compel the whale to give you up. And the whale fights back. Hard."

Jonah looked up, only to see Oliver with a look of total confusion on his face.

"Where's the whale?" Oliver asked. "You got that close to a whale? And why did you let him swallow you? And how in the world did you get out of the belly of a whale?"

Jonah chuckled, and warmly looked at his friend.

"I'll explain it to you on the way home, buddy," Jonah said. "It wasn't a real whale."

Oliver nodded, knowing that Jonah meant what he said. Oliver didn't instinctively trust too many people outside of his mother, but he had quickly formed a bond with his new neighbor. Oliver was able to look past Jonah's past and his weaknesses. Somehow, in the world as Oliver saw it, Jonah had become his reliable friend and companion, someone who accepted him as he was with no judgement.

The three did a few more chores, but Jonah wasn't done with his questions for the day. As he worked at re-stocking shelves, he spotted Katie across the aisle.

"So what is it about living around here?" Jonah asked.

"What do you mean?" Katie asked.

"I don't know exactly," Jonah said. "I can't really describe it. But I've noticed that living here is different from living anywhere else I've been. The people are different. The towns are different. Even the land is different."

Katie stopped what she was doing and peered at Jonah. She could tell he wasn't asking the question mockingly.

"The Coal Region has a unique history," Katie explained. "It prospered on the blood and the sweat and the resolve of the coal miners. But there was animosity and distrust between the miners and the mine owners from day one. Mine owners got rich on the backs and lives of generations of workers who barely made enough to survive. People died in mine accidents and of disease, miners were barely paid and cheated at that. Their families were cast out of their homes once the miner was no longer useful. Mine managers were murdered in revenge, suspected union organizers were hung..."

"Wait," Jonah said. "What? Murdered? Hung? Where?"

"Not too far from here," Katie said. "Some in Jim Thorpe, some in Pottsville. There were others. Violence was a way of life for a long time. You never heard of the Molly Maguires?"

Jonah thought about the question.

"I've been to a bar called the Molly Maguires," he laughed. "Back in my drinking days, of course."

"Not the same thing," Katie said with a smirk. "Though I'm not surprised."

"Wait, I drove by a restored village a couple of weeks ago when I first got here," Jonah said. "Supposedly a movie about the Molly Maguires was filmed there."

"Eckley Miners' Village," Katie said. "Now you're getting closer."

"So who were the Molly Maguires?" Jonah asked.

"The Mollies were an Irish organization in the 1800s," Katie explained. "To their supporters, they fought for fair wages and safe working conditions for the miners. But to their detractors, they were thugs who murdered any number of mine supervisors in a decade of terror."

"So what's the truth?" Jonah asked.

"Who knows?" Katie said. "Probably a little of both. Depends on who you ask."

"So OK," Jonah persisted. "But that was generations ago. What does that have to do with today?"

"The spirit of the Molly Maguires – and the divide between the haves and the have nots – is still felt here today," Katie continued. "Almost every family here has a relative that was killed in a mine accident or suffered a fatal case of Black Lung Disease. They've seen the coal industry die off and the heartache it caused to so many towns and so many people. King Coal was both their livelihood and their nemesis. They lived and died by the same sword. The hated it and survived by it at the same time. So that fierce, independent, defiant, distrusting-until-you-show-me attitude... there's a long history to that. A lot of people have never left the Coal Region. That's why it's The Bubble. Many people who live here never leave the confines of The Bubble."

Jonah thought about that for a minute.

"Don't we need an ain'a right about now?" he finally asked.

Katie gave Jonah an exaggerated smirk, then threw a towel at him.

"Shut up," Katie said. "Ain'a that."

A few minutes later, Harvey's Cadillac came growling down the road. After parking the car and helping his wife back into the house, he came down and closed up shop for the day.

"You all go home," Harvey said. "Mrs. Kershaw has me worn out, and the day isn't done yet. I'm sure I'll be rubbing her feet tonight."

No one argued, but Jonah's face curled in a knot envisioning that picture. Jonah drove Katie and Oliver home. Katie hopped out of the car, stared back at Jonah for a moment or two and appeared ready to say something. She shook her head as if changing her mind, turned and walked into her house. The rest of the trip, Jonah did his best to explain the concept of a metaphor to someone who lived his life thinking in very concrete terms.

Jonah spent his afternoon and evening relaxing. He pulled out his laptop and did some online reading about the contentious and controversial history of the Molly Maguires and the coal barons. He was struck by the divergent views of writers and historians, even to this day. And he began to understand the unique nature of Northeast Pennsylvania, one that still bore the scars of its past in an oddly proud way.

The Coal Region grew up in conflict, Jonah thought, *and some of that still endures. It likely will be here for many more years.*

Jonah finally settled in. The house was quiet that night.

Too quiet, Jonah thought. *The proverbial calm before the storm.*

CHAPTER 12

Jonah carefully scanned Dr. Sheffield's office. Still nothing out of place, the office immaculately clean.

Always the same, he thought, *nothing ever changes. The model of stability and consistency while her patients get tossed and turned by their own minds.*

"So you moved, you got a job, and you made some new friends," Dr. Sheffield said. "You've made quite a number of changes in your life recently."

Jonah squirmed in his seat. Even though his psychiatrist didn't sound apprehensive in her statement, he was pretty sure there was some inference of misgiving. Dr. Sheffield was always suspicious of too much change too soon in her patients' lives.

"I feel more normal than I have for a long time when I'm at Kershaw's," Jonah responded. "I've never felt more accepted by a group of people since..." Jonah paused. "Since I don't know when. Since I was a kid. Since before all this started."

"I understand that," Dr. Sheffield acknowledged. "It's not easy being accepted when you're battling your own issues. I just want to make sure you process all the changes in your life appropriately."

Jonah again shifted in the too cushy chair and looked at the various photos and framed degrees on the wall. The degrees were about the only personal information one could glean about the psychiatrist. Jonah again noted all the photos were generic scenes of various destinations around the world. No indication that Dr. Sheffield had actually visited any of them. Jonah figured it would do no good to ask.

"I understand your concern," he finally said. "But really, I'm good..."

Dr. Sheffield made some notes in her ubiquitous notepad. Her facial expression remained unconvinced.

"Of course," Jonah added, purposely nonchalantly, "the house I bought is haunted."

Dr. Sheffield stopped writing in mid-sentence. She shut her notebook and raised her head to stare directly at Jonah, who was debating whether to smile or not.

"Excuse me?" she asked abruptly.

Jonah laughed.

"Well, at least that's what I've heard," Jonah continued. "Some of the towns' folk believe the old lady who used to live there never left."

"And what do you think?" Dr. Sheffield pressed.

"I have to admit I've seen some strange things," Jonah said. "Boxes knocked over, cushions piled up on top of one another. And the clock in the living room always stops at 3:33 in the morning."

"Perhaps you need a new clock," Dr. Sheffield said, with only a hint of sarcasm in her voice.

"Already thought of that, doc," Jonah countered. "Bought a new one, but the same thing happened. Maybe that's when they change shifts at the electric company."

"Jonah," the psychiatrist said in her most clinical voice, "I don't want to sound alarmist, but are you sure these things are happening, or are you imagining they are? You know they don't sound very serious, but sometimes that's how hallucinations begin."

Jonah stared at Dr. Sheffield. Dr. Sheffield stared back. The unstated contest lasted several seconds, before Jonah turned away. Dr. Sheffield tried to maintain an objective, non-judgmental gaze. Part of her had much more concern than she indicated to Jonah. Better to over-react than wait too long and find out this was the beginning of a much more serious episode than it initially appeared.

"Dr. Sheffield," Jonah finally said, breaking the silence. "I may be crazy, but I'm not crazy about this. I don't know if the house is haunted, honestly. Some people have told me it is, some people have told me it isn't. Some things that have happened. Well, maybe I just didn't stack the boxes very well. But other things – I'm pretty sure I didn't pile all the sofa cushions on top of one another for fun before I went to work. So unless someone is breaking into my house to just re-arrange the furniture, I'm not sure what's going on."

The psychiatrist studied Jonah carefully. This was delicate territory, and she needed to proceed cautiously.

"You know, Jonah," she said. "The scientific community generally does not believe that ghosts exist."

"Well," Jonah said in his best cynical voice, "most of them probably don't have one living with them."

Dr. Sheffield did her professional best not to frown, but she wasn't sure she fully succeeded. Jonah realized his doctor was not appreciating his sarcasm.

"Look," Jonah finally said. "I'm not saying the place is haunted. I haven't seen any spooks in white sheets floating around. And no, before you ask, none of my own demons have made an appearance. I'm just telling you what the neighbors think and what I've seen. Maybe someone is pranking me and I don't know it. Who knows?"

"OK," Dr. Sheffield said, becoming a little calmer. "I'm glad you're staying rational about this. But I want you to be careful about internalizing anything your friends say. Maybe you need to be a little more careful about spending time with them."

"I work with them," Jonah chuckled. "And besides, one of them is autistic, another has MS. None of us – myself included – are exactly banging on all eights. Give us a little space, Doc."

"All right," the psychiatrist finally backed down, and spent a few minutes reviewing Jonah's medications and discussing whether any changes were necessary. While she considered some modifications, she ultimately stayed the course. While Dr. Sheffield was somewhat concerned, there wasn't enough evidence to warrant any significant re-appraisal – yet. But she needed to watch for any additional signs of degradation.

"See you again in three weeks, Doc," Jonah finally said, lifting himself off the chair and heading out. He stopped before he opened the door and turned back. "And don't worry. I know that's your job, but

I'm not falling off the cliff."

She nodded and Jonah left the office.

As soon as the door closed, Dr. Sheffield re-opened her notebook and made detailed observations. She wanted as much documentation as possible if this was the first step in yet another breakdown. Jonah had a long and checkered past, and nothing could be taken for granted, even if on the surface, this sounded like a lot of town gossip and overactive imaginations. Before she left that night, she input her notes into her PC. She needed to watch Jonah's actions over the next few appointments carefully.

As Jonah walked out to his car, he could hear a voice, distant but distinct, in his head.

"She doesn't trust you," the voice said. "Never has, never will. You can't trust her."

"Shut up," Jonah said. "No one asked you. And your opinion isn't wanted or needed."

CHAPTER 13

Hot summer days and weeks move laconically in much of small-town America, and Clayburn and the Coal Region were no different. Time seems to takes a little longer to move when there's no mad rush to complete a task or reach a destination.

Nevertheless, between work and the continuing task of finishing the set-up of his house, Jonah found the weekend arrived relatively quickly. Kershaw's closed at noon on Saturday, so Jonah decided he needed to give himself a history lesson about the area now that Katie had piqued his curiosity.

"I think I'm going to find out more about King Coal and the Molly Maguires," he said to Oliver. "I'm going to Jim Thorpe. Do you want to come along?"

"I better not," Oliver said. "Mom likes to go to Mass on Saturday night. I don't want to mess up her routine."

"*She* has a routine?" Jonah said incredulously. "She doesn't get that from you, does she?"

"I don't think so," Oliver answered.

"All right," Jonah said. "Go to your Mass. Say a prayer for me."

"I always do," Oliver answered. "Actually, I usually say several for you."

"Good. I need them."

Oliver walked into his house. Mrs. Paskiel met him at the door with Daffodil yipping at her heels. Mrs. Paskiel waved to Jonah as he pulled away. He stopped at the gas station down the street and filled his Malibu, then headed out to explore the mystique and bloody history of Jim Thorpe. He turned on his radio and classic rock filled the cabin.

We all came out to Montreux
On the Lake Geneva shoreline
To make records with a mobile
We didn't have much time
Frank Zappa and the Mothers
Were at the best place around
But some stupid with a flare gun
Burned the place to the ground

Smoke on the water, fire in the sky
Smoke on the water

"Nothing like a little Deep Purple to get us started," Jonah said as he hummed the song's famous four-note riff. Soon, he had found his way to Route 209 and threaded the sides of hills and mountains to reach his destination.

Formerly known as Mauch Chunk, Jim Thorpe is a beautiful historic town of about 5,000 people cut out the side of a mountain and teeming with small gift shops and specialty stories. It also serves as the county seat for Carbon County, so the tourist-oriented commercial district is intermixed with attorney's offices and the local court house.

Founded in 1818, the town thrived for decades as a railroad and coal-shipping center, with an advantageous location along the Lehigh River. Prior to the development of the railroad system, coal was transported down the river through barges and an elaborate system of locks. Mauch Chunk also served as a popular 19th Century tourist destination. For a time, it was one of the wealthiest municipalities in the country. But Mauch Chunk, whose name was derived from the term *Mawsch Unk*, or "Bear Place," in the language of the native Munsee-Lenape Delaware peoples, became collateral damage of the slow demise of the coal industry. By the mid-20th Century, the town leaders were searching for a new economic driver.

Enter the saga of Jim Thorpe one of the most renowned athletes of the early 1900s. The first Native American to win an Olympic Gold

Medal, Thorpe also played professional football and baseball. He was stripped of his Olympic medals after it was discovered he played two years of semi-professional baseball prior to competing in the 1912 Olympics, a decision that was heartbreaking to the athlete. The International Olympic Committee restored his medals in 1983, thirty years after his death. Thorpe was also named the greatest athlete of the first 50 years of the 20th Century by The Associated Press, and he was part of the inaugural class inducted into the Pro Football Hall of Fame.

After Jim Thorpe's death in 1953 from heart failure following a long battle with alcoholism, Thorpe's widow and third wife, Patricia, was angered when the government of his native state of Oklahoma refused to erect a suitable memorial in his honor. A number of communities around the country made offers to commemorate Thorpe, but the most attractive came from the boroughs of Mauch Chunk and its neighbor, East Mauch Chunk. It has been suggested by none other than Jim Thorpe's son that Patricia's motivation was less about ensuring her husband's legacy than it was lining her own bank account. Considering the primary motivation of the borough was to revitalize its own fledgling economy, this was clearly a deal where everyone followed the money.

Mauch Chunk and East Mauch Chunk merged, and renamed their new municipality Jim Thorpe in the legendary athlete's honor. Shortly thereafter, the newly minted municipality obtained Jim Thorpe's remains from his wife and constructed a monument, which still stands today. The memorial contains his tomb, two statues of him as an athlete, and historical markers that describe his life story. It sits on mounds of soil imported from Thorpe's native Oklahoma and from Stockhom Olympic Stadium, where he won his Olympic medals. Perhaps the only remotely close link Jim Thorpe has to his namesake town is that he began his sports career about 100 miles southwest of the location while attending the Carlisle Indian Industrial School in Carlisle, Pennsylvania, not far from Harrisburg, the Pennsylvania state capital.

While Patricia Thorpe delivered her husband's remains, she was unable to fulfill the second part of her deal. Supposedly, she had met with then National Football League Commissioner Bert Bell, and together, they had designs to locate the Pro Football Hall of Fame in Jim Thorpe. However, Bell died before the supposed deal could come to fruition, and the NFL chose Canton, Ohio instead. There was also talk of construction of a hospital specializing in cancer and heart issues – Jim Thorpe suffered from both – but that also never materialized.

Nevertheless, renamed with a new purpose, Jim Thorpe slowly became the tourist attraction that it has developed into today. It didn't come as quickly as town officials had hoped, but boutique shops and historic attractions now line the main street. The Lehigh River still runs through the bottom of the valley in which Jim Thorpe sits, attracting a variety of water enthusiasts. Nearby, the Glen Onoko Falls – three falls located near Jim Thorpe on state game lands – offers both natural beauty and imminent danger. A fatality occurs there nearly every year due to the precarious paths around the falls.

The story, however, doesn't quite end there. In addition to tourism, the name change and the arrangement negotiated with Thorpe's widow has sparked controversy.

On June 24, 2010, one of Jim Thorpe's sons, Jack Thorpe, sued the town for the return of his father's remains. Jack Thorpe cited the Native American Graves Protections and Repatriation Act, which is designed to return Native American artifacts to their tribal homelands. The trial judge ruled in 2011 that Thorpe's son was not due any monetary award, and that for the lawsuit to continue, it would have to be joined by other members of the Thorpe family and the Sac and Fox Nation. Shortly thereafter, Jack Thorpe passed away. Following that, Jim Thorpe's remaining sons and the Sac and Fox Nation of Oklahoma joined the suit. In 2013, the U.S. District Court ruled for the Thorpe family. However, that ruling was reversed by the U.S. Court of Appeals and the U.S. Supreme Court refused to hear the appeal. Thus, for the foreseeable future, Jim Thorpe's remains will stay on the side of a mountain greeting residents and tourists to Jim Thorpe, in Carbon County, Pennsylvania, more than 1,300 miles from his birthplace in

Oklahoma.

Route 209 turned into Broadway as Jonah entered town. Jonah snaked down the hill through the heart of the town, and found the public parking lot by the train station and visitor's center. Parking was six dollars for the day, and the lot was wedged between the Lehigh River and the railroad tracks.

Jonah had learned much of the history of Jim Thorpe before he arrived, though he was sure to pick up additional bits and pieces of it as he traveled through the borough. He was intrigued and enchanted by the small town, as are many visitors traveling there for the first time.

Jonah decided he would start his history lesson at the Asa Packer Mansion, which overlooked the Lehigh River perched on a steep hill in the corner of the town. There was only one way up the incline – walking a series of steps that slowly led to the entrance of the magnificent building.

Might as well give the coal barons the first crack, Jonah thought. *They built the town.*

Asa Packer was an American businessman and founder of Lehigh University. As owner of the Lehigh Valley Railroad Company he pioneered the use of railroad construction and made his fortune transporting coal in rail cars. He later served two terms in the U.S. House of Representatives and unsuccessfully made a bid to win the Democratic nomination for President in 1868, losing to Ulysses S. Grant. His enduring legacy is the Asa Packer Mansion, a classic structure located on a terrace overlooking the Lehigh River. Packer's son, Harry, owned a mansion that was built next door and still also stands proudly today. The Asa Packer Mansion is an extravagant three-story, 17-room home, with the main roof capped by a cupola. The Mansion was named a National Historic Landmark and is owned by the borough of Jim Thorpe. It is financially maintained by the Jim Thorpe Lions Club. The Harry Packer Mansion operates as an Inn. Its claim to fame lies in the oft-told story that its exterior design served as the model for The Haunted Mansion ride located in the Disney theme parks.

Jonah took the guided tour, noted the immense safe located in Asa Packer's office from which his employees were paid each week. He marveled at the elaborate wood work, period furnishings, fine china and lavish construction. He found it fascinating that, during Packer's lifetime, 13 of the 28 millionaires in the United States lived in Mauch Chunk.

But what was the human cost? Jonah wondered. *On how many bodies and lives were those fortunes built? And how much does that matter?*

He was also bemused by Asa Packer's youngest daughter, Mary Packer Cummings, who didn't let her lifelong religious fervor get in the way of a marriage of convenience to allow her to gain control of her family's massive riches. As the last direct heir to the Packer fortune, Mary, as a woman, could not control her millions at the time unless she was married. So she entered into a six-month arrangement and paid the gentleman a nice sum when he abandoned the marriage and re-located to Florida.

Amen, Jonah thought. *And hallelujah!*

Ultimately, Jonah decided the mansion was way out of his price range and moved on.

After the grandiose tour of the mansion, Jonah turned his attention next to 128 West Broadway. He walked up the hill along the various shops on the south side of the street, checking in on a store that specialized in various types of jerky. He drew the line at python, but did try several other samples.

After a short hike, he came to his destination, the Old Jail Museum, a two-story building built in 1869, whose original purpose was to serve as the Carbon County Jail. The fortress-like structure was grandiose and imposing. For Jonah, this was the primary reason he had come to Jim Thorpe. The jail, in many ways, represented the final fate of the Molly Maguires, the end of their reign – whether it be as standard-bearers of the oppressed working class, or as terrorists on a spree of violence. He forked over the seven-dollar admission fee, and a few minutes later, was one of a dozen guests ushered through the building by the tour guide. Jonah thought the aging, white-haired man who walked with a slight limp may have been one of the original residents. The slight remains of an Irish accent in his speech was an ironic bonus to the tour.

The structure contains 72 rooms, including 27 cells, as well as basement dungeon cells that were used for solitary confinement until the facility closed as a prison. The warden's living quarters were spread across the first two floors in the front of the building. The warden's apartment included a large living room and dining room on the first floor, with two bedrooms and a sitting room on the second.

The tour guide then revealed the women's section of the prison, a small sliver of the facility on the second floor with only three cells. The prison could only hold a maximum of six women at any one time.

I guess women didn't commit as many crimes back then, Jonah decided. *Or at least, they didn't get caught as often.*

The tour methodically moved to the men's section of the facility, a cellblock designed as a smaller version of the famed Eastern State Penitentiary in Philadelphia. The men's section was comprised of two stories with a wide central hallway. Jonah noted a gallows standing at the end of the open expanse. The guide led the group through the cell block down a back set of stairs to the dungeon, where solitary confinement kept generations of prisoners in total darkness for up to three days. In the winter, the large coal furnaces in the center of the block – designed to heat the entire prison – broiled the dungeon to near hellish temperatures.

Good evening, Clarice, Jonah thought.

The tour returned upstairs into the cell block and gathered around the gallows. The tour guide then turned his attention to the most infamous episode in the old prison's history.

"From June 1877 through January 1879, this facility was the site of some of the most notorious incidents in the history of American criminal justice," the old man began. "The Irish were driven from their homeland by poverty and famine. Many of them settled here in Northeastern Pennsylvania, only to face extreme prejudice. In shop after shop, they found signs that read, 'No Irish need apply.'"

The tour guide looked at his guests.

"They finally found employment in the coal mines," he said. "But it was hard, dangerous work that paid little. To add insult to injury, they rented their homes from the coal companies, and their pay came in the form of company scrip that could only be used in company stores. There, they paid inflated prices for the goods they needed to survive. Oftentimes, the miner ended up in debt to the coal company, a debt from which it was nearly impossible to escape. And if a miner was killed in an accident, his widow would have three days to move from the company housing or replace her husband with a new employee – inevitably one of her children if she had a son of age – and that age could be as young as seven years old."

The tour guide paused.

"The Molly Maguires were supposedly named after a widow named Molly Maguire, who after being evicted by her landlord led worker movements in the 1840s. The Molly Maguires were formed in 1843, then came to the United States and fought for fair working conditions against the mine barons here in the Coal Region. They were immediately identified as a threat. They were accused of a number of violent incidents that disrupted coal mining operations, though a number of historians now suggest that mining bosses may have staged many of these events themselves. Why? Because the coal barons wanted to maintain firm control of the mines and their employees. They were committed to stamping out any and all signs of potential union activity. Eventually, the Molly Maguires were arrested for murder."

The tour guide paused to clear his throat.

"On June 21, 1877, a day that is now known as the Day of the Rope, four Irish coal miners were hanged at the same time on gallows erected inside this cell block. The gallows that I am standing under are an exact reproduction of those tools of death. Alexander Campbell, Edward Kelly, Michael Doyle and John Donahue all lost their lives," the tour guide continued solemnly. "Thomas Fisher was hanged on March 28, 1878, and James McDonnell and Charles Sharp met their fate on January 14, 1879 on the very same gallows."

The tour guide paused dramatically once again. Jonah looked up to make sure there weren't any bodies dangling above him. In his fascination with the overall story, Jonah missed the similarity in names between one of the convicted Molly Maguires and the former resident of his house.

"Today," he continued, "those who have researched this era believe the Molly Maguires were brought up on false charges and that both the state and federal governments abdicated their powers and responsibilities. The investigation was started by the coal and railroad companies – private corporations. They were conducted by Pinkerton – a private detective agency hired by the coal companies. The arrests were made by the Coal and Iron Police – a private police force. And the cases were prosecuted by private attorneys who were employees of the coal companies. The Commonwealth of Pennsylvania provided only the courtroom and the gallows. Do you think these miners really received a fair trial?"

The two visitors besides Jonah shook their head from side to side in a resounding no. Jonah remained uncommitted.

"All of the men declared their innocence," the tour guide said. "But one went further than that. Before his hanging, Thomas Fisher – who was held in Cell 17 just to your left – rubbed his hand on the dirty floor of his cell, then placed it firmly on the wall. He proclaimed for all to hear, 'There is proof of my words. That mark of mine will never be wiped out. It will remain forever to shame the county for hanging an innocent man.' A short while later, he was hung by the neck until he was dead."

The tour guide paused momentarily. "The handprint was originally thought to be that of Alexander Campbell's, but our additional research has led us to believe that it belonged to Thomas Fisher. Here that handprint remains more than 130 years later."

The tour guide looked across the cell block.

"Past wardens tried to eradicate it by washing it, painting it, even taking down the wall and re-plastering it," he said emphatically. "Despite that, the handprint has survived and remained for generations, a lasting testament to the Molly Maguires' innocence.

"Many years later while this facility was still operating as a prison," the tour guide concluded, "a guest asked the warden if he believed in the handprint. The warden responded, 'I shouldn't believe in the handprint, and neither should you. But there it is. So what do you believe?'"

The old man paused once more.

"This is the end of our guided tour," he concluded. "Feel free to walk about the cell block and explore for yourself. But I leave you with one question: do you believe in the hand print? I know I do."

The tour guide dramatically walked out of the room, leaving the tour to explore. One by one, each guest peered into Cell 17. The handprint was difficult to see, high up on the wall and circled in green. Nevertheless, there was clearly something there. Jonah waited until last, then looked intently through the bars of the cell. He wasn't sure what to believe. Then, a blast of heat pulsated from the cell, with enough force to push Jonah backwards a foot or two. He returned to the cell and looked inside again. He heard an otherworldly laugh, and for a moment, he was sure he saw the hand on the wall clench into a fist. Then, a shadowy figure appeared in the cell. It moved toward Jonah, who jumped back from the closed cell door.

"Jesus," Jonah said.

The rest of the guests were already leaving the cell block and didn't look back. Jonah looked at Cell 17 one more time. Nothing appeared amiss any longer. Jonah turned and followed the cell block to the exit, but he swiveled his head backwards several times.

As Jonah finally stepped into the gift shop, he saw an advertisement for ghost tours held in the Old Jail Museum, with claims of Molly Maguires still roaming the facility.

Jonah decided he had seen enough of that tour already.

CHAPTER 14

After Jonah left the Old Jail Museum, he again wandered among the shops, this time heading downhill on the other side of the street. He finally stopped at 15 Broadway, the home of a wonderfully named shop called The Emporium of Curious Goods. The Emporium was a store that truly lived up to its name, stuffed full with items ranging from tarot cards to incense, gargoyles to Wiccan paraphernalia, spell books to Tibetan humming meditation bowls, Victorian-style lamps to New Age merchandise, dragons, knives, books, and all things Gothic. Jonah checked more than once to make sure he hadn't somehow stepped into Hogwarts.

He wandered through the store, examining various items along the way. He saw a portrait of Barnabus Collins, but didn't stop to study it. He picked up a pen carved in the shape of a dragon, but figured that wouldn't match the décor at Kershaw's.

He was intrigued by a hand-written sign in the middle of the shop with the headline, "Have You Seen Our Cat?" Jonah stopped to read it. As it turned out, a gray cat had been seen on the premises for nearly 100 years by both owners and customers alike. The cat had become so ubiquitous that the shop keeper had named the friendly spirit, Spooky.

Only in the Coal Region would the cats even come back as ghosts, Jonah thought. *Probably started as a white cat coated in coal dust.*

He slowly moved further back into the store, where he encountered yet another hand-written sign. This one told the history of the building, which was as unique as the shop. It was originally built as the Victorian Palace Theater in the early 1920s, but never thrived. Sure enough, as Jonah looked around, a small stage still inhabited the back part of the premises.

Jonah finally selected a Celtic Wall Cross carved out of olive wood. Jonah read the description, which noted that olive wood was native to the Holy Land and had been cultivated since ancient times.

"Well, that should help," he said.

He spent a few more minutes perusing the merchandise, eventually reaching the checkout to make his purchase. He did so, and walked out the shop ready to head back to the car. But a few store fronts down, at a building with a sign that advertised psychic readings, Jonah saw an African-American woman of undefinable age – she could have been anywhere from 30 to 50, Jonah thought – and a mercurial gait as she glided out the front door onto the top step of the entrance. She turned and stared at Jonah, with such intensity as to make him uncomfortable. It was as if she had come out of the shop at that very moment looking for Jonah and fully expecting to find him. But Jonah couldn't pull his eyes away from her.

"You are troubled," she said. "I have been sent here for you."

Jonah looked at her more closely. The woman had a perfectly smooth glass-like complexion, with dark brown eyes that matched the color of her skin. Her hair was hidden in a colorfully wrapped scarf, and she wore a flowing lavender maxi dress. She had an ethereal quality about her that was both beguiling and disturbing at the same time. Jonah was tempted to check if her feet actually hit the floor, or if she merely floated through space.

"And you are?" he finally asked.

"My name is Aadya," she said in a charming accent of indeterminate origin. "And you are Jonah. I am a psychic and I can sense your soul is searching for answers."

Jonah squirmed uncomfortably, not exactly sure how to answer that. He did wonder how she knew his name, but chose not to challenge her.

"Exactly what are you proposing to do about my soul?" he finally asked. "A lot of people have tried to help that over the years, with little success."

"I don't propose to do anything with your soul," Aadya assured him. "But I can help you see your path forward. Would you like a reading?"

"Ummm...," Jonah hesitated. "I've never had one. I don't think..."

Aadya descended the two steps separating her from Jonah, took him gently by the hand and started to lead him through the entrance to the building. Jonah resisted, but only mildly.

"I do the readings in the back of shop," she said. "I have read people's fate and fortunes for many years. I sense my spirit guides have brought me to you. I wasn't scheduled to be here today originally, but I could feel I was needed."

Jonah looked suspiciously at the psychic.

"And how much is your spirit guide telling you to charge me?" he asked cynically.

Aadya stopped and looked at him seriously. Jonah was sure for a moment that her eyes pierced directly into his brain. Then, after a long few moments, a half smile crossed the African-American woman's face.

"You do not worry about the money," Aadya said. "You decide what my words are worth. If you find no value in them, you pay me nothing. Otherwise, you weigh the importance of my message and the significance to your current situation. Pay me accordingly."

Jonah looked at the psychic. She seemed perfectly content and confident.

"Fair enough," he agreed. *This will be a cheap reading,* he thought.

Aadya led him through the front room, which seemed to be designed as a waiting area. A few over-padded chairs and a corner table with a lamp constituted the only furniture in the room, but on the walls hung oversized images of faeries, angels and gargoyles. Aadya led Jonah to the second room in the back of the building. The room was draped in so much fabric that it resembled a large tent. Aadya pulled back one of the curtains and led him into an inner chamber with a small table and two chairs in the middle of the space. Candle light illuminated the chamber, the flickering shadows dancing across the dark-colored fabric. Purple? Grey? Jonah couldn't tell for sure. A moonstone pendulum carved into the shape of a fourteen-point

Merkaba star dangled from the ceiling.

Aadya wordlessly motioned Jonah to sit on the cushion-backed chair to the right. He did so, perusing the items on the table in front of him and laying his hands on the surface. Crystals of various colors were scattered haphazardly on the tablecloth, glistening in the candle light. A deck of tarot cards sat unopened in a box on the table's edge. The smell of incense – *not traditional incense*, Jonah thought, *something sweeter that he couldn't quite identify, perhaps some combination of cherry, vanilla, and violet* – filled the space.

Aadya glided onto her chair in a single motion that appeared effortless and elegant. For a minute or more, Aadya remained silent, alternately studying her subject, gazing into the darkness, or gently touching the crystals on the table. Her eyes appeared interminably deep. Then, she thrust out her right hand and fiercely took Jonah's into her own, squeezing hard enough to make her client grimace. After a few seconds, she again let go and looked into Jonah's eyes, boring into his mind.

"You are troubled, Jonah," the psychic said, "and well you should be."

Jonah squirmed and considered his response.

"I've been troubled for a long time," Jonah finally said. "That's hardly newsworthy."

Aadya pondered her subject once more. Then, she seemed to reach some clarity in her own mind.

"I see four woman surrounding your aura," Aadya continued. "They represent the light and the dark. Some shine brightly, others have dimmed. One I can barely see, but still she remains."

Aadya paused. Jonah remained silent, trying to figure out the identity of the four women to which the psychic could be referring.

"The woman I can barely see is related to you somehow," she continued. "An aunt, a sister... "

"My mother," Jonah interrupted. "She passed away a short time ago. But we had a – a falling out years before that. We were never really close since then. We tried, but we were never able to get over it completely."

"Ah, indeed," Aadya said. "But she still loves you, and she has forgiven you for what you did."

"I know," Jonah said. "She told me."

"She is trying to protect you, but her power is not as strong as the others," Aadya said. "She is powerless against forces much stronger than her."

Aadya went silent for a few moments, focused intently on the crystals on the table.

"There is another," Aadya said. "She is hard to describe. I do not quite understand this. She is part of you, but not part of you. She is real, but not real at the same time. She means you ill. She is intent on her own devices, and you are the vessel to achieve them. Without you, she is nothing. Does this mean anything to you?"

The psychic looked at Jonah, who didn't answer at first.

"I know her," Jonah finally said. "She's the devil I know. She's the demon I hate."

Aadya nodded in understanding and didn't press the issue any further.

"She has been dormant for a significant amount of time," Aadya said. "But she is not so far away as you might hope. She waits. She is on an endless vigil, waiting for the right opportunity. Beware this one. She means you harm."

"No question about that," Jonah muttered. "We've gone more than a few rounds."

"And now comes a third," Aadya said. "You have quite a number of women in your life."

The psychic smiled.

"That's not always necessarily a good thing," Jonah said.

"But here, you have one that is a positive force in your life," Aadya said.

"Have I met her?" Jonah asked, raising his eyebrow.

"Indeed you have," she smiled. "But only recently. You have not yet discovered what you mean to each other. But you will. Of that, I am sure. She is the light in the darkness to which you must turn. She represents your best hope, Jonah Frost. She will be the one loyal to you under all circumstances."

Jonah was still processing that information as Aadya again became silent, gazing into her crystals. She raised her head once again, but this time, her calm visage was shattered by a clearly disturbed look that flashed across her face.

"And then there is the fourth," Aadya said. "She is the real evil here. She is why I was brought her to warn you. She is malevolent with a long and dark past. She also has only just come into your life, but she did all she could to lure you here. She believes she can control your soul and use you as a vessel for ill."

"I don't think I've met her," Jonah said. "I kind of think I would have remembered her."

"You have indeed met her," Aadya insisted. "Though she has not fully revealed herself to you yet. She is not of this Earth. Or perhaps, better to say, she is no longer of this Earth, but she yearns to return and believes you are the perfect channel to accomplish her goal.

"She is trying to block me from seeing her," Aadya added. "She grows more powerful by the moment. Beware, Jonah Frost. She is a danger to you and all around you. She is even more powerful than the malignant spirit of which you are familiar. Are you sure you do not know her?"

Jonah thought back to the strange occurrences at his house and Oliver's earnest warnings. He remained silent.

Aadya stopped suddenly, threw her body back in the chair and grimaced in pain. Her hands came up and cupped her head. It was a dramatic change from the serene expression that Jonah had witnessed earlier. He heard a sizzle, and looked down at the table. One of the crystals was slowly melting.

"How is that possible?" he asked.

"She will attack anyone that stands against her," Aadya screamed in pain. "I am a threat to her plan. Leave, Jonah Frost. You have been forewarned."

"But I haven't paid... "

"Leave now!!!!"

Jonah stood and hurriedly left the enclosure. He looked back and saw Aadya at the opening to the back room staring back at him. The whites of her eyes contrasted with her dark skin, sweat dripping down her face. Jonah was struck by the fear in her eyes. He pulled a fifty-dollar bill out of his wallet and laid it on one of the chairs just inside the entrance.

Jonah walked out the shop and headed back down Broadway to his car. Halfway down the block, he broke into a jog, then to a run.

"Fucking crazy," he said to himself. "I have to get out of here."

He finally reached his Malibu, slammed it into gear, and crossed the railroad tracks back out onto the road. He had to head south on Broadway to return home. He climbed the hill and saw that Aadya had returned to her front step, still in deep distress. Her eyes followed Jonah's car intently up the road. Jonah passed her without looking back and drove out of town, as fast as the winding roads allowed. Aadya stood outside of her shop for many minutes, her gaze peering into the distance in the general direction of Jonah's travels. Silently, she walked back inside, dread filling her thoughts.

For Jonah's part, he drove a good long time to clear his thoughts and convince himself – to one degree or another – that what he had seen was some illusion, hoax, or a figment of his imagination. Whether he truly believed that or not was up for debate. But it was easier than the alternative. He finally had to stop because he was hungry. Jonah grabbed a quick bite to eat at a fast food restaurant, taking a long time to finish his simple meal. Finally, he pointed his car back toward Clayburn.

He returned home as the sun was fading and dusk was emerging. He got out of his car and looked across the street. He saw Oliver standing by his bedroom window upstairs, like a silent sentinel ensuring the safety of his friend and neighbor. He waved, and Oliver gave a tentative wave back. Oliver's eyes went from Jonah to the house, an odd look of concern on his face.

Jonah pulled out a Celtic cross he had bought at the Emporium, and held it into the glow of the streetlight so Oliver could see it clearly.

"See, I'm good," he mouthed, waved goodnight, and walked into the house. The first thing he did was find a nail and hang the cross on the wall.

CHAPTER 15

Jonah slept restlessly that night, flopping from one side of the bed to the other. Aadya's words of warning continued to swirl through his head. It took some time, but he finally fell into a fitful slumber. Nevertheless, something disturbed his sleep the entire night.

Sometime in the midst of the darkness, Jonah dreamed – or at least thought he dreamed – of six children singing:

Ring-a-round the rosie,
A pocket full of posies,
Ashes! Ashes!
We all fall down

He saw them in the distance, through some sort of fog, or perhaps they were just blurry. Jonah couldn't tell. The children formed a ring and moved in a circle, over and over, oblivious to the viewer. Suddenly, they stopped and looked off into the distance in obvious fear. A dark figure – a woman, menacing but her appearance again obscured – came into the picture. She overshadowed the others, threatening them with merely a glare. The children scattered and hurriedly disappeared from view.

The woman stared after them for a moment to ensure the children had left, then seemed to become aware that she was being watched. She turned slowly, then looked directly at Jonah. She moved forward deliberately with clear vile intent. She was a dark figure still. Jonah could not make out exact details, but she was overwhelming in both her size and her malevolence. Hatred oozed through her pores. She came face-to-face with Jonah, seemingly inches from him, and opened her mouth, revealing sharpened teeth...

Jonah sat straight up in bed. The bedroom was dark except for the soft glow of the alarm clock. It read 3:33 a.m. Jonah noticed in the shadows that his bedroom door was open. He was sure he shut it before going to bed. He got up, closed and locked the door and climbed back under the covers, wrapping them around himself tightly.

He lay disturbed anew for some time. Then, exhausted, he finally fell into a deep sleep.

CHAPTER 16

Several hours later, Jonah awoke with a dull headache. Daylight now filtered through the windows into the house. He walked into the kitchen and added two extra-strength Tylenol to his normal medications. He made himself a cup of coffee and sat down in the living room. Glancing over to the clock on the end table, Jonah noticed it was flashing 3:33.

He shook his head.

Every freaking day and night, he thought. *"What's so damn special about 3:33?*

He glanced back at the cross on the wall. While it still hung, it was now turned on a 45-degree angle. He walked over to straighten it again, put his hand out, and pulled it back quickly.

"What the hell?" Jonah cried, grabbing his hand with the other and shaking both of them vigorously.

The cross was hot to the touch. Jonah checked his fingers, but saw no mark. He approached the cross one more time, much more cautiously. This time, as he reached out and touched it lightly, he discovered the cross was room temperature. Nevertheless, Jonah could have sworn he saw some chafing on the cross that wasn't there before. He straightened the cross to its proper angle, and backed up a few steps waiting for something to happen. All remained quiet.

"I don't know what is going on around here," Jonah muttered to himself. "But this is bullshit."

Later that morning, once Jonah's head stopped throbbing, he decided another road trip was in order. He was still shaken by the reading of the psychic, and the red-hot cross did nothing to allay his fears. Plus, there was one more place that was crucial to Molly Maguire lore. This time, however, Jonah decided company was in order, so he walked across the street and knocked on Oliver's door. A few seconds later, Mrs. Paskiel answered attired in a dress and an apron, shaking off remnants of flour from both of her hands. Daffodil stood by her owner, licking Mrs. Paskiel's hands of whatever sweet goodness still could be found.

"Oh Jonah," she said happily. "You caught me baking. Oliver does love his chocolate chip cookies."

"I can't blame him," Jonah answered. "I kind of like them myself."

"Well, I'll be sure to package a box up for you if I can keep them away from Oliver long enough that he doesn't eat them all," Mrs. Paskiel laughed. Jonah thought Mrs. Paskiel likely ate her share as well, but kept that thought to himself.

"So is Oliver busy today?" Jonah asked, getting to the point of his visit. "I thought I'd take him on a road trip."

"A road trip?" Mrs. Paskiel said in surprise. "Oh, for heaven's sake. I don't know if Oliver has ever done such a thing. I'll have to ask him."

Jonah chuckled. "Don't worry, Mrs. Paskiel," he assured her. "I'll get him back in one piece."

"Oh dear, I know you will," she said. "Let me go call for him. He's probably in his room. That's where I usually find him."

Just as Mrs. Paskiel began to turn, Oliver appeared behind her. She jumped in surprise. "Oh my goodness, you scared me half to death! Jonah wants you to go with him today. Is that all right with you?"

"Sure," Oliver said, a slight smile on his face. "Where are we going to go?"

"How about Centralia?" Jonah asked.

Oliver looked at his friend curiously.

"There is no Centralia anymore," he said matter-of-factly.

"True enough," Jonah admitted. "How about we see what's left of Centralia?"

"OK," Oliver agreed, with only a hint of hesitation in his voice.

Mrs. Paskiel shook her head and headed toward her kitchen.

"You boys sure have an unusual idea of fun," she said, then turned her attention to her son. "Just don't fall into a smoking pit! I don't want you to get barbecued."

"I won't," Oliver assured her. "I don't think you can get barbecued that way anyway."

Mrs. Paskiel smiled knowingly at her son, then switched topics.

"I'll have cookies for both of you when you get back!" she promised. "I'll have more than I expected to, because Oliver won't be here stealing them when I'm not looking!"

"We'll bring our appetites," Jonah assured her.

Jonah and Oliver headed outside and walked toward the car.

"Where else would our appetites be?" Oliver asked.

"A figure of speech," Jonah said, then looked over at Oliver's uncomprehending face. "Oh, forget it. You'll have plenty of cookies to eat when you get home."

"If Mom doesn't eat them all first," Oliver added.

Jonah looked over at his friend, who gave him a sly smile, then climbed in the car and buckled his seat belt.

"Are we going to invite Katie?" Oliver asked.

Jonah looked at Oliver for a second, then remembered Aadya's reading from the day before about the positive woman in his life.

"That's not a bad idea," Jonah said. "I don't know if she'll come or not, but we can ask."

He pulled his cell phone out of his pocket and looked up Katie's contact. She picked up on the second ring.

"Hey," he said. "What are you doing?"

"Getting ready to go to the costume ball," Katie answered sarcastically. "It's Sunday morning. What do you think I'm doing? I've barely had my coffee."

Jonah smiled. "You want to go with me and Oliver on a road trip?"

"Where are you going?"

"Centralia."

Jonah noted a discernible pause on the other end of the line.

"Why?" she finally asked, more than a hint of a sneer in her voice.

Jonah laughed out loud. "Because it's there," he said. "And besides, you got me interested in the history of the Coal Region. You have any better ideas?'

Katie's paused once again.

"Well, you know, it's not really there," she said. "Not anymore."

"Yeah," Jonah said, "Oliver already has pointed that out to me."

Katie chuckled.

"Oh, why not?" she finally said. "It's either that or clean the apartment."

"OK," Jonah said. "Pick you up in a few."

Katie stared at the phone for a few seconds after Jonah hung up. "How does he talk me into these crazy schemes?" she asked, smiled in spite of herself, and went to get dressed.

"I guess pajamas just won't do," she muttered as she began to pull off her top.

Four minutes later, Jonah roared up in front of Katie's apartment and blew the horn. She walked out shortly thereafter, still adjusting her jeans and climbed into the front passenger seat. Oliver had already re-positioned himself comfortably in the back.

"So you want to see a town that no longer exists?" Katie asked quizzically.

"Humor me," Jonah smiled.

"Whatever," she responded. "Consider yourself humored."

Jonah's Malibu left Clayburn and followed the Northeastern Pennsylvania roads toward the region that was once Centralia. Located on Route 61 in Columbia County, today Centralia is the ultimate ghost coal town. The borough was a relatively thriving community from its beginnings in 1866. Residents made their living primarily through the anthracite industry, and its population peaked at more than 2,700 in 1890.

In his Google search, Jonah had learned that, in the 19th Century, Centralia was a hotbed of activity by the Molly Maguires. In fact, Alexander Rea, the supervisor of the mine operations for the Locust Mountain Coal and Iron Company, was robbed and murdered traveling from Mount Carmel to Centralia, the town he founded. This act ultimately helped lead to the prosecution of the Molly Maguires, though it was unclear if any of them were truly involved in the homicide.

"So it's because of you we're going to Centralia today," Jonah said to Katie, looking over to her with a half-smile.

"Well, I doubt we'll find any Molly Maguires there today," she responded dryly. "But we can look if it makes you happy."

As the coal industry began to wane, so did the fortunes of Centralia. Its population had dropped to under 2,000 by 1950, and soon thereafter, a tragedy that would ultimately doom the town occurred, unbeknownst to its residents for many years.

While there is still disagreement over the exact cause, the most popular theory points to a decision by the Centralia Borough Council to hire five members of the volunteer fire company to clean up the town landfill, located just outside the borough limits next to the Odd Fellows Cemetery. On May 27, 1962, the firefighters, just as had been done in previous years, set the dump on fire and let it burn for some time. But that year was different: the landfill had been relocated to an abandoned strip mine pit and the fire was not fully extinguished. An unsealed opening allowed the fire to enter the abandoned coal mines below Centralia. No one noticed and the fire festered for years without being discovered.

But from there, the fire spread. For well over a decade, the residents of the town were unaware of the cauldron burning beneath their feet.

It wasn't until 1979 that the full breadth of the disaster became clear. As a routine measure, a gas station owner inserted a dipstick into one of his underground tanks to check on the fuel level. When the dipstick came back hot, a thermometer was inserted – and it was discovered the temperature of the gasoline was 172 degrees. Two years later, a 12-year-old boy fell into a sinkhole four feet wide by 150 feet deep that suddenly opened beneath him. He was saved by his 14-year old cousin, but the plume of steam seeping from the sinkhole contained a lethal level of carbon monoxide. By the early 1980s, vegetation was dying and smoke seeped from yards and roadways. Homes were abandoned and demolished. Only a few hardy homeowners resisted the government's buyout and subsequent eviction. While some fringe conspiracy theorists surmised the government overstated the danger of the fire to gain mineral rights to the alleged large and highly desirable coal deposits that still lie beneath the town, anyone who traveled through the town at the height of the fire witnessed a site eerily unnerving and unearthly.

And yet, this was not the last indignity the town suffered. During its Centennial celebration in 1966, town officials buried a time capsule, to be opened in 2016 at the 150th celebration. The plan was to distribute the items in the capsule back to the families that originally donated them. Though the capsule survived the fire, potential thieves excavated the capsule in 2014 and tried to break off the locks. The would-be burglars were unsuccessful, but the commander of the local American Legion decided to open the capsule early and check for anything missing. When they did so, the found the contents floating in water, with much of what was placed inside covered in mold. While a few items survived relatively unscathed, much of the historical treasure – just as the town – was mostly destroyed.

Jonah drove through the broken, empty streets, the macadam cracked and uneven. Only 10 houses remained. As the mine fire had moved, Centralia was not quite as spooky and as ghostly as it was when the fire raged directly under the center of town. New vegetation and nature has reclaimed much of what was once the borough. But a sense of loss still pervaded the environment.

Jonah parked on one of the decaying remains of the town's streets. He could imagine the row homes and the residents going about their business, blissfully unaware of the inferno raging under their feet. But now, both the road and the adjoining sidewalk were slowly surrendering to nature as it inexorably worked to reclaim the land. The three friends got out of the car and walked the lonely streets of the lost town.

"This is so...quiet," Katie said softly. "Weird."

Jonah nodded.

"What happened to all the people who lived here?" Oliver asked.

"They moved," Katie answered. "Some of them moved to Ashland, which is the next town over, or over to Mount Carmel. Others just left the area. A few hearty souls stayed."

"This place feels so haunted," Oliver said, "like so many people left, but their souls stayed."

Jonah turned and stared at Oliver, who stayed focused on the area around him. He remembered people telling him that those on the autistic spectrum saw the world differently, and he thought this was a moving example. Oliver was clearly attuned to the lost souls of Centralia in a way Jonah would never achieve. Jonah wondered if Oliver could sense or even see the ghosts of the past wandering across the ruins.

The three eventually made their way to the aptly named "Graffiti Highway," a former section of Route 61 that was closed when it became too damaged to accommodate traffic. Massive fissures appeared in the roadway, leading the state to close the road and re-route the highway. But since then, for more than 20 years, former residents and other visitors have used the near mile of abandoned road as a macabre artist's palette, spray-painting various messages along the path that range from the profane to the romantic. The Graffiti Highway has become a path of living history, despite constant warning from the Pennsylvania State Police that spraying graffiti on the stretch is illegal – a warning that has for the most part gone unheeded.

"Did you want to leave a message?" Jonah asked Oliver.

"Why would I do that?" Oliver responded. "It's against the law."

"And why would you encourage Oliver to break the law?" Katie added, laughing.

Jonah paused, then smiled.

"My mistake," he finally said.

In addition to the few homes remaining, the Assumption of the Blessed Virgin Mary Ukrainian Catholic Church still stands in the distance, just across the old borough line and far enough away from the fire to remain safe. And in the midst of the desolation, a perfectly kept cemetery stands behind gates and a fence. Jonah, Katie and Oliver climbed back into the car and made the short trip to the cemetery, parking outside the gates. Then, they again exited the car and looked over the expanse of the St. Ignatius Cemetery.

Flowers decorated a number of the graves. Jonah and his friends stood and peered across the rows of tombstones. The inhabitants of the cemetery remained some of the last residents of Centralia. He wondered if this would be the fate of other old coal towns as they decayed and the population moved to more economically prosperous locales. Would the residents of the graveyards be the last citizens of lost towns? Then he remembered Father McDermott, the priest who had cursed the town after being roughed up by several Molly Maguires.

"I guess that old priest did know what he was talking about," Jonah said.

Katie viewed the cemetery then turned toward Jonah.

"You can't believe everything you read," she said. "Notice his cemetery is still here, but not his church. His prediction turned out to be wrong."

Indeed, Father McDermott's St. Ignatius parish was located inside the Centralia burn zone. The school was closed in 1981, and while services continued to be held inside the church until the mid-1990s, eventually too few parishioners braved the fires and resulting carbon monoxide to sustain the beleaguered sanctuary. The last service was held in the church in 1995, and the building was razed in 1997. Father McDermott apparently overlooked the fact that if the town disappeared, there was little reason for his church to remain.

The three walked through the remnants of the town for a few more minutes, climbed into Jonah's car and left Centralia. On the way out, they passed a monument at the edge of town, a bell mounted on a stone and brick base, dedicated to military veterans.

Centralia had fought its own war, and lost.

Let the ghosts of Centralia remain where they belong, Jonah thought. *It's a fitting graveyard.*

By the time Jonah, Oliver and Katie returned to Clayburn, Mrs. Paskiel's kitchen was bursting with chocolate chip cookies, enough to satiate the appetites of all those returning from a walk through a ghost town. They ate heartily if unhealthily that evening.

CHAPTER 17

Jonah recognized this old woman. She was a familiar but unwelcome face. They had many, many encounters, dating back to at least his teenage years. He had seen her the night he injured his mother and was taken to the hospital. He battled her in the emergency room. Since then, he had come to recognize her for what she was. He had named her Regan, inspired by *The Exorcist.* She was his own personal demon.

"Did you miss me?" the old woman hissed. "It's been a very long time. Too long."

"You aren't welcome here," Jonah answered. "You're not real. I've learned how to deal with you."

"Have you now?' Regan replied. She was interminably old, and Jonah knew, not of this world. Indeed, she did not exist outside of his own mind. She was his own sick demented creation. "But have you learned who SHE is?"

"Who are you talking about?" he mocked. "Are you back to your old tricks?"

She laughed, part in triumph, part in remorse.

"She's here for you. Beware!" Regan cautioned.

"That's a tired story," Jonah said, "and a lie."

"Not this time," Regan hissed. "Look inside yourself and see the truth. The psychic already warned you. She's the true evil."

Jonah was jolted back. He remembered Aadya's words about the one who strived to possess his soul.

Suddenly, the old woman turned and shrieked. Regan was seemingly pushed violently off to the side. Yet another old woman, this one not quite so ethereal and not so ancient, appeared. Jonah did not recognize her, though he thought it might be the same woman as the night before. Now, however, she was far more defined. While his familiar demon was bone thin, his newest demon was large and imposing, and not quite so...decayed. Jonah thought it was curious she wore glasses and the remnants of a paisley dress, which somehow had been transformed into something dreadfully threatening and macabre in its own right.

"Who the fuck are you?" Jonah demanded. "I don't know you."

"It's who you are that matters," the stranger said. "You will get to know me much better. I've been waiting for you. You have been a difficult fish to find and catch."

"What are you talking about? he said. "And why the hell are you wearing glasses. What? Hallucinations are near-sighted now?"

Jonah smirked, proud of himself.

"Do you think you're funny?" the woman said, her voice growing deeper and more threatening, almost a growl. "This is only the beginning. We are going to accomplish great things together."

Regan re-entered the conversation. "Get away from him," she scowled. "He's mine."

"Not anymore," the figure said. "You're old news. You're a figment of his imagination – weak and helpless. You are no longer needed now that I'm here."

The stranger turned toward Jonah, baring her sharpened teeth, blood dripping from her mouth. Jonah recoiled. He had seen those teeth before.

"If two women are going to be fighting over me," he said defiantly, "I wish it wouldn't be you two old hags."

"You have no choice," the second woman said menacingly. "I'm coming for you, and I'm going to have you."

"I don't think so," Regan said, rushing the new demon.

The stranger flung her arm as if swatting a fly. Even though it made no contact, Regan was hurled away. She grabbed desperately at thin air, and in an instant, disappeared, shrieking in her own terror.

Jonah then thought he heard a cacophony of voices. While he heard his familiar nemesis crying, "Nooooo...," he was sure he heard both younger and older voices in the background. Some cried, "Help!" while others sounded like they said, "Be afraid!"

Jonah wasn't sure what to make of this development. For years, Regan had been the demon he battled. But now, she seemed to be in some odd way his protector.

But isn't that how she always casts herself? Jonah thought. *She can't be trusted. Is this one of her tricks?*

Yet somehow, this felt differently.

Jonah now eyed this new adversary. From what portal of hell did his second nemesis arise? He faced the strange woman.

"What do you want from me?" Jonah demanded.

"Much," the apparition said. "But there's nothing you can give me. I will take what I want and use you how I will."

"Not if I can help it," Jonah said in defiance.

"You can't," she said mockingly. "Sniveling little thing that you are. You will bend to my will in good time. You'll be my toy, and I will play you as I please."

The strange woman snickered, then suddenly, opened her fist to reveal dagger-like fingernails. She hurled herself toward Jonah, seeming to breach the barrier between the other-world she occupied and Jonah's space. She flew closer and closer, a grotesque violent expression distorting her face. Jonah tried to back away, but was blocked by the headboard on his bed.

The woman was nearly upon him, a foot, now inches, in what appeared to be a slow-motion scene evolving in front of him. The stranger lifted her hand to strike, brought it down...

Suddenly, Jonah awakened and hurled himself up from the bed in a scene reminiscent but more desperate than the night before. He was drenched in sweat, crouching in a posture ready to defend himself. He looked around the darkened room, searching frantically for the woman to identify the direction from which she would attack.

"Where are you, you son of a bitch?" he screamed.

She was not there. Jonah slowly came to his senses, realizing he was standing in his bedroom – alone.

"It was a dream," he said. "A dream. What a fucking dream. A goddam nightmare."

Jonah looked at his clock. It was 3:33 a.m.

What the hell? he thought.

But there was a nagging part of him disturbed that it felt so real.

He turned on the light, climbed out of bed, walked to the bathroom and reached for a towel to wipe himself dry.

"Jesus Christ," he said. "It felt like she was right in my face."

Jonah did not get back to sleep for a long time. Across the street, Oliver tossed and turned, wondering why his own rest was so uncharacteristically disjointed and interrupted. He finally slipped out of bed and looked across the street. He could have sworn there was a blackish otherworldly glow surrounding Jonah's house.

"What in the world is that?' he wondered aloud. Suddenly, Oliver could have sworn a pair of malevolent eyes stared back at him in the mist.

Oliver shook, ran back across the room, and slid underneath the covers. He didn't come back out until he heard his alarm ringing well after daybreak.

CHAPTER 18

When Jonah and Oliver arrived for work the next morning, Harvey already had the truck loaded and was waiting for his employees. As Jonah had discovered, a good part of Kershaw's business involved deliveries, and Harvey did his best to ensure his small business accommodated the significant number of customers who took advantage of this service.

"Got an early morning run to Nesquehoning," Mr. Kershaw said. "The customer needs this delivery right away."

"Nesqu-who?" Jonah asked. "I don't have to pronounce that, do I?"

Harvey laughed.

"Nesquehoning," he said. "You don't have to say it as long as you can find it. It's right on 209."

Jonah nodded, happy the directions didn't include any large tree landmarks.

"Heigh ho, heigh ho, it's off to work I go!" he sing-songed, climbed into the truck, and sputtered out of town.

"He doesn't look like one of Snow White's dwarves to me," Harvey muttered, then ambled back into the store.

Jonah came back ninety minutes later and parked, the vehicle backfiring as he turned off the ignition, leaving no doubt of Jonah's return.

"You gotta wonder how long the old man thinks this hunk of junk is going to last," Jonah muttered to himself. "I guess they don't give up on their vehicles that easily. Or their trucks."

Jonah walked into the store, where Oliver and Katie were busy filling the shelves with new inventory. Since Harvey was never short of stock, that involved moving and shuffling the items already there to make room for the products that had just arrived. Harvey had an eclectic sense of his customer's tastes. There was everything from a cream for achy joints to insecticide, ready-to-eat camping food to pet snacks, every kind of tool to multiple versions of industrial lubricant. Yet, even though it seemed Harvey had lost his mind in ordering, he rarely misjudged the tastes of those who came into his store.

Jonah joined in the work. A short while later, the three finished up and there was a short lull in the day.

"Are you going to the block party this weekend?" Katie asked her two co-workers.

"My mom takes me every year," Oliver said. "She gets her two favorite things there – food and gossip. Or maybe it's gossip and food."

Oliver smiled craftily. Jonah looked at him in astonishment.

"Did you just crack a joke?" he asked.

Oliver giggled.

"I'm having a bad influence on you!"

Katie looked at Jonah.

"What about you?" she asked. "You going for food and gossip?"

"I don't know anything about a block party," Jonah admitted. "What is it?"

Katie rolled her eyes.

"You don't know about the block party? You really didn't grow up here, did you?" she said in surprise. "The fire company holds it every year as a fundraiser. They close off the street and turn the area around the station into a huge festival – thus, a block party, get it? There's food, games and music. It will be going on all weekend."

"Sounds like the biggest thing to hit Clayburn since I've been here," Jonah said. "How can I miss it? Are you going?"

Katie hesitated. "It's a little far to walk," she finally said. "I'll go if I can find a ride."

She turned away in embarrassment.

Is that designed to be an opening? Jonah asked himself. *Not exactly subtle, but I'll take it.*

Jonah paused. He glanced over at Oliver, who was grinning from

116

ear to ear and nodding. He scowled at his friend for just a second.

"If you want, I can take you," he finally said to Katie.

Katie turned. "You don't have to," she said. "I don't want you to feel obligated..."

"No, I want to," he finally stammered. "I don't know anyone here. It will be good to go with someone. I'll feel out of place otherwise."

"Are you sure?"

"Don't push it," Jonah said. "I already said yes."

Katie smiled demurely, and the three went back to their work.

•   •   •

Jonah had just returned from yet another delivery and was at the counter with Katie and Oliver when the front door opened and the entrance bell rang. An old man entered the store and looked at the three clerks.

"It's the retard trio," 80-year-old Chester Mountz, muttered. Jonah had seen this customer before. His appearance was as miserable as his personality, unkempt and surly in every aspect of his life. "Any of you have enough brains to get me a five-gallon drum of driveway sealer."

Before the three employees could answer, Harvey stepped out from the back, seemingly out of nowhere. He had a discernible frown on his normally smiling face.

"Chester, we're out of stock on that item," he said curtly.

"What are you talking about, Harvey?" Chester asked. "I see the drums right there in the back." The customer pointed past the counter.

"Those are reserved for someone else," Harvey said, defiantly. "Now the next time you come back, if you do so with a better attitude, I'm sure we'll have what you need available."

Chester looked at him with a mix of disdain and shock.

"But I need it today . . ," he stuttered.

"You should have thought of that before you opened your ugly mouth," Harvey answered. "Now you'll have to get it somewhere else. Maybe you can get some from the Walmart in Hometown."

"But, but...," Chester sputtered, his face turning red.

117

"No buts," Harvey interrupted. "I expect you treat my employees with respect. They work hard and they do their job. And every one of them is more civil and has twice the brains than you ever did."

Chester stared at Harvey, who remained stern and intractable. Chester turned and stomped out of the store.

Jonah peered at Harvey, his mouth agape.

"Can you afford to do that?" he asked him.

"Can't afford not to," Harvey said. "I don't have much time left on this Earth. I'd rather build up some credits while I can. And Chester's been an asshole for years. Time for him to get his due."

Harvey returned to the back of the store and chuckled.

"That felt pretty good," he said, and began to whistle. "Now if I could only get Mrs. Kershaw straightened out that easily."

•   •   •

The week sped by, or sped as fast as it could in Clayburn. By mid-week, the entire town was talking about the block party, and by Friday, there was no other topic of conversation to be had. Jonah was bewildered by the level of excitement a block party could generate, but he could do little but be swept up in the wave.

"You'd swear the president was coming to town," he said in astonishment more than once.

"Quit complaining," Katie said. "This is the biggest thing in town since they put up the Christmas decorations."

"Well, if it's competing with Christmas," Jonah said, "I'm not saying another word."

Katie gave him a look that Jonah knew told him he had taken his incredulity to the limit.

The Clayburn Volunteer Fire Company No. 1 Annual Block Party was held Friday night, Saturday starting at noon until well into the evening, and Sunday afternoon. Foster Street between 2nd and 3rd, from the fire company down through the rest of the block, was closed for the weekend. Nearby residents needed to use the alley behind their homes or park on the side streets. In return, they received front-row seats to the festivities without ever having to leave their porch. The block party was a major community event and a significant source of revenue for the fire company, in which Clayburn took great pride.

One hoped there was no fire emergency that weekend, not because the company's apparatus was blocked in – they had made accommodations for that – but more likely because it would be difficult to locate a sober firefighter until Monday. It was a given that the century-old brick building that served as the fire house would be the home for many passed-out firefighters over the weekend. Fortunately, nearly every volunteer fire company in the area held a block party throughout the summer, and the stations had an unwritten agreement to cover each other when their turn came. So even if the Clayburn engine driver was too intoxicated to see, the town would not be allowed to burn to the ground, thanks to the generosity of more sober firefighters from nearby towns.

A large tent was erected outside the fire station, and the unit's kitchen worked at full capacity. Elsewhere down the block, wooden stands with various carnival games shared space with mobile food trucks, a kids' bounce house, stands for community organizations, and a stage for the musical entertainment. Of course, for the adults, there was a roped-off beer garden under a separate tent that would be heavily utilized.

The band lineup leaned heavily toward country. An oldies band had slipped in there as well, but that was the extent of the variety. Jonah's classic rock had no chance of entering the festivities. There would be no Bob Dylan, Janis Joplin, Beatles or Jimi Hendrix at the Clayburn block party. A Northeast Pennsylvania block party was a far cry from Woodstock.

Since Kershaw's was open until six on Friday afternoon and re-opened the next morning at 9 a.m., Jonah and Katie decided Saturday was the best day for Jonah's baptism to the local tradition of the block party. The shop closed at noon, and no one had to work Sunday morning.

They arrived later that afternoon around five. Jonah noticed that Katie had applied makeup for the event, a rare occurrence, but decided not to make mention of the fact. As he pulled his Malibu up to the festival, he noted parking spaces were at a premium, with street parking packed for blocks and makeshift lots overflowing. Jonah stole a space as another car pulled out, only a block or so away from the celebration.

The two took an easy stroll to the event. It was a hot, humid July night, so they both wore shorts and T-shirts. Katie was dressed in a pretty blue top only slightly revealing, while Jonah had found a Led Zeppelin shirt for the occasion. There was nothing worse than rain for the community block party, so while the heat wasn't ideal, it was far better than the alternative. Though they took their time, just as they were about to skirt the barriers that closed the road, Katie appeared a bit flush.

"You OK?" Jonah asked.

"Just my MS acting up a bit," she said. "I have to get used to the temperature. Can we get to some shade?"

The tent was too far away, but fortunately, there were a few empty tables close by. Katie sat down, and Jonah brought her a bottle of water. After a few minutes, she seemed significantly improved.

"Sorry about that," she said.

"Not your fault," Jonah said. "We are both at the mercy of our conditions. Glad you're feeling better."

Jonah and Katie looked around. The block party was already well attended, but more people would arrive as the evening went on. The place was a noisy combination of music, the clanging and buzzing of games, neighborhood children running and dodging through the crowd, and a rambunctious crowd sharing stories and re-igniting acquaintances.

"Let's get something to eat," Jonah said. "I'm starved."

While you could buy hamburgers and hot dogs if you wanted, block party purists in Northeast Pennsylvania enjoyed a variety of ethnic dishes and eschewed the more traditional picnic fare. The menu was full of potato and sauerkraut pierogis, haluski, potato pancakes, halupki, kielbasa and other items not easily found at an event outside of the Coal Region.

"I don't even know what half these things are," Jonah complained. "You think they could list this stuff in English?"

Katie laughed heartily.

"Here, I'll help you pick something out," she said. "You're NOT coming to a block party in Clayburn and eating a hamburger."

"Not even with cheese?" Jonah asked.

"No, absolutely not," Katie asserted. "Heathen."

Katie coaxed Jonah into a halupki (cabbage stuffed with ground beef in a tomato sauce), potato-filled pierogis, and an order of haluski (a combination of noodles, cabbage, onions and butter).

"Is there anything you can't drench in butter up here?" Jonah asked.

"You can put vinegar on your fries if you order some later," Katie answered. "I'll help you eat them."

Jonah looked at her and opened his mouth to say something.

"Shut up and eat," Katie interrupted.

Jonah followed Katie's instructions, and soon was digging into his plate-full of Polish-Slovak delicacies. He agreed the food was delicious, even as he wiped tomato sauce and butter from his face on a regular basis.

"Glad I shaved today," he commented. "Or I'd have a face-full of greasy stubble. I hope they don't run out of napkins."

Afterward, Jonah and Katie took a leisurely stroll through the game area, Jonah especially cautious with Katie after her earlier episode, despite her protestations that she was feeling fine. Neither managed to win a bottle of soda at the ring toss, but Jonah claimed a stuffed SpongeBob plush for Katie by puncturing enough balloons with his crack dart-throwing.

"Never trust me with a sharp object," he said.

"I'll remember that."

Jonah and Katie eventually caught up to Oliver and Mrs. Paskiel. Oliver could hardly contain his enthusiasm and had difficulty trying to stop flapping his arms in excitement. Mrs. Paskiel was in her element, bouncing from person to person saying hello to nearly everyone within arm's reach, hugging them tightly beyond comfort, and, most importantly, catching up with all the news and gossip to be had. After tonight, she would likely have a month's worth of scuttlebutt to report.

"Why, hello you two," Helen said, when she spotted Jonah and Katie and eyed them closely. "Don't you look like a cute couple? Ain'a, Oliver?"

Oliver nodded in agreement.

Uh-oh, Jonah thought, *we just became the headline of the nightly report. Nothing beats this for the lead story.*

Jonah gave Katie a half-smirk of a smile. Katie wasn't sure if it was it was because of the suggestion they were a couple, or still a reaction to the "ain'a." She didn't care. In response, Katie nestled her head on Jonah's shoulder. Jonah glanced over to her but didn't pull back, and in fact, shifted slightly toward her.

"Are you having fun?" Oliver asked.

"It's great," Jonah said. "As soon as I get all this grease out of my gut, I'll feel even better."

Katie pulled her head up and gave him a whack.

"What?" Jonah responded mockingly.

"Oh, you city boys," Mrs. Paskiel said. "You have to learn to eat some real down-home cooking. Don't worry, we'll toughen up that sensitive stomach for you before long."

"That's what I'm afraid of."

Mrs. Paskiel gave both Jonah and Katie a big hug whether they wanted it or not, then *shooshed* Oliver away from them, beckoning him to come with her.

"Let's give them some privacy," she mock-whispered conspiratorially to Oliver, though her voice was easily heard by Jonah and Katie. Mrs. Paskiel then shifted her attention to the newly-designated couple.

"Now you two have a good time," she said. "It's so nice that you found each other. You both deserve some happiness in your life!"

With that, Mrs. Paskiel headed to her next target, waving happily to the pair.

"Have fun!" Oliver said over his shoulder as he was swept along by the whirlwind that was his mother.

The day turned to dusk and one by one the lights came on, illuminating the block party the length of the entire street. By then, the band had kicked into high gear and had attracted an appreciative crowd. Jonah had never witnessed a scene quite like this one: an old-fashioned slice of Americana, with people enjoying the moment and each other, with games, music and food that hadn't changed in decades. He felt like, in some ways, he had been transported for just a short time, back into the 1950s.

Where's Chuck Berry when you need him? a part of Jonah thought ruefully.

Harvey and Mrs. Kershaw sat on lawn chairs off to the side of the stage. They waved appreciatively at Jonah and Katie. Harvey had somehow managed to sneak a beer out of the beer garden – Yuengling Lager, of course, manufactured in nearby Pottsville and apparently the only acceptable brew in Northeast Pennsylvania – and he toasted them, taking an exaggerated mouthful. No one was going to stop him, and the police looked the other way. This *was* the block party, after all.

Jonah wasn't much of a dancer, but when the band started playing Kenny Chesney's "Me and You," Katie dragged him to the front of the impromptu dance floor. Jonah didn't object. She wrapped her arms around him, and joined other couples nearby in a slow dance.

Ordinary no, really don't think so
Not a love this true
Common destiny
We were meant to be
Me and you

Jonah tentatively put his arms around Katie and looked into her eyes. For once, they were focused directly on him.

"It's been a long time since anyone danced with me," she said softly. "Hold me."

Without another word, Jonah wrapped his arms tightly around her and held her for as long as the song lasted, and then some. The two spent the rest of the block party arm-in-arm. Jonah didn't pay much attention to what was going on around him for the rest of the night.

A few hours later, Jonah pulled his Malibu up to Katie's apartment.

"Thank you," Katie said with sincerity. "For everything."

"Did you have fun?" Jonah asked.

"More than I have had in a long time."

"Me too."

Jonah and Katie peered into each other's eyes, silently and awkwardly. Music from Jonah's radio played in the background – this time, the Eagles. Jonah had enough of pure country for one night, but he didn't stray too far as he played the classic rock of one of the most famous bands of all time. At this moment, it was the perfect choice, "Take It Easy," written by Glenn Frey and Jackson Browne.

Well, I'm a-standin' on a corner in Winslow, Arizona
Such a fine sight to see
It's a girl, my Lord, in a flat-bed Ford
Slowin' down to take a look at me

Come on, baby, don't say maybe
I gotta know if your sweet love is gonna save me
We may lose and we may win, though we will never be here again
So open up I'm climbin' in, so take it easy

Katie started to lean toward her date, Jonah lightly touched her arm as he moved forward, and the two met each other for that long-awaited first kiss. They didn't let go of each other for several minutes.

"I'll see you at work?" Katie asked imploringly.

"You will," Jonah affirmed.

Katie got out of the car, climbed up the short stairway to her apartment, and turned and smiled before she walked inside. Jonah waved, and headed home. Life has just become much more interesting in Clayburn.

•   •   •

Jonah unlocked the front door of his house, and stepped inside. He had barely flicked on the light switch, when out of the corner of his eye, he saw an object flying toward his head. He ducked, only to watch a book bounce off the wall behind him. He looked over at the bookshelf and watched several other volumes fall off the shelf.

"Pissy?" he said out loud. "Or jealous?"

He heard a low, rumbling laugh.

"Just making sure you don't forget me," a low ominous voice growled.

Jonah looked around the house, but the voice was as mercurial as the wind.

"Who are you?" Jonah demanded. "How can I forget you if I don't know you in the first place?"

Again, he heard a voice. Was it in his head? Or did it boomerang around the house? Or both?

"You can call me...Evelyn."

"Evelyn? Are you kidding me? What kind of name is that for a ghost?" Jonah screamed. "Get the fuck out of my head and out of my house! You are not welcome here."

The voice laughed once more, and went quiet.

CHAPTER 19

That night, both the house and Jonah were restless. The house cracked, groaned, and creaked. Voices of an old woman, young children, and even adult men drifted through the darkness. Another book – maybe two – fell off the shelf.

Jonah thought he heard water running in the bathroom. He distinctly discerned the sound of footsteps walking through the house, up the steps, across the floor above him, back downstairs, and then into the kitchen. A few seconds later, cabinets and doors opened and closed. He finally got up and investigated, only to find all in order. As he returned to his bed, he was sure he saw a shadow pass in the darkness.

Later, he heard ominous noises from the basement. Laughter filled with vitriol, wails that emanated with tones of desperation and terror. Jonah opened the basement door, flipped on the light switch, and peered down the stairs. He tentatively placed one foot on the top step, then pulled it back. There was something too sinister for Jonah to continue. He turned off the light, closed and locked the door and again returned to his bedroom.

He finally heard Evelyn's voice once again as the clock struck 3:33.

"You are only beginning to feel my power," she said. "I plan on being here for many, many years and you will do what I wish. We will have a very long and productive partnership. I have great plans for us."

Then Jonah heard a more familiar voice.

"I told you to watch her," Regan said. "I told you so."

"Both of you," Jonah finally screamed. "Out! Now! I'm tired."

Jonah again arose, walking through the house and turning on every light.

"How the fuck am I supposed to sleep around here?' he said bitterly.

As 4 a.m. approached, however, the house fell quiet. Jonah, exhausted, finally collapsed back in bed and slept until late that morning.

CHAPTER 20

Jonah spent the next morning investigating every nook of the house. It was time to put this mystery to rest. Jonah tried to convince himself there was some logical reason for the strange occurrences and disturbing nightmares. Oliver came over early Sunday afternoon, and after Jonah described what happened, Oliver offered to help with the search.

"What are we looking for?" Oliver asked.

"I don't know," Jonah admitted.

"Then how will we know when we find it?"

Jonah looked at his autistic friend.

"Now is not the time to make sense," Jonah concluded. "When we come across whatever it is, we'll know. I'm sure of it."

"OK," Oliver said, but he was still confused. He continued to search, not knowing exactly whether he would recognize the object of their hunt, but trusting Jonah that he would.

The two looked under sofas and in kitchen cabinets. They searched the walls, the floors and even the ceilings for hidden compartments. Once, Jonah opened a drawer and set off an ancient mousetrap, making him jump backwards so hard he nearly knocked himself out on the wall behind him.

"I guess the old woman had mice," he muttered.

Katie called to check on him. She could tell immediately that something was bothering him.

"I'm pretty sure this house is haunted," Jonah finally told her.

Katie was silent for a long minute. Jonah could hear her breathing heavily on the phone.

"Listen," she finally said, "if you want to forget about what happened last night, that's fine. You don't have to make shit up. I'm a big girl."

She was ready to hang up, but Jonah pleaded with her to stop.

"No, no, no, that's not it at all," Jonah said mortified, then described all the occurrences since he moved in, as well as Oliver's tale of those who had looked at the house earlier.

"You're serious?" Katie finally said.

"As a heart attack," Jonah assured her.

"You're not having one of your mental breakdowns?"

"No, absolutely not," Jonah answered.

"I didn't set off some trigger in your head?" Katie persisted.

"Don't give yourself that much credit."

Jonah imagined he could see Katie's half-smirk through the phone.

"Don't worry," she said. "You're not all that and a bag of chips either. But come over and pick me up. If we're looking for ghosts, then all the members of the freak show might as well search the place together. This sounds like a quest made for us."

Jonah didn't hesitate.

"I'll be right over," he said. "Thank you for believing me."

It took only a few minutes for Jonah to get to Katie's apartment, grab a quick kiss, and bring her to the house. But when they returned, Oliver was pacing nervously back and forth.

"What's wrong?" Jonah asked.

"This place gives me the creeps," Oliver said. "I can feel some sort of presence in this house. And I could have sworn I just heard a baby cry."

Jonah and Katie looked around the room, but neither saw anything nor heard a sound.

"I believe you," Jonah said. "Let's try to get to the bottom of this."

The three continued the search with renewed vigor. They searched the two main floors, plus the attic, leaving the basement for last. Jonah still felt uncomfortable in the cellar and only tentatively began his descent into the dimly lit space. He paused after reaching the second step, with Katie and Oliver finally coaxing him down the entire way.

Katie found a switch on one of the support beams that turned on additional lights, allowing her to better view her surroundings.

The basement was nearly bare. The old noisy heating unit stood in one corner, quiet during the heat of summer. While many homes in the Northeast still burned coal, Jonah's house was heated by fuel oil. Old Miss Donahue must have tired of shoveling coal at some point and converted to a more convenient option. The electric water heater stood nearby. A few uneven wooden shelves lined the walls. Several dust-encrusted cans and bottles, some empty, others containing unknown substances – Jonah didn't even want to know what they could be – still lined a few of the planks. Jonah remained perplexed and disturbed by the patchwork quilt of concrete on the floor. It made no sense to him that someone would finish the floor in such an odd and uneven fashion.

While Jonah stood mostly frozen in the middle of the room, Oliver wandered aimlessly still trying to figure out the object of his pursuit. Meanwhile, Katie systematically explored the dismal space. A few minutes later, in a nook obscured by the steps, Katie stopped.

"I think I may have found something," she announced.

Jonah and Oliver walked back to Katie's location, both of them somewhat reluctantly. Katie had discovered an old wooden desk, dusty and filled with cobwebs, pushed back into the shadows. It took some effort, but Katie finally opened one the drawers. She reached in gingerly and very carefully pulled out its contents. As she leafed through the material, it turned out to truly be a curious find. Six old local newspapers had sat in the drawer, presumably for decades. They were dated September 12, 1961; June 13, 1963; February 11, 1966; March 18, 1969; November 12, 1973; and April 3, 1977. All had yellowed and become brittle with age.

"What the hell?" Jonah said. "Why keep six random newspapers from decades ago?"

"No idea," Katie said. "This is very odd."

"This place is getting weirder and weirder," Jonah said. "She was a crazy old lady, that's for sure."

"I wonder just how crazy," Katie said. "Why these dates?"

"Who knows?" Jonah said. "No rhyme nor reason."

Oliver shook his head and flapped his arms nervously.

"All I know," he said, "is I always felt very nervous around her. My mom told me not to come near the house when she lived here."

"Did she think she the old lady was going to eat you?" Jonah asked, forcing a joke.

Oliver looked at him.

"I don't think so," he said flatly. "I don't think I would taste very good."

"Only with a lot of salt," Jonah cracked.

"Salt?" Oliver asked, shaking his head back and forth. "I don't think that would help."

"Just kidding," Jonah said. "I shouldn't have started."

Katie looked in the desk again, forcing open another drawer. This one was empty except for a few old pens and pencils. But when she opened a third, she looked up at Jonah and Oliver.

"Hold on," she said," there's something else here."

As Katie reached her hand further into the drawer, her two friends inched closer.

"Be careful it's not a mouse trap," Jonah said. "I've caught one of those already."

Katie glanced back toward him with that look that said, "Really?" She pulled out a book, dog-eared and dusty. She wiped away the thick layer of debris that had collected on the cover and read the title and author aloud.

"The Molly Maguires by Wayne G. Broehl Jr.," she said. As she flipped through the book, she noted there were various sections highlighted and bookmarked, with a number of pages turned down on one corner.

"The Molly Maguires again?" Jonah asked. "Why do they keep showing up wherever I go?"

At that moment, a guttural rumble shook the house.

"What the..." Jonah said, scanning the entire basement.

Katie finally gathered up the yellowing newspapers and the book and stood up.

"Let's go upstairs and look at these more closely," Katie said.

She carried the brittle newspapers carefully and laid them on the kitchen table. The three examined the newspapers page by page, but found nothing that would link them to Miss Donahue. None of the content had anything in common, nor did the dates make any sense in any sequence.

However, when they paged through the book – as it turned out, written by an acclaimed former Dartmouth professor – the readers found a striking similarity. The old woman bore the same last name as John "Yellow Jack" Donahue, one of the Molly Maguires executed at the Carbon County Jail, and his name was highlighted in the book. It was the detail Jonah overlooked during his tour of the Old Jail Museum. Now, the parallel was obvious. Could it be more than coincidental?

"Donahue," Katie said intrigued. "Do you think she was a descendant?"

"Who knows?" Jonah said. "There has to be what, a hundred years between the time he was hung and the time she was born?"

"Probably not quite that much," Katie said. "But still, what does this all mean?"

"I have no idea what to think," Jonah said. "I'm not sure any of this makes any sense whatsoever."

"I don't think those newspapers or that book is making all the racket in the house," Oliver finally said, chiming in. "I'm pretty sure they haven't been moved in years."

"No, you're absolutely right," Katie said. "But we've definitely perturbed someone who finds value in them."

"Whatever the hell is going on," Jonah said, "they give me the creeps. Let's put everything back downstairs where they belong."

"I'll take them down," Katie said. "I know how much you dislike your basement."

Katie carried the newspapers and book back into the dank cellar. She made a note to herself that she wanted to study the book further to see if she could unravel some of the mystery of what was happening in this house. As she began down the steps, she thought she heard a low rumble. She looked around, but it had passed. After setting them into their original location in the desk, she headed upstairs again, only to find the basement door closed. The basement light began to flicker. She pushed on the door harder, but it didn't open. She was just about to scream for help, when the door slid open by itself. Katie walked through the door, looking at it especially closely as she passed.

"Did either of you close this door?" she asked Jonah and Oliver, who had not appeared to move.

"What are you talking about?" Jonah asked. "Of course not. Why would we close it when you were down there?"

"I didn't," Oliver assured her.

Katie looked back at the door

"Forget it," she said. "Just another weird thing about this place."

The house continued to be particularly unfriendly that day, as if something – or someone – was perturbed by the curiosity of the inhabitants. There was an occasional bang, a wisp of a scent, a faraway scream, but nothing concrete. A slightly acrid odor wafted through the house, just enough for those inside to notice. Oliver became particularly disturbed.

"I think I need to go home," he finally said. Jonah understood the feeling. Oliver hastily said goodbye and walked out the door. As he headed toward his house, he saw Daffodil jumping from window to window, barking in the direction of Jonah's house and clearly agitated.

As the day waned, Jonah looked at Katie.

"Will you stay with me tonight?" he finally asked. "I don't want to be alone."

"Sure," Katie said. "Do you have any ideas of what we might do? Watch a movie? Play Monopoly?"

Jonah gazed at her, studying her with new appreciation.

"I have a couple of thoughts," he said, smiling, "all more interesting than that."

Jonah slipped his hand through Katie's and together they headed toward the bedroom. Jonah looked around the house.

Whatever happens for the next hour, he thought, *I'm busy.*

Indeed, whatever happened for some time after that, Jonah and

Katie were blissfully unaware.

Later that night, the two cuddled tightly. The house remained in a state of disquiet and they were now both acutely aware of the hostile rumblings. As the night went on, Katie could feel the effects of her MS – her joints became sore, her leg stiffened.

"What the hell?" she said to herself. "What is going on?"

"Are you OK?" Jonah asked, awakened by Katie's distress.

"I will be," she answered. "Not sure why my body is acting up now."

"Maybe I was too much for it," Jonah said slyly.

"Don't give yourself too much credit," Katie said, echoing Jonah's sentiment from earlier.

Even later that night, Jonah and Katie were awakened by a six loud knocks in quick succession on the bedroom door.

"There's no one else here except us," Jonah said. Nevertheless, he climbed out of bed and walked across the room. When he opened the door, the hallway was empty, but he was sure he heard mocking laughter in the distance.

It was 3:33 a.m.

"What the hell is it about that time?" Jonah asked.

Jonah and Katie cuddled even more tightly.

"I think you might be right," Katie finally said quietly. "This place might be haunted."

"You think?"

Eventually, Jonah and Katie fell back asleep in each other's arms in spite of the general discontent surrounding them.

CHAPTER 21

The beginning of the week had been uneventful, both at home and at work. Jonah began to breathe a sigh of relief, thinking whatever may have had designs on him and his house had gone looking for more palatable targets.

Maybe I didn't give Evelyn enough of a rise, he thought. *Or maybe she didn't like the competition. Whatever, I'm not complaining.*

Jonah and Katie's budding relationship began to fully bloom, and they spent more and more time together during and after work. However, on Wednesday, Katie's MS acted up and she missed her shift at Kershaw's. She was so tired, she could barely get out of bed.

"Sometimes this happens," she assured Jonah. "I just need a day to rest. It's nothing to worry about."

After some additional assurances, Jonah finally accepted her explanation, but promised to stop by immediately after work. He drove off to Kershaw's and he and Oliver kept the store operating with Harvey as best they could.

"You know," Harvey said, "I miss that girl when she isn't here. She's the one that knows where everything is."

"I miss her too," Jonah said.

Mr. Kershaw looked at him knowingly and rolled his eyes.

"Young love," the old man muttered. "Don't worry, son. You'll get over that."

A few minutes later, the door to the shop swung open, the familiar attached bell ringing to alert the staff that a customer had arrived. Jonah walked to the counter to greet the visitor and was somewhat surprised to see a young African-American man surveying the shelves.

Schuylkill County even today remains predominantly white, with about 95 percent of the population Caucasian. What diversity the county can claim is generally represented among the residents in the City of Pottsville, which was more than a half-hour away. Jonah could probably count the number of African-Americans in Clayburn on...

Actually, Jonah thought, *this is the first person of color I've seen in town at all.*

Jonah must have hesitated a moment too long, because the customer finally grinned broadly.

"Don't worry," he said, "I'm not lost."

Jonah chuckled.

"Sorry," he said. "You just caught me by surprise."

"Happens a lot around here," the customer responded, extending his hand. "I'm Myles."

He and Jonah shook.

"Nice to meet you, Myles," Jonah said. "I'm Jonah. Looking for anything in particular?"

"Yeah, I need a new flashlight," Myles said. "Mine got run over."

"By a vehicle?" Jonah asked.

"Is there any other type of transportation?" Myles shot back.

The two men shared knowing smiles, and Jonah led his customer to the aisle where the flashlights were located.

"We have quite a variety," Jonah said. "Mr. Kershaw loves his flashlights."

Myles thanked Jonah and spent a few minutes evaluating his choices. He eventually selected a Fenix PD35, a lightweight flashlight known for both its power and durability.

"Good choice," Jonah said as he rang up the sale.

Myles nodded and the two chatted for a few minutes. Myles was a relative newcomer to the area as well, and Jonah and he found much in common in what they have discovered thus far. The two promised to see each other again in the near future. Jonah and Myles shared a friendly goodbye before the customer left the store.

Later that day, Oliver was helping Harvey in the back of the shop when an older man walked into the store. Jonah again was staffing the counter.

"Good afternoon," Jonah said.

"Afternoon, son," the senior citizen acknowledged. "I have a list of plumbing supplies I need. The missus has assigned me a project."

"Ahh, the old honey-do list," Jonah chuckled.

The man snorted. "That's a long, long list at my house," he said. "Keeps growing all the time. I'm sure I'll never see the end of it. There are days I wonder why I retired."

"I've heard that story before," Jonah said. "Let me go put this together,"

Jonah circled around toward the back of the store to compile the order.

"Say," the customer said. "Aren't you the one that moved into the old Donahue house?"

Jonah stopped and turned back. He had learned in his short time in Clayburn that news traveled fast, if nothing else in the town reached that speed.

"As a matter of fact, I am," he acknowledged.

The old man chuckled.

"She was a piece of work, the old woman who lived there before you," he said.

"You knew her?" Jonah asked, returning to the counter.

"I should say so," the man said. "Stanley Tazik."

"Jonah, nice to meet you. How did you know her?"

"Well," Stanley said, "I was acquainted with her mostly back in my unmarried days, if you know what I mean. I would venture to guess quite a few men knew her then. She was quite the wild one."

"Miss Donahue was wild?" Jonah asked incredulously. "I have a hard time believing that."

"Oh, believe it," Stanley asserted. "She was an odd duck. Never much of a looker and plenty of meat on the bones, but once her parents passed away when she was a teenager, she had a parade of men in and out of that house."

"Really?" Jonah asked, still stunned at the revelation.

"Yes indeed," the old man said. "She took over the house and never moved away. Didn't get married, though she had her share of company. But she blew hot and cold. It was a revolving door, then she'd get in a mood and the door was locked for weeks and months at a time. However, by and by, she was eventually back open for business. Probably went on for 20, 25 years. I visited her a few times, I admit, but she seemed to lose interest in me pretty quick. I guess I wasn't her type."

"Hard to believe we're talking about the same woman," Jonah said, then finally moved toward the back of the store. "Let me go back and get your stuff."

"Yep," Stanley said. "That was Evelyn. Back in her day, she was quite the talk of the town."

Jonah stopped, frozen in his tracks, and whirled around once again.

"What did you say her first name was?" he asked.

"Evelyn," Stanley said. "Evelyn Donahue. I thought you knew that."

"No, no I didn't," Jonah answered softly. "I never did know her first name. She didn't seem to be on a first name basis with a lot of folks. But that explains a lot. I'll be right back."

Jonah went back to collect Stanley's order, leaving the old man at the counter wondering what was so interesting about Evelyn Donahue's first name. It took a few minutes for Jonah to return with a box filled with items. By then, he seemed to have regained his composure.

"If you don't mind, I have another question," Jonah said, as he wrote up the bill.

"Sure," Stanley said. "Can you put this on my account?"

"No problem," Jonah said. "Tazik, correct?"

"That's the one," Stanley said. "T-A-Z-I-K. Only one left in town. Used to be a lot more of us, but the rest either moved out or died off."

"I've heard that story a few times," Jonah said.

"Yes," Stanley continued. "This town is only a shadow of what it used to be."

Jonah looked through Harvey's files and found the account named "Tazik," pulled out the slip and noted the items being purchased. Finally, he returned to the topic of Evelyn Donahue.

"Did anyone else ever live at the house?" Jonah asked.

"At Evelyn's?" Stanley guffawed. "No, she was funny about that. Once her parents passed and she inherited the place, she lived alone the rest of her life. Even the men she invited in were escorted out once they were done with business. No exceptions. Absolutely no overnights. Even with her favorites."

"I hear you," Jonah said.

"Of course," Stanley added. "She had quite an effect on some of her men. A few of them dropped over dead for no reason. She must have had a few tricks up her sleeve I wasn't aware of."

Jonah processed this information carefully.

"She has quite a legacy," he finally agreed.

Stanley cocked his head. "Why are you so interested in her anyway?"

Jonah thought about it. Any talk about ghosts would be dismissed as the ramblings of a documented crazy man and quickly become the talk of the town. No sense fueling the fire.

"No real reason," he said. "I've just found some of her stuff as I've cleaned up the house, and I was wondering about her."

"Well, don't wonder too much," Stanley advised. "As she got older, she got meaner. By the end, she was pretty much a hermit, and a nasty one at that. You saw her in the store and she just scowled and turned away. I don't know if she talked to anyone for the last 30 years of her life. And if you did get a word out of her, it wasn't pleasant."

"I'm not surprised," Jonah said. "Well, you have a good day."

"You too, young man," Stanley nodded. "Don't let Evelyn get to you. She's dead and buried."

Stanley left, closing the door behind him.

"If only that were true," Jonah muttered.

CHAPTER 22

Jonah stood outside Dr. Sheffield's office, hesitating. Exactly what should he tell his psychiatrist that wouldn't set off more alarms than had already been rung? Jonah decided that Dr. Sheffield didn't need to know everything.

Transparency can sometimes be a dangerous thing, he thought.

"So how's it going in the new house?" Dr. Sheffield asked.

"It's going fine," Jonah said conversationally, trying to show as little emotion as possible. "All good."

"What about your ghost?" she asked.

Jonah waved casually.

"That was overblown," he said. "I think I listened to too many stories from the locals. I'm not concerned about all that haunted stuff anymore."

Dr. Sheffield looked at her patient skeptically.

"You seemed pretty certain the last time we met," she said.

"I was new in town," he said. "I was letting everything get to me. There's no ghosts. Ghosts aren't real. I know that. You told me so."

Dr. Sheffield thought these answers were much too rehearsed and far too convenient, but realized she wasn't going to get any more information from Jonah. She made a few notes and moved on.

"So what else is new?" she asked.

"I have a girlfriend," Jonah said.

"My," Dr. Sheffield said, not being able to completely hide her surprise. "Now that's unexpected. You haven't had a relationship in quite a while."

"It's been difficult to find someone who can look past my issues," Jonah said. "Katie knows all about them and doesn't care."

"What attracts you to her?" the psychiatrist asked.

"She's pretty," Jonah said. "She's honest. She's funny. She's caring. And she knows what pain feels like."

"What do you mean by that?" Dr. Sheffield asked.

"She has MS," Jonah replied. "Had it for a few years. She's been isolated, snubbed. She can feel it progressing, even if her doctors aren't so sure."

"You know MS can be extremely disabling," the psychiatrist said. "Medical treatment has advanced, but the disease can be very difficult in its late stages. Can you handle that?"

Jonah shrugged.

"I guess every form of refuge has its price," Jonah said.

Dr. Sheffield smiled.

"The Eagles. Lyin' Eyes," she remarked. "I see you're back to your classic rock roots."

"You remembered," Jonah said.

"Of course," Dr. Sheffield remarked.

"Well, anyone can be a fan of The Eagles," Jonah responded. "They've been around for some very important moments in my life."

"I'm sure they have," the psychiatrist agreed. "I think a number of people can say that."

Dr. Sheffield eyed her patient more carefully. She considered her options.

'There's an awful lot of changes taking place in your life," she finally said. "Do you think you can handle all of them?"

"Of course I can," Jonah responded, a little too quickly and smugly for his psychiatrist's liking.

I wonder, Dr. Sheffield thought to herself. *He's not telling me everything.*

The session continued on, Jonah bobbing and weaving through Dr. Sheffield's questions, the psychiatrist trying to find what was really going on inside her patient. As the time began to wind down, Dr. Sheffield came to a decision.

"I'm going to tweak your meds just a bit," she told her patient.

"Really?" Jonah said in dismay. "Do we have to?"

"It's so slight I don't even think you'll notice the difference," she assured him. "I just want to give you a little bit of defense against all the stresses you're facing."

Jonah reluctantly agreed.

"You're the doctor," he said.

By the time the session ended, both psychiatrist and patient were somewhat frustrated. It was a relief to both of them when their time finally came to an end and Jonah uttered the expected last words.

"See you again in three weeks," he said.

As Jonah left, Dr. Sheffield watched him exit the room. She felt no more assured than she did at the conclusion of the last session.

CHAPTER 23

The work week was slowly counting down. Noon on Saturday would be arriving shortly and Kershaw's would be closing for the weekend. But Jonah wasn't anxious to go home. In fact, he wanted to go anywhere but home, which no longer felt warm and inviting. As the days had progressed, the house had again begun to rumble with odd occurrences.

"Let's get away from Easley Avenue and Clayburn for a while," Jonah said.

Katie didn't need much urging. The longer she stayed at Jonah's house, the more it seemed that the surroundings somehow exacerbated her MS symptoms. Once she stayed away for a few days, she began to feel better. She didn't want to admit it to herself, but even Jonah noticed to trend.

"Any ideas?" Jonah asked.

Katie thought for a minute or two.

"Have you ever been to Knoebels?" she finally asked.

"Knoebels?" Jonah asked. "I've seen billboards for it. What is it? An amusement park?"

"Yes," Katie insisted. "It's less than hour from here."

"I don't know," Jonah said. "I haven't been to an amusement park in years."

"Come on," Katie insisted, "It'll be fun. You won't have any worries for a few hours. We can even take Oliver if you want."

Jonah shrugged, half in agreement, though still somewhat unconvinced. Oliver was working in the back room, so Katie raised her voice so he could hear her.

"Oliver," she began, "how would you like to go to Knoebels with us?"

Oliver popped into view quickly with a big smile on his face.

"Can I?" he asked.

Katie looked at Jonah. Seeing the anticipation on Oliver's face, Jonah felt his enthusiasm level grow.

"Do you think his mom will allow it?" Jonah asked.

Katie chuckled.

"It's Knoebels," Katie said knowingly. "Everyone goes to Knoebels."

"I don't go to Knoebels," Jonah objected.

"You're weird," Katie cracked. "And besides, since that's where we're headed, you do now."

Jonah shrugged.

"I guess I do," he finally said. "Does that officially make me a Skook?"

Katie laughed out loud at Jonah's mention of the self-identified moniker of many local residents.

"Yes," she admitted. "You're now officially a member of Schuylkill County."

"I'm not sure that's a badge of honor," Jonah cracked.

Katie gave him that look that Jonah already too well. Jonah, Katie and Oliver headed toward the Paskiel household.

It didn't take long for Jonah to convince Mrs. Paskiel to allow Oliver to tag along. Somehow, the word "Knoebels" in Northeast Pennsylvania has some magical connotation, because the typically overbearing and overprotective mother immediately broke into a huge smile.

"Oh, Oliver hasn't been there in forever," she said. "He always did love it when we went. Here, let me get you some money for the rides and some food. Oliver loves all their food! I have to pull him away sometimes so he can get on the rides!"

Jonah held back a laugh, picturing Mrs. Paskiel – who placed a high premium on enjoying a variety of culinary treats – tugging Oliver away from the concession stand.

"I don't think we'll make it back in time for Saturday night Mass,"

Jonah warned.

Mrs. Paskiel waved her arm dismissively.

"Sometimes you have to make exceptions," she laughed. "You know there was a time we all had to go to Mass on Sunday morning. I know Oliver doesn't like to change his routine, but I don't think he'll mind."

Remembering Oliver's rationale of not wanting to disrupt his mother's routine when he declined the invitation to Jim Thorpe, Jonah glanced back knowingly at his friend. Oliver, however, was oblivious to any irony, visions of Knoebels already dancing in his head.

So armed with Mrs. Paskiel's blessing, Jonah turned to Katie and Oliver.

"Into the vehicle!" he proclaimed, laughing. "Next stop, Knoebels!"

Katie smirked, Oliver complied, and the three hopped into the Malibu and began the pilgrimage to what is touted as America's largest free-admission amusement park. From almost anywhere in the Coal Region, you find your way to either Route 54 or Route 61 to spend a day at Knoebels. With Katie as the navigator, they chose the Route 54 path route and traveled west. Large, colorful billboards promoting Knoebels all along the way assured Jonah they were headed in the right direction. Katie indicated they were almost there when they reached the cemetery on the outskirts of Elysburg. About two miles later, they came to the traffic light at the intersection of 54 and 487, turned right, and a short distance later, were met by all things Knoebels. They passed the Three Ponds Golf Course (owned by Knoebels), the entrance to the Knoebels' campground and the Knoebels lumber yard before finally taking another right that led to the entrance to the park.

Knoebels on a Saturday afternoon in the summer is a mass of activity, filled with families, company picnics, children's groups and out-of-town tourists. Jonah had to park a good distance from the actual park, but a shuttle came by a few minutes later and took the three of them to the entrance.

Founded in 1926, Knoebels Amusement Resort still today attempts to retain the feel of a small, family-friendly park while continuing to grow and add new rides and roller coasters. Admission and parking is free – you could walk through the park all day if you chose and never pay a cent – and on weekends, you have to buy rolls of tickets and pay for individual rides. Only during the week can you purchase wristbands that allow for unlimited use of the attractions – with or without coasters, depending on your level of bravado. Unlike the concrete behemoths of the super-parks, Knoebels still boasts a combination of stone and macadam paths that wind through a park lined with trees and dotted with benches and pavilions. Several bridges crisscross a creek that runs through the middle of the facility, with printed messages on each that memorialize past flood levels when storms caused the waterway to overflow its banks.

On a typical day, the initial crowd at the park tends to thin later in the day as families with small children leave for home. However, many local residents arrive at the park after 5 p.m. – especially on weekdays when wristbands are discounted – keeping the park active until well after dark. Knoebels contains more than 60 rides, an original 1913 carousel, a nationally-famous wooden roller coaster, exhibits, and shops to satisfy anyone of nearly any age, as well as enough food to quell even the most voracious appetite. So it's easy to spend the entire day if you can fend off exhaustion.

Jonah, Katie and Oliver walked pass the various pavilions hosting company and family outings and entered the main section of the park. They soon passed the Skloosh, a ride that featured a boat in the shape of a cut-out log that takes a 50-foot drop into a tidal wave of water. Some guests chose to stand on the observation deck just above the landing spot and manage to get soaked just as thoroughly as those on the ride.

"Is the Skloosh related to the Skook?" Jonah asked sarcastically.

Katie gave him an elbow to the ribs in response.

"You're going to lose your honorary membership talking like that," she cracked.

To the left of the visitors' location was the Crystal Pool, a mega-sized pool filled with nearly 900,000 gallons of water that has served as a Knoebels' staple for decades. To the right was the Impulse, a blue and yellow roller coaster with four upside-down twists and a 90-degree freefall. The three visitors then bore to left, finding the iconic Grand Carousel that has served as a signature ride at Knoebels for many years.

Jonah stood in line at the ticket booth and bought enough tickets to last the afternoon.

"What do you want to do first?" he asked. "Your call, Oliver."

Oliver chose the Italian Trapeze, where the rider was strapped into a swing-like seat and hurled in a circle at faster speeds and greater heights as the ride went on. Jonah wasn't a big fan of "spinny" rides, but his younger companion loved it. Jonah could see the pure joy on Oliver's face, one of the first times that his friend saw Oliver in his own element, unfettered by the rest of the world.

From there, they took on a variety of attractions of greater or lesser adventure, from the Cosmotron to the Super Round-Up to the Flying Turns and the Giant Flume. Jonah watched the happiness and innocence of Oliver's expressions – the awkward, uncertain man who sometimes struggled with everyday life allowing his inner 12-year-old to roam through the park with utter and unbridled enthusiasm, no longer caring about the stares or looks he might be getting from others. If he said something awkward or too directly, if he laughed too loudly, or if his arms flailed a bit too wildly, no one cared. Jonah smiled and put his arm around Katie. He himself hadn't felt this happy or complete in many years.

"Can we ride it again?" Oliver asked as he ran off the Paratrooper, a ride that let his feet swing free as he soared toward the treetops.

"Sure," Jonah said. "Go ahead. Katie and I are going to sit down and take a break."

It took significantly longer to walk through the park than Jonah and Katie anticipated. Visitors are allowed to bring their dogs onto park grounds, as long as they are friendly and leashed. It soon became apparent that Oliver planned on stopping and doting over each and every canine he discovered, and on this day, there seemed to be any number of them roaming the Knoebels' landscape. Jonah lost count after 20, and there were at least that many more for whom Oliver needed to spend quality time.

"These dogs are like stop signs in Clayburn," Jonah said to Katie at one point. "Never-ending."

Katie rolled her eyes and chuckled.

Jonah again marveled at the transformation of his friend; the socially-challenged man was perfectly comfortable around dogs of every shape and variety. Even more fascinating, the animals seemed to respond universally positively to Oliver's touch and voice.

"He's a freaking dog whisperer," Jonah said softly to Katie.

Katie nodded in agreement.

"Isn't it wonderful?" she said.

"Yes it is," Jonah agreed, then wrapped his arm around Katie even more tightly.

When he returned to the rides, Oliver finally drew the line, however, at the Phoenix, the park's vaunted wooden roller coaster that has served as a staple of thrill-seekers for many years. Katie, however, convinced a reluctant Jonah to ride along as Oliver took a seat on the myriad of benches to watch. The two stood in a long and slow-moving line until they finally reached the ride.

"How bad is this coaster?" Jonah asked, just as the ride was taking off.

"Oh, it's not that bad," Katie chuckled. "I survived it."

As the ride picked up steam – rather quickly, at that – Jonah felt his rear end leave the seat, with only the safety bar keeping him from flying straight off the contraption. The car vibrated and banged as it flew across the wooden tracks, rattling and shaking its occupants to and fro. The ride didn't last more than two minutes, but it felt much longer than that. Throughout the entire ride, Jonah disconcertedly never quite regained his proper place in the chair.

"Every one of my bones is rattled," Jonah complained as he walked down the ramp to the viewing area where Oliver waited.

"Oh, stop your bitching," Katie said laughing. "You need your bones rattled once in a while."

Oliver was smiling broadly as they reached him.

"Was that fun?" he asked.

Jonah looked at him.

"It was...memorable," he said.

Katie again jabbed him in the ribs.

"Oww," he said. "They're already sore from the ride."

By now, however, Oliver had a different agenda.

"Can we get something to eat?" he asked.

"As soon as my stomach stops doing flips," Jonah initially objected, but finally demurred to Oliver's wishes.

They ended up at Cesari Pizza, ordering a half-plain, half-pepperoni pie. They took a seat at a table under the adjacent pavilion and placed the placard with their order number in clear sight. While Oliver and Katie waited, Jonah got up and grabbed several orders Tri-Taters – a fried triangular potato with the consistency of a hash brown – and Pierogies at the "Round Stand." The Round Stand was the original park food court, and still serves as the unofficial "center" of the Knoebels' park. Eventually, the server delivered their pie, complete with paper plates and napkins.

"This is amazing pizza," Jonah concluded as he hungrily consumed a piece and wiped the cheese from his mouth.

"It's the best," Katie agreed. "It's one of the unexpected pleasures of the park."

Jonah responded by taking another oversized bite. After the three finished their meal, they took a short walk around the park to scope out the rest of the rides. They walked by the Christmas Cottage, where Jonah dared Oliver to put his tongue on the frozen pole outside.

"I don't think that's a very good idea," Oliver opined, touching the icy pole slightly with his finger.

"No, it's not," Katie said. "Don't listen to him. Didn't you ever see *A Christmas Story?*"

A few more rides ensued, including the Looper, a classic ride which sent its riders upside down or back and forth depending on how you maneuvered the controls. They returned to the Impulse, a more modern roller-coaster than the Phoenix with a long climb and a terrifying drop. Oliver again chose to skip this, but Katie dragged Jonah onto the ride, again against his objections. It took a few minutes for Jonah to get his bearings after the Impulse, which left Katie laughing hysterically.

They walked through the Mining Museum, Knoebels' tribute to the anthracite coal industry and ended up at the Black Diamond, an attraction where you sat in a mine car that moved through the haunted coal mines of Pennsylvania. Jonah's attention was piqued halfway through the ride when Centralia showed up.

But a few seconds later, Jonah froze.

In the blackness of the ride, Jonah was sure he saw the image of Evelyn – or was it Regan? Or both? Jonah couldn't say for sure. The image seemed to change back and forth. The old woman – or women – smirked for a moment, then broke into a deep, evil laugh. The image remained fuzzy, blurred. Jonah still couldn't positively know from one moment to the next the identity of his tormentor. His heartbeat surged as the ride continued forward. He swung his head backward and looked again. Nothing. Was it real, or was it in his mind? He had no way of knowing and he didn't want to consider the possibilities.

When the ride was completed, Jonah got off and walked away in silence.

"Is everything all right?" Katie asked.

"Fine," he said. "Just fine."

But it wasn't. Jonah knew it. Something evil lurked. It was right around every corner, just waiting for a moment of weakness. Whether it be Evelyn or Regan or both, they were patient, they were cunning, and they were persistent. One or the other would jump when they had the opportunity. Even in his happiest moments, he had vulnerability.

Can I maintain that level of vigilance? Jonah wondered. *Just one slip...*

Before they left, Katie coaxed Jonah and Oliver to ride the Scenic Skyway, a 15-minute trip where guests rode what looked like a park bench attached to a ski lift. The ride crossed the street that served as Knoebels' main entrance and gently climbed the side of the adjacent mountain until reaching the top. It then turned around in a wide semi-circle and made its way back down the slope, providing a stunning view of the entire amusement park. As the sun had already begun to set and lights now illuminated the park, the view was twice as spectacular.

The ride was the perfect antidote for Jonah. He relaxed and put his arm around Katie. The two snuggled as Oliver gleefully and obliviously looked about at the various sites, *oohing* and *ahhing* the entire way until Katie couldn't help but giggle. Jonah smiled, and for a few minutes, allowed himself to enjoy the moment.

A short while later, the three headed back to the car and left the park. Jonah was quiet on the way back to Clayburn as his anxiety returned and he kept re-living his experience in the haunted coal mine attraction. With every incursion, Jonah felt his hidden nemesis was coming closer and closer. But even he struggled with how much was real and how much was an invention of his diseased mind.

If I don't know, he thought, *how will anyone else believe me?*

Katie tried to figure out what was bothering him, to no avail. She finally settled on some mindless chit-chat, but even with that Jonah offered little but short, cursory answers. Mercifully, Oliver had fallen asleep in the back seat and was blissfully unaware of Jonah's turmoil

Jonah dropped Katie off at her apartment. He didn't offer to come back, claiming he was exhausted. Jonah then took Oliver home, then went back to his own house. He opened the door, then slammed it shut in anger.

"Keep it here, you bitch," he said. "Whoever and whichever one you are, this is our battlefield. Right here."

Had Jonah been listening closely, he might have heard the words, "Challenge accepted," whistle in the breeze.

CHAPTER 24

Jonah awoke the next day and began his morning ritual. He came downstairs and poured himself a glass of water. His medications were carefully parsed in a weekly dispenser, the best and most reliable way he had found over the years to keep the various pills organized in a way that ensured he took the right prescriptions at the right time. He opened the Sunday morning compartment and dropped the pills into his hand.

He looked down at the medications. Something didn't seem quite right. He was sure he usually had six pills in the morning, but today he only had five.

He thought again.

Maybe I counted wrong, he said to himself. *Wait, Dr. Sheffield adjusted my meds. That probably changed the number of pills.*

That must be it, he rationalized, coming to a conclusion unsupported by the facts.

"I know I put these in here right," he said. He shrugged, threw the pills in his mouth, and swallowed them at once. Over the years, Jonah had mastered the art of taking multiple medications at once.

Mental illness is an insidious enemy. It takes advantage of even the smallest opportunity to overwhelm its host. Did Jonah forgot to add a pill to the dispenser? Was it removed by someone – or something – else? Did it fall on the floor and no one saw it? It didn't matter. It was an opening, and the disease that lay relatively latent slowly began to take advantage of the moment of doubt.

There were ways Jonah could have checked. He could have looked at the other compartments in his dispenser. He might have gone back and checked his prescriptions. He could have picked up his phone and called his therapist's office, at the very least reaching her answering service. He did none of these. The demons in his head – real or imagined – convinced him otherwise.

Everything is fine, Jonah said to himself. *Just didn't count right.*

One missing pill didn't necessarily spell disaster. Missed dosages happen frequently for a variety of reasons. Oftentimes, the next scheduled dose will be enough to steer the patient back to normalcy. But missing a pill was just one factor that played in Jonah's mind and began his brain's descent into darkness. There was the ever-increasing threat of Evelyn. And the constant voice of Regan. The other odd happenings of the house. Jonah's mental health had demonstrated just the smallest cracks of breaking down. But it was a start – just enough, like the small pebble that begins to roll down the hill, collecting more stones and dirt along its path, then pushing rocks and boulders and worse until the avalanche is in full force. It was the opening for which the forces working to take advantage of him had waited.

Jonah spent an uncertain day in his house. He would see a shadow in the corner of his eye and quickly turned, only to find nothing. He thought he caught wisps of images of Evelyn – or was it Regan? He heard voices, but couldn't make out the words. He thought he heard the sounds of both children and adults, cries of both warning and suffering. He tried to close his eyes, but the images invaded his cerebral cortex.

He became more anxious and on edge as the day progressed. Katie tried to call once, twice, even a third time – Jonah wasn't sure how many times. He didn't answer.

Just everyone leave me alone, he thought to himself. *That's all I want.*

Jonah walked around the house jerkily, stopping and starting, jumping in alarm at real and perceived sounds.

"What was that?" he would cry, then wasn't sure if he had heard anything at all. He would investigate, but never found evidence of an intruder. Jonah would then hear a noise in another part of the house, running to that location to no avail.

He started innumerable tasks without ever finishing them. At one point, he started to cook a chicken breast, but never turned it over. He walked away and started re-arranging a drawer of clothing in his bedroom. When the smoke alarm sounded because of the charred meal, he ran into the kitchen and quickly threw the pan into the sink.

Oliver knocked on the door. Jonah didn't answer. Persistent to a fault, Oliver kept knocking. And knocking. He was not to be denied.

"Jonah," he would cry, "are you in there?"

Finally, Jonah had no choice but to answer the door. Oliver must have knocked a couple of hundred times, but despite sore knuckles, he kept it up.

Jonah cracked it open only slightly.

"Are you OK?" Oliver asked plaintively.

"Not feeling well," Jonah said softly. "I'll see you tomorrow."

Jonah closed the door again, giving Oliver no chance to ask another question.

Oliver stood at the door unsatisfied. A few minutes later, he finally turned away and started walking back home. He glanced back and stared at Jonah's house several times. There was something unnerving there, but Oliver couldn't identify it. But the more Oliver looked at the house, the more uninviting and menacing it became.

He eventually circled around and crossed the street, returning to his house, fearful of what he had just witnessed. He walked up to his room, and watched Jonah's home like a silent sentry the rest of the day. Daffodil joined him, barking occasionally at something only she could see. The structure appeared to become darker as the day wore on. Oliver knew something was deeply amiss, though he had no words to describe what he felt. He felt helpless and afraid.

·　　　　·　　　　·

Another pill was missing on Sunday evening, and by Monday, two pills had disappeared from the dispenser. Jonah never noticed. He took them without thinking and proceeded with his day. He picked up Oliver and then Katie for work.

"I tried to call you yesterday," she said. "Multiple times. You never answered."

"Sorry, wasn't feeling well," he said.

Katie looked at him with concern.

"You could have let me know," she said. "Are you better today?"

"I feel great today," he answered. "Like I'm a new man."

Indeed, Jonah seemed to have a lift in his step the entire day. He walked – no, nearly jogged – around the store singing to himself. Katie, Oliver and especially Harvey tired of hearing Jonah's renditions of songs from Deep Purple, Led Zeppelin and The Animals.

There is a house in New Orleans
They call the Rising Sun
And it's been the ruin of many a poor boy
And God I know I'm one

"Can't stand that music in the first place," Mr. Kershaw muttered when Jonah left the room, "and it's even worse when he can't hit a note to save his life."

That didn't stop Jonah. He continued to sing loudly and out of tune, finally finishing his latest rendition.

Oh mother tell your children
Not to do what I have done
Spend your lives in sin and misery
In the House of the Rising Sun

Between songs, Jonah joked and laughed incessantly. He came up and unexpectedly hugged Katie on several occasions, just a bit too tightly. It was the first time he had ever shown her that type of affection at work, and she wasn't sure what to make of it. Harvey, however, didn't seem to mind.

"Never saw anyone so happy to come to work," he finally said begrudgingly.

Several deliveries needed to be made, and Jonah loaded up each order with nary a complaint. Oliver and Katie watched curiously as Jonah climbed into the vehicle, firing up the banged-up truck like it was a race car. He gave an exaggerated wave to Oliver and blew Katie a kiss. Then, he nearly laid rubber as he pulled out of the store driveway.

"He's in good mood," Oliver said matter-of-factly.

Katie followed the truck with her eyes, concern clearly identifiable in her demeanor.

"Yes he is," she said. "Too good."

"What do you mean?" Oliver asked. "Is there such thing as too good a mood?"

"I don't know," Katie answered, hesitation in her voice. "Something just doesn't feel right."

Oliver just looked at her blankly. He didn't know what Katie meant. Katie wasn't sure herself. But Katie knew what she was thinking.

How do you go from sick and solitary one day to ridiculously giddily happy the next? she asked herself. *This was so unlike the Jonah I know. This is a different person altogether.*

Jonah came back a few hours later, still unnaturally ecstatic. While he laughed and joked easily, he seemed self-absorbed, easily distracted, and nearly oblivious to those around him. After another hour, Jonah was finally on Harvey's last nerve.

"When you get him home, can you settle him down?" he asked aloud to both Katie and Oliver. "At my age, there's only so much good mood I can take."

Harvey sauntered slowly into the back room.

"Of course, Mrs. Kershaw will take care of too much good mood as soon as I walk in the front door," he muttered.

When Kershaw's closed for the day, Jonah dropped off Oliver and then went back with Katie to her apartment. They were barely inside when Jonah grabbed Katie, pulled her against him and kissed her passionately.

"I missed you too," Katie said uncertainly.

Jonah picked Katie up with ease – something he had never done before – and carried her to the bedroom. He set her down, and torn off her blouse and bra, pushed her down and pulled down her jeans and panties.

"Jonah?' Katie asked, but by then he was stripping off his own clothes and was quickly on top of her. He took one of her nipples into his mouth roughly.

"A little more gentle please," Katie whispered. "That hurts."

The sex was rough, aggressive. Jonah stared at and past Katie at the same time, a stone look on his face.

When they finished, Jonah got up, put his clothes back on and left the room. Katie took her time before she went into the living room and sat next to him on the sofa.

"Are you all right?" she finally asked caringly.

"I'm great," Jonah said. "Never been better."

Did he just lie, Katie asked herself, *or does he really believe that?*

Looking at Jonah carefully, Katie couldn't tell. It was the first time since she met him that she couldn't read what he was really thinking. That bothered her more than any of his actions.

Jonah ordered Chinese take-out for dinner. By the time he returned with their meal, Jonah's mood had amped up from merely happy to ebullient. The two ate, Jonah talking wildly and unusually fast, bouncing from topic to topic so quickly that Katie could hardly keep track. Jonah flipped subjects from plans to fix up his house to stories about his work deliveries to tales of his past to ideas of how they would spend the rest of their lives together. Katie never remembered Jonah talking so much before or being so difficult to follow. She eventually became too exhausted to even try.

Jonah cleaned up the dishes while Katie sat wearily – and warily – on the couch.

"Hey, do you wanna...," Jonah looked over at Katie. "No, I guess not. You look kind of tired. I guess I should go home and let you rest. I have a lot to do at home. Maybe I'll...no, probably not, I have to do that other thing instead..."

Jonah made less sense as he went on, and when he finally kissed Katie and left for home, it was a relief.

"I don't know what the hell is wrong with him," she muttered to herself, then laid down and fell asleep, exhausted from his company.

After the short drive, Jonah walked into his own home. It was quiet, though his head was not. Thoughts ran in and out at a thousand miles per hour.

"Slow down," Jonah tried to tell himself, but his own words were drowned out by the other voices in his head.

"I'm coming," he heard the familiar voice of Regan. "You need my help."

"Get out of my head," Jonah said. "I don't need you."

In the distance, he heard deep, malevolent laughter. This time, it was not Regan.

"She's coming for you," Regan cut in. "Be afraid."

•   •   •

By Tuesday morning, Jonah's pill dispenser was empty.

"Huh," he said to himself. "I must have already taken them."

Had he thought about it logically, Jonah would have known that couldn't be true. He had gone from his bedroom to the bathroom to the kitchen, with no earlier opportunity to take his medications. But mental illness is clever twice over when playing tricks on the mind, and by now Jonah's brain was poisoned by a toxic mix of madness.

Jonah literally ran out the door into his car. He honked wildly on the horn until Oliver ran out and climbed into the back seat.

"Why are you blowing your horn?" Oliver asked. "I was coming. Same time every day."

"Just making sure you're awake."

"That doesn't make any sense," Oliver noted. "Have I ever not been awake?"

"Always a first time," Jonah said flippantly, then zoomed off too fast down the streets of Clayburn.

"Mom wouldn't let me sleep if I tried," Oliver said.

Jonah zipped up to Katie's house, slamming on the brakes at the last minute.

"Be careful!" Oliver objected, to no avail.

Jonah jumped out of the car and barreled into Katie's apartment, nearly dragging her out.

"I'm coming, for Christ's sakes," she finally said. "What is wrong with you?"

"Just excited to get to work," Jonah replied.

"No one is that excited to get to work!" Katie said. She climbed in the car and looked back at Oliver, silently questioning him about Jonah's condition. Oliver raised his arms in ignorance.

At work, Jonah was a whirlwind from the time he arrived, even more frenetic than the day before. Harvey exhorted him to slow down and take a break.

"Son, we have the whole week to get our work done," he exhorted. "There won't be anything to do if we finish it all in one day."

Mr. Kershaw looked at Katie and Oliver when his pleas went unanswered.

"I don't know what's gotten into that boy's trousers," he finally said, "but I hope it climbs back out soon."

Near the end of the day, Jonah felt his phone vibrate.

"Who could that be?" he asked himself. "Everyone I know is here."

He pulled the phone out of his pants pocket and looked at the screen. It was a text message from a gibberish series of numbers. He opened the text.

"I AM WAITING FOR YOU."

Who the hell is that? Jonah wondered. *Must be a wrong number.*

He took his phone over to Katie. "Look at this," he said.

Katie looked at his phone. "Look at what?"

Jonah turned the phone toward him. The text was gone. "There was just...," he paused. "Forget it. It was nothing."

Am I seeing things? Jonah thought. He was sure the text was there a moment before.

After work, Jonah stayed at Katie's for only a short time. She couldn't stand his constant, frenetic activity and he felt trapped and caged. He finally returned home that night well before dark. He glanced up in the sky before entering the front door. Storm clouds brewed nearby.

Jonah walked into his living room only to find his house nearly broiling. Somehow, the air conditioners had been turned off and the heat had been switched on and set to 90 degrees.

"Jesus," he said. "What the hell is this?"

"It's hell. You have that part right," Jonah thought he heard someone say in a whisper. He turned, but no one was there.

Jonah went to the windows and turn the air-conditioners back on, then walked into the hallway to turn off the thermostat. He heard a loud laugh in the living room. He rushed back in and saw a full-fledged figure standing by the television.

It was Evelyn, this time clearly identifiable. She no longer wore the glasses and paisley dress from his first meeting, but had transformed herself into a archetypical demon with discolored, greenish skin and a black gown streaked with blood red.

"It took you long enough to get back here, you ingrate," she said. "I've been waiting for you since I sent you that message."

"That text was from you?" Jonah asked. "How..."

"Stupid questions from a stupid man," Evelyn cut him off. "Your fancy phones are easily manipulated. I'm glad you're finally able to see me. I've been waiting for you to wake up and see the real world around you."

"What do you want from me?" Jonah asked.

"Want from you?" Evelyn asked. "Oh, your puny diseased mind has no idea what I have in mind. You have more in common with me than you think. I have great plans for us."

"I have nothing in common with you," Jonah protested. "And I certainly am not interested in your plans."

Jonah thought he heard muffled cries in the background. Evelyn turned to an unseen subject.

"Quiet if you know what's good for you," she said. The sounds went silent.

Who is she talking to? Jonah wondered.

Evelyn swung menacingly back toward Jonah.

"You," she said as if she had momentarily forgotten he was there. "I brought you here for a purpose. A noble purpose."

"This is my home," Jonah said. "You're dead and gone. You have no purpose here. Go back to hell where you belong."

Evelyn laughed heartily.

"I'm just getting started with you," Evelyn said. She raised her arm, and somehow a kitchen knife appeared in her hand. She brought her arm forward. At the last second, Regan appeared and knocked Evelyn off-balance. The knife flew across the room, to the left of Jonah's head and landed in the wall behind him.

"You stupid wench," Evelyn screamed. "I was only going to scratch him so he knew I was serious."

Regan looked at Jonah. "See," she hissed, "she wants to hurt you. She'll kill you."

"I have no intention of killing him, you vapid whore," Evelyn screeched. "You on the other hand, that's a different story. I have no need of grousing hallucinations."

The two grappled, and suddenly, disappeared. Jonah swiveled his head backward and saw the knife still implanted in the wall. He walked away, leaving it there. The boom of thunder rolled across Clayburn, following a few seconds later by a streak of lightning.

"Shit's getting real now," he said. "Let's rock and roll. I'm ready to face both of them."

His mind, already reeling as it freed itself from the calming influence of his medications, began to churn madly. Outside, the storm clouds burst open and a hail of rain pounded the town as the thunderstorm made its presence known.

It was not the only maelstrom brewing in Clayburn.

CHAPTER 25

After a few more days, Jonah no longer even checked his medicine dispenser. He had forgotten how out-of-touch his prescriptions made him feel – cloudy, foggy, disconnected from his real emotions. On the other hand, getting off his meds made him free, uninhibited. He could feel life, almost touch it. He could see the deeper reality within himself and all around him. The colors of his emotions swirled through his brain. He could detect the vibrancy of the world at the touch of his fingertip.

Who needs medication? Jonah thought. *I feel better than I have in years.*

Jonah now firmly believed he could face his demons directly. And he had, again and again. His encounters with Evelyn and Regan had become more frequent and more violent. Evidence of his battles across the house were apparent. The house lay in disarray. Gashes decorated the walls. Bottles, pans and kitchen knives littered the floor. A chair was overturned

"You will bend to my will!" Evelyn threatened.

"I will bend over so you can kiss my ass," Jonah said. "This is my house and you're not welcome."

A vase flew across the room, smashing on the wall behind Jonah.

"Your aim sucks."

"I would hit you if I wanted," Evelyn laughed. "But I need you undamaged."

In his altered mental state, Jonah didn't appreciate the danger which he faced. In his mind, he was the courageous, unbeatable, indefatigable warrior. He failed to see that his bravado was misplaced.

He had a hard enough time telling the difference between what was real and what was in his head – maybe everything was real, maybe nothing. He jousted with Evelyn, with Regan, sometimes with both at the same time. He couldn't really tell on which side Regan actually stood. Regan didn't like Evelyn, but it wasn't clear that she cared for Jonah either.

On occasion, Jonah would get into a screaming match with Evelyn, Regan or both.

"You, get out of my house," he would screech at Evelyn, then turned to Regan. "And you, get out of my head!"

"You'll have to make us!" they would cry in unison.

"You sons of bitches," Jonah would cry, take a wild swing and hit nothing but air. "I will kill you both."

Oliver would sometimes hear Jonah's voice from across the street. He didn't hear Regan, but he could hear another woman's laughter. Eventually, he would put his hands over his ears and shut his blinds. He didn't know what Jonah was doing, wasn't sure what battles he was fighting, but it frightened him. He was scared for himself, scared for his friend. His mother would look out the window for a moment, then turn away.

"I don't know what has gotten into that boy," Mrs. Paskiel would mutter. "He seemed to have his head screwed on right until now."

Daffodil stood at the window for hours and barked at the house across the street.

Jonah became increasingly erratic at work as well. He would start the day hyperactive and overjoyed, then return from a delivery haunted and morose. His conversations were broken and staccato. He rarely could stay on one topic for more than a minute at a time. He would circle to multiple other matters, return momentarily to the initial subject, then jumped off to another faraway place. He would start tasks, then leave them unattended and half-finished, only to return to them hours later. He was nothing like the Jonah his co-workers and friends had enjoyed just a few weeks before.

"Are you sure you're OK?" Katie kept asking, more and more concerned.

"Absolutely," Jonah assured her. "Never been better."

Katie knew that wasn't true. This was not the man she loved. She suspected Jonah had stopped taking his medications and wondered exactly what was going on in his house. She hadn't been over since these episodes had started, and Jonah hadn't invited her. He still came to her apartment, but his visits were shorter and less frequent. The two slowly began to drift apart, in part because Jonah was so distracted, in part because Katie was becoming scared of his unpredictable behavior.

Harvey was also keeping a wary eye on his employee. Jonah was still generally doing his work, though somewhat chaotically. He unfailingly completed all the deliveries, and there were no complaints. In fact, if anything, Jonah was completing his trips faster than ever.

"You're not speeding, are you?" Harvey asked one day when Jonah returned in what seemed like far too short a time.

"Of course not," Jonah said. "Do you think this old bucket of bolts could actually speed?"

"That vehicle has served me well for a very long time," Harvey chuckled.

"That's obvious," Jonah said. "I'm not sure which is older, you or the truck."

"Trust me," Mr. Kershaw chuckled. "I have many years on that vehicle."

With that, Jonah sprinted into the store and continued his frantic pace.

"Can't make heads or tails out of what's eating that boy," Harvey said, shaking his head. He was nearly as concerned as Katie for Jonah's well-being, but didn't know how to reach him in a meaningful way.

Later that day, Jonah was out on another delivery.

"I'm very worried about him," Katie admitted to Harvey.

"I am too," Mr. Kershaw said. "But I'm not sure what to do. He's doing his job, he's not causing trouble. When I ask him if there's anything he wants to talk about, he says he's doing great."

"That's what he tells me too," Katie said. "But I know better. He's far from great."

"I hear you," Harvey said. "I hear you loud and clear."

At that moment, Harvey heard his truck barreling and backfiring down the street. A few seconds later, Jonah pulled into the lot, screeching to a stop.

"He's going to beat the hell out of those brakes," Harvey grumbled. He looked over at Katie. "I don't think that's enough to call him on the carpet, though."

"No," Katie said. "He was tough on brakes when he was doing fine."

Harvey chuckled. "We'll just have to keep an eye on him. He's a good kid, and he's still in there somewhere. Hopefully, he'll come back out soon."

Despite Harvey's hopes, Jonah continued to degrade over the next several days. His nights at home also became more and more frenetic if that were possible. Oliver would watch through his window as Jonah ran past one window then the next, swinging a baseball bat wildly at his foe. Occasionally, Oliver caught a glimpse of a shadow or a dark female image wildly mocking and laughing. He heard glasses crash against walls and Jonah screaming unintelligibly. A woman would scream back. These antics went on until late into the night, long after Oliver had fallen asleep. Oliver's mother had mastered the art of not noticing what she didn't want to see, so after some time, completely ignored the activities across the street. But she had to shush Daffodil regularly as the dog continued to bark and growl throughout both day and evening at whatever was occurring at 225 Easley Avenue.

By morning, Jonah came out of the house disheveled with bloodshot eyes. He seemed to take a deep breath once he stepped outside, and straighten himself out as best he could. He honked the horn and Oliver ran out of the house. Jonah's appearance even broke through Mrs. Paskiel's façade and she began to show her concern, at the very least for the safety of her son.

"Are you sure it's still safe to go with him?" Mrs. Paskiel asked cautiously, peering out the window at Jonah sitting jerkily in his car.

"He's my friend," Oliver said. "Jonah would never hurt me."

Oliver's mother wasn't so sure, but she let him go anyway.

"If you ever think otherwise," Mrs. Paskiel said earnestly. "You let me know right away."

"I will," Oliver promised.

As Jonah pulled away, Mrs. Paskiel watched, her anxiety deepening.

"That's not just a case of Saint Vitus Dance," she said, shaking her head. "I've never seen anything like this."

Jonah zoomed down the streets of Clayburn silently, picking up Katie and pulling into Kershaw's, still without a word. He hopped out of the car, ran into the store, and pulled out the orders for delivery that day. He ran about the store, haphazardly filling boxes, throwing them in the truck, and leaving before anyone could get in a proper hello.

"What in the hell has gotten into him now?" Harvey asked.

"No idea," Katie said. "He's getting worse every day."

Business at the store went on as normal until Jonah returned from a delivery shortly after lunch. He was wild-eyed and sweaty, his body language shaky and uneven.

"Are you OK?" Katie asked.

"I just have to sit down for a while," he said.

Jonah brushed past her and hurried into the back room. Katie heard him going up the stairs to the second floor of the building into a section used only for storage. She heard a door slam. She followed Jonah, tried to open the door to the room he had entered, and found it locked. However, she heard him talking fervently inside.

"No, they're not," he said. "You're lying. You don't belong here."

Katie heard silence for a moment.

"NOW!" Jonah screamed. "Get the fuck out!"

Katie wasn't sure what to make of what she heard, but she ran downstairs.

Inside the room, Jonah continued his argument with Regan. "What are you trying to do? I don't need you."

"I am trying to protect you," Regan hissed. "They're after you. She's after you. They all want you dead."

"They're not after me, they're my friends," Jonah protested. "And I will deal with her myself."

"How's that working out for you?" Regan cackled. "All I see is her kicking your ass all over the house."

"Shut up," Jonah said. "Just shut the hell up."

"And as for the ones downstairs, they PRETEND to be your friends," Regan said. "What are they doing behind your back? You don't know, do you? They're plotting against you."

"Fuck you!" Jonah screamed. "You have no fucking idea."

"They are out to get you," Regan continued. "Just like that ogre in the house."

"That's different," Jonah argued. "These people will never hurt me. Evelyn is my enemy – just like you."

"You say that now," Regan hissed. "I have always been here for you. Wait, just wait. They'll hurt you, they'll turn against you. You watch my words. You'll discover I'm the only one you can trust.'

Jonah paced nervously, erratically about the room. He hardly heard the door open behind him, Harvey in the lead with the key with Katie right behind. Jonah whirled around and stared blankly at them.

"How did you get in here?" Jonah asked furiously, then did his best to bring himself under control. "I have to get out of here."

Jonah bolted past them, ran down the stairs, out of the shop and into his car. He tore his car out of the small parking lot, his tires squealing as he zoomed down the street. Back at the shop, Harvey and Katie looked at each other with concern.

"I'm afraid he's near the breaking point," Harvey finally admitted.

CHAPTER 26

Jonah drove to his house, stopped, and looked through his windshield toward the front door. He saw Evelyn smiling ghoulishly in one window, Regan hissing in the other. By now, sweat poured down his face, his body shaking.

I can't do this, Jonah thought. *Not right now.*

He turned away from the house, shifted his car back into drive, and left Easley Avenue once again. He drove aimlessly for a mile or so, then ran across Jack's, a former row home that had been converted at some point into a dive bar. The illuminated sign outside the establishment had seen its better days, but the watering hole appeared to be open for business – about the only requirement that Jonah needed.

What was it about me not drinking? Jonah said to himself. *That was a stupid idea. I really need some alcohol. Actually quite a bit of alcohol.*

Jonah parked his Malibu on the street outside the neighborhood tavern, stepped out and looked in either direction. It wasn't clear for whom or what he was checking, but the street and sidewalk were both clear. He slipped into the building and took a seat at the far end of the taproom along the wall.

The room was dark and windowless, the walnut-stained bar dominating the space. A couple of small tables were wedged against the wall against the door, and a pool table had somehow been impossibly jammed into one corner. The bar seated about 20, but only about half the stools were occupied. The patrons were a mix of men and women ranging from their 20s through their 70s and beyond. Two couples sat together, while the remaining customers were scattered about the bar.

The bartender was about Jonah's age, perhaps a few years younger, tall and rail-thin with wavy blonde hair.

"You Jack?" Jonah asked.

"Jack's grandson," the bartender answered. "Trevor."

"Family business?" Jonah said, half as a statement and half as a question.

"Something like that," Trevor answered.

"What do you have on tap?"

"Yuengling Lager."

"Of course you do," Jonah said. "I'll have a Yuengling and a shot of Patron. And keep them coming."

"Rough day?" the bartender inquired.

"Something like that."

Trevor shrugged, poured Jonah his drinks, and made change from the twenty dollar bill his customer had placed on the counter. As the bartender walked to the other side of the tavern to serve another patron, Jonah heard a familiar voice in his head.

"That's it," the female voice cackled. "Drink yourself silly. Do you think that you won't hear me that way?"

"Go away," Jonah said quietly, gritting his teeth. "I just need a few minutes to think."

"Think!" Regan howled. "Think? What do you have to think about? Will you find your inspiration at the bottom of that glass? Go ahead and try. Pass out. See if I care. Do you think that will really help?"

Jonah swung around violently to face his tormentor, but Regan wasn't there. The rest of the guests at the bar looked over to see what was causing the commotion. Jonah waved his hand in apology, and the observers returned to their drinks.

"What's the matter, Jonah?" Regan mocked. "Don't like to show me off in public?"

"Leave me alone," Jonah muttered.

Jonah downed his shot of Patron and signaled for another.

"Tequila," Trevor said as he poured the second shot. "The devil's poison."

"I hope so," Jonah muttered. "I'm going to see if it works."

Jonah sat in the corner, trying to keep his battle with Regan inconspicuous. But the voice in his head was persistent, aggravating, infuriating... the result of madness, driving Jonah deeper and deeper into the abyss. Occasionally, one of the patrons looked over at Jonah as he snapped at Regan or appeared to be talking to himself.

"Another nut fell off the damn tree," a man said to his wife as he turned his body away from the newcomer. "Can't get away from them wherever you go."

The woman nodded in agreement, shaking her head in disgust.

By his third beer and fifth shot, Jonah had left sober behind and was seeing the world through a dizzy haze. Regan still poked at Jonah, but he was more likely to laugh at her than argue.

A heavy-set woman with dark brown hair who had been eyeing Jonah from across the bar stood up and approached him with her beer. Jonah watched her warily as she came closer. She hadn't washed her hair in several days, and her complexion was mottled. She appeared to be in her early 40s, but in Jonah's state, it was hard to be sure. He could have been off by ten years in either direction.

The woman sat down on the stool next to Jonah and smiled.

"Summer teeth!" Regan hissed in Jonah's ear. "Some 'er here, some 'er there!"

Jonah shrugged as if shaking Regan away, but somehow resisted the urge to speak.

"Hi honey," the woman said. "What brings you here tonight?"

"Rough day," Jonah answered. "Rough week."

"I'm Carol," she continued. "You want some company?"

"Not really," Jonah said.

Regan cackled.

"Of course you do!" she said. "She's just your type."

The woman sidled up to Jonah.

"Look, you're the best thing that's come into this bar in quite a while," she said softly. "Why don't we head to your place and get to know each other a little better."

Regan's voice in Jonah's head became even louder.

"Go ahead and fuck her," Regan whispered. "Enjoy yourself! Then you can get rid of that little skinny tramp of yours."

"Shut the fuck up," Jonah said aloud to Regan then turned to the confused woman.

"Carol," he said, "there's not enough alcohol in this bar to get me drunk enough to take you home."

Carol mouth dropped open in astonishment. She stood up indignantly.

"Asshole," she snapped, turned and walked back to the stool she originally occupied. Several men around the bar tried to hold back smirks and giggles at the turn of events.

After a few minutes, the bar quieted down and things seemed to return to normal. But Regan continued to haunt Jonah, and her target became more and more agitated. Even the alcohol couldn't repress the madness from bursting through the thin veneer of normalcy.

"Drink all you want. You can't keep me away from you," Regan laughed hysterically. "I'll always be part of you, whether you like it or not. Passed out, fully awake, intoxicated or not, it makes no difference to me. I'll haunt you in your dreams."

"I hate you, you mother fucker," Jonah screamed. "Get out! Get the fuck out!"

He started swinging wildly, losing his balance and falling off his bar stool in the process. He hit the wood floor hard on his side, stayed down for a minute, then slowly worked himself back into a standing position. When he finally succeeded, the bartender was staring at him across the counter.

"You're cut off, buddy," Trevor said. "Time to pack it in for the night."

Jonah opened his mouth to object, but Regan interrupted him.

"Fuck him," she said. "Next thing you know, he'll be calling the police. Or pulling a gun on you. You don't need that shit. He's probably one of them. Stay here and he'll be trying to kill you too."

For once, Jonah thought Regan's advice was sound. He regarded the bartender, put his hands up in both surrender and apology, straightened himself out as best he could, and staggered out of the establishment. He stumbled to the car, climbed inside, and for a fleeting second, wondered how he would make it home.

"You'll be fine," Regan whispered. "I'll be your navigator."

"Shut the hell up," Jonah muttered. "You'll run me into a goddam tree on purpose."

One way or another, Jonah made it back to his house in one piece, though his parking left something to be desired. Oliver watched from his bedroom as Jonah slowly and unevenly walked to his front door, unlocked it, entered his home and shut the door behind him. Jonah did not look back as he typically did to acknowledge his friend and neighbor.

Then, a few minutes later, Oliver saw flashes of light flare across Jonah's living room and heard the echo of a horrifying shriek.

Inside 225 Easley Avenue, Jonah was greeted by the terrible sight of Evelyn in all her ghastly glory. Jonah was not in the mood. He picked up a vase, threw it at her, walked to the bedroom and passed out.

•   •   •

The next day, Jonah somehow awoke in time for work, dressed haphazardly, and even managed to pick up Oliver and Katie on his way. His head throbbed, his face was unshaven, his eyes bloodshot.

"Is that alcohol I smell on your breath?" Katie asked.

"Maybe," Jonah said.

"I thought you didn't drink," she challenged him. "You told me it didn't mix well with your meds."

"Sometimes you need a drink," Jonah said defensively.

Or six, Katie thought.

"Are you sure you're fit for work?" Katie challenged him.

"I'm perfectly fine," Jonah insisted.

Jonah pulled his Malibu into Kershaw's, but was slow getting out of the car. He stumbled into the store lethargically and immediately sat down. Harvey took one look at him and shook his head.

"That boy looks like the dogs dragged him all over the county," he said to Katie. "I thought he didn't drink."

"I didn't think so either until now," Katie answered.

Jonah had one delivery to make that morning. He slowly packed the truck with help from Oliver, and drove off ever so slowly down the street. He didn't return for four hours, more than twice as long as the trip should have taken. When he finally reappeared and parked the truck, he didn't come back into the store. A few minutes later, Katie, Oliver and Mr. Kershaw heard Jonah shouting angrily outside. They rushed out the store to see what was happening.

When they reached the parking lot, they saw Jonah standing outside the truck with the door open, screaming and flailing his arms wildly.

"Leave me the fuck alone," he said. "Between you and that other bitch, I can't take it anymore. No one is out to get me except you two bastards and I'm sick of it..."

Jonah paused as if listening to an answer.

"You're fucking lying," he shouted even louder. "Get away!"

At that moment, Jonah turned and saw the shocked faces of Mr. Kershaw, Katie and Oliver.

"Oh shit," he said, fear suddenly spreading across his face.

Jonah ran to his Malibu, hopped in and started the car.

"Jonah, wait!" Katie cried, to no avail. "Let me help you."

He ignored her, roared out the parking lot and disappeared down the street.

"He's in trouble," Mr. Kershaw said. "I'm afraid he needs more help than we can provide."

CHAPTER 27

Jonah returned to his house, and shortly thereafter, 225 Easley Avenue turned into a war zone. Jonah ran from room to room, shutting and locking doors, closing curtains and blinds, and otherwise cocooning himself inside. As he scrambled about the house, he was hounded, first by Regan, then by Evelyn, and finally by cries of both young and old voices he could barely discern.

"What the hell is going on in here?" he cried. "Leave me the fuck alone!"

"You and I are bound for eternity," Evelyn cried. "Together, we are the spawn of Satan. You must continue my work. There is much to be done."

"She's wants you dead," Regan hissed.

"That dumb cow has no idea what she's talking about," Evelyn said. "That's the last thing I want. You are my heir. She is your albatross. I will help you get rid of her for good."

Jonah screamed.

"I'm not shit to either of you," he responded angrily. "I've had it! Get the hell out of my house!"

Suddenly, Jonah hurled himself toward Evelyn. The spirit slashed her arm across her body, catching Jonah in the jaw and sending him crashing across the room. Jonah landed hard against the wall, gashing his forehead. It took Jonah a minute to return to his senses. He wiped the blood from his face with his hand, then dried his hand on his pants. The bleeding slowed to a trickle, leaving his face stained.

"That son of a bitch means business," he growled. "Well, so do I."

"Stop fighting me, you moron," Evelyn implored. "I need you

healthy and strong."

"I told you," Regain whispered. "You can't trust her. You can only trust me."

"I can't trust either of you," Jonah muttered. "I can't even trust myself."

Jonah staggered to his feet, stumbled into the kitchen and grabbed a chef's knife. He turned to pursue Evelyn, but she had followed him and stood right behind him. He thrust the knife forward, deep into her stomach. He pulled it back out, but the wound closed on its own and Evelyn laughed heartily.

"I'm already dead, you idiot," she shrieked. "Do you think you can kill me again?"

Jonah staggered backwards.

"I can try," he said defiantly. "I'll keep trying until I succeed."

Evelyn's body shook as an unnaturally deep guttural laugh echoed across the room.

"You can't get rid of me," she snapped. "I'm here for you. You and I are bound together in a sacred quest."

"I told you she wanted to hurt you," Regan screeched in Jonah's year.

"You, shut up," Jonah said. "You aren't real."

"And she is?" Regan said mockingly. "She's DEAD!"

Jonah stumbled even further backwards, ultimately falling and curling up in the corner of the kitchen. The synapses in his mind fired this way and that trying to comprehend the situation. But as his brain's chemicals swirled in a toxic imbalance, Jonah could make no sense of the world, his current circumstances, or his life. He slumped further down toward the floor.

"What the hell is happening to me?" Jonah cried. "What the hell is going on?"

"I've come for you," Evelyn cried. "You can't hide from me. I am your destiny."

"I'm not hiding from you," Jonah said defiantly. "And you are definitely not my fucking destiny. This is my house! Get out and climb back into your hole, you old bat!"

"You tell her," Regan shrieked. "She's out to get you."

"No one asked you!" Jonah stomped. "You're not welcome here either."

He swung his fists, first at Evelyn, then at Regan, equally ineffectively.

"Aarrgh," Jonah growled. "One of you is dead and the other isn't real. How the fuck am I supposed to fight either one of you?"

"Don't bother," Evelyn mocked. "I can kill you any time I want. I should have done it already. But I have bigger plans for you. Much bigger plans, flawed and weak as you are. But I'll toughen you up with time."

Regan re-appeared in front of Jonah.

"See," she hissed. "I told you. She wants to kill you. She just said so. I'm the only one you can trust."

"I don't believe either one of you," Jonah cried. "I have to figure out how the hell to get out of here."

Jonah got up and hurtled himself around the room, banging into walls and tripping over furniture. His shirt ripped, so he tore it off. His body was bruised across his entire torso.

"Bring it, bitch!" he screamed. "I'm not afraid of you."

Jonah ran wildly here and there, swinging at ghosts and hallucinations, picking up whatever was in his reach to throw. His movements were manic, disjointed, and uncoordinated. He likely would have hit his target only by pure luck, though it would have made no difference. Sweat poured down his face and chest and he screamed maniacally. Evelyn laughed, Regan screeched in his ear. Evelyn would snap her fingers, and the TV remote would fly off the table toward Jonah. Jonah ducked, only to be hit by some other object.

"Son of a bitch," he hissed. "I'm tired of getting beat up."

Jonah finally worked himself into exhaustion. His heart pounded, his legs shook, his shoulders ached. He fell to the floor, then crawled across the carpet. He needed a refuge from the assault he was sustaining. Even through the lens of his addled mind, he knew he had to escape. He reached the coat closet, opened it and maneuvered himself inside. Once there, he slammed the door shut and jammed it closed with his foot.

"Do you think you can get away from me in there, you worthless piece of scum?" Evelyn cried. "I can wait an eternity for you."

"Shut up," Jonah whimpered. "Just go away."

"You think I'm going to show you sympathy?" Something heavy banged against the door. Jonah closed his eyes and sat still in the dark.

"She's going to kill you," Regan shouted in his ear.

"Go. Now," he snapped. "You're not wanted either."

Jonah was frozen. His mind spun even further out of control. He couldn't tell where he was, what day to was, even who he was. The noise outside the closet ebbed and flowed, occasionally shaking him from his stupor. He had no more strength to move. He finally forced himself into a fitful sleep, though he dozed for no more than 10 minutes at a time. Evelyn roared. Regan screamed. Cackles of laughter, children's cries and men's wails filled the air. Occasionally, something crashed against the wall or smashed on the floor. Jonah's phone rang over and over. He didn't dare leave the small room to answer. His body was paralyzed with uncertainty. The night came, but Jonah couldn't tell. The closet remained dark no matter the time. Eventually, his body overloaded and he passed out. Evelyn and Regan chased him into his dreams.

Jonah never answered Katie's phone calls or heard Oliver knocking on the door that evening. He laid catatonically in his closet, barely moving.

·　　　　·　　　　·

The next morning, Jonah didn't come out of his house, nor did he pick up Oliver or Katie for work. Oliver walked over to Jonah's house, lifted his hand to ring the doorbell, but pulled back. Somehow, he knew it would be to no avail and a sudden fear shook his body. He finally started walking to work, knocked on Katie's door and together they headed toward Kershaw's. Their concern was palpable, but they didn't know what to do.

They sat in the store considering their next action until Harvey came in the front door. Immediately, the two began to talk in panicked tones, describing Jonah's lack of communication to either of them and the eerie silence that had enveloped his house since the previous evening.

"Well, what in tarnation do you want me to do?" Mr. Kershaw finally asked.

"I have a key to his house," Katie finally said urgently. "Will you please go and check on him?"

Harvey stood there, grumbling for a few seconds. Finally, he nodded his assent.

"I wouldn't do this for just anyone, you know," he finally said. "But for you..."

Katie hugged him appreciatively. "Thank you."

"If the wife comes looking for me, tell her I'll be right back," Harvey said. "Whatever ails her today can wait a few minutes."

Mr. Kershaw ambled over to his house, pulled his Cadillac out of the garage, and drove down the street.

"Do you think Jonah's all right?" Oliver asked.

"No, I don't," Katie answered. "I don't think he's been all right for quite a few days. But I think things have gotten worse. I have a really bad feeling about what's going on."

Her body shook involuntarily and pain shot through her forehead.

"Damn MS," she whispered. "I know I'm stressed, but I have to hold it together."

Oliver fought through his instincts to withdraw, took Katie's arm and helped her to a chair. Then, he thought hard about what to do next.

•　　　　　　•　　　　　　•

Jonah awoke to the doorbell ringing, followed by a loud knocking on his front door. His eyes were encrusted shut. He wiped them hard with his hands until he could pry them open, but when he did so, he saw nothing but darkness. For a moment, he had no idea where he was. Then, his nightmare came back to him. He moved his legs stiffly and pushed open the closet door.

Evelyn still stood in the middle of the room. She laughed when she saw Jonah.

"The little sniveling rat has finally come out of his hole," she bellowed. "I've been waiting patiently for you – or at least as patiently as I can."

"You're as loud, as fat, and as obnoxious as ever," Jonah said, as defiantly as he could. His legs were weak, however, and he stumbled as he tried to cross the room to the door. He saw Harvey at the door, inserting the key.

"No," Jonah tried to cry, but to no avail. His voice was thin and reedy, then went silent altogether.

Don't come in, he thought. *I don't know what she'll do to you. It's not safe.*

Jonah saw the knob turn and the door open slowly. Harvey stepped through and stopped in his tracks. His eyes traced the outline of the room, which was now in shambles: furniture overturned, the upholstery torn and thrown about. Tables thrown across the room, their legs broken. Glass smashed across the carpet. The screen on the television shattered. Harvey spotted Jonah next, looking desperate and half-dead. He stepped toward him, only to follow Jonah's eyes to the corner of the room, where Evelyn now stood menacingly.

"Who the hell are you?" Harvey said. "How did you get in here?"

"Another intruder," Evelyn howled. "You are not welcome or needed!"

Regan suddenly appeared directly in front of Jonah. "What are you going to do now?"

"Get out of my face," Jonah yelled. "I have to help Harvey before that bitch hurts him."

Harvey glared at Evelyn, then at Jonah, who seemed to be trying to scream at him, though no sound came from his mouth. Harvey then turned back to face the ghost demon.

"I don't know who or what you are," Harvey said commandingly, "but you don't belong here. You need to leave this house now."

"Get out?" Evelyn cried and thrust her finger toward Harvey. "You are the one who is unwanted here."

A malevolent mask of hatred enveloped Evelyn's visage and she channeled an energy of pure evil toward her victim. Suddenly, Harvey felt a tightness in his chest. He brought his hand over his heart and staggered backwards. The pain emanated across his body, down his arms and legs. The old man stumbled out the door. He swayed for a few seconds, then fell unconscious to the ground.

"NO!" Jonah screamed, finally finding his voice. "Not Harvey!"

He tried to get up, but couldn't get his legs to work properly. He crawled across the floor, Evelyn cackling in the background, Regan howling in his ear.

"See," Regan scowled. "I told you. You'll be next. She's a cold-blooded killer."

"Shut the fuck up, would you?" he finally said. "I have to get to Harvey."

"What's the matter?" Evelyn cried. "Can't help your friend?"

Jonah glared at the specter, pure hatred in his eyes.

"Stay out of my way, you son of a bitch," he hissed. "I will find a way to kill you."

Jonah somehow remembered to grab his cell phone laying on the floor. He made it to Harvey, who was sweaty and breathing unevenly.

"Hold on, Mr. Kershaw," Jonah said. "I'm getting help."

With great effort, Jonah focused on his phone. He slowly pressed 9-1-1, then SEND and put the phone to his ear.

"This is 9-1-1," the operator answered. "What is your emergency?"

"We need an ambulance," Jonah finally said, forcing out the words. "I think Harvey Kershaw is having a heart attack."

"Address?" the 9-1-1 operator continued.

"Oh shit," Jonah said. For a few seconds, he couldn't wrap his mind around the question.

"225 Easley Avenue," he finally blurted out.

With that, Jonah dropped the phone and collapsed next to Harvey. Evelyn laughed in victory as Regan faded from view.

"You're mine now, you sniveling defective," Evelyn roared. "You can't save your friend, and you certainly can't save yourself."

Evelyn turned her head as she heard the sirens in the distance. Oliver and Katie heard them at the shop as well. Katie immediately had a sick feeling in her gut. Horror-stricken, she tried to call Harvey, then Jonah. Her calls went unanswered.

"The truck," Katie said.

Both she and Oliver jumped into the shop's delivery vehicle. Katie turned the key. Nothing. She tried again, and the truck again refused to start. She looked at the dashboard. The fuel tank read "E."

"Son of a bitch," Katie cried. "What a time to be out of gas."

She got back out the truck, Oliver right behind her, and together they began to run toward Jonah's house. The farther they went, however, the more Katie's symptoms worsened.

At the house, Evelyn took note of the coming commotion.

"I'm not ready to reveal myself quite yet," Evelyn said as she heard the sirens blaring louder as they came closer to the house. "Not yet, but soon."

Evelyn disappeared, leaving her trail of destruction for others to discover.

CHAPTER 28

A few minutes later in a surprisingly fast response, the ambulance arrived, though to Jonah it still felt like a lifetime. Jonah had regained consciousness and finally forced himself to stand. He tried to look as presentable as possible. Realizing he was shirtless and his body was bruised and battered, he stumbled back into the house. Evelyn was nowhere to be found. Jonah walked tentatively to the bedroom, picked a gray t-shirt out of his dresser and pulled it over himself. He stepped into the bathroom, washed his face quickly cleansing it of both dried blood and grime, and ran a comb through his hair. Then, he came back outside, and closed the door.

No need for them to look in there, he knew. *I can't explain it anyway.*

Putting on as much of an air of normalcy as possible, Jonah managed to not draw much attention to himself as the ambulance arrived and the crew focused on the emergency at hand. The EMT worked to stabilize Harvey as much as he could and the ambulance workers moved him onto a litter as quickly as possible. They needed to get Harvey to the hospital without delay. Jonah didn't say much, trying to keep himself under control, answering most questions with short phrases. He smartly kept Evelyn out of the conversation, and merely talked about how Harvey had grabbed his chest and fallen as he left the house.

"I had overslept," Jonah explained. "Mr. Kershaw came looking for me. I came to answer the door, and I found him here on the porch. I called 9-1-1 right away."

Regan looked over the scene, cackling in Jonah's ear, but Jonah tried to ignore her as best he could.

Keep it together, he kept saying to himself. *Get Harvey help and get these people out of here.*

Harvey finally opened his eyes as they hoisted him on the stretcher and lifted him into the ambulance. Just before he disappeared into the vehicle, the old man weakly winked at Jonah. It was not reassuring in the least. All Jonah could think about was the pale look of death as it crept over Harvey's skin.

Jonah watched the ambulance pull away. He stood frozen on the porch. He heard Evelyn's voice laughing inside the house.

"These intruders aren't going to be able to save you forever!" she bellowed. "You're all mine. Just come back inside so we can finish our business."

Regan appeared in front of him. "See, I told you! What are you going to do now? If you don't do something soon, she'll kill you just like she killed him."

Jonah sat motionless. He pondered his options. Finally, he got up, stumbled into the house and grabbed his car keys. Evelyn has re-appeared and now moved toward him, but he dived out the door, slamming it closed behind him. He ran off the porch and across the small lawn, moving onto the street and into his car as quickly as possible.

"Let her stay in there," he pleaded to whatever higher power in which he still believed. "I have to get away from that bitch. Now."

"But you can't escape me!" Regan cackled from the back seat. "I'm inside you."

"Get out of my face," Jonah screamed. "I'm leaving whether you like or not."

Regan simply laughed.

Jonah put the key into the ignition, and began to turn the key when his passenger door swung open. He looked over, only to see Oliver climb into the car and sit into the seat next to Jonah.

"What are you doing here?" Jonah managed to sputter.

"I saw them putting Mr. Kershaw into the ambulance," he said as he latched his seat belt closed. "I ran all the way back here from the store. Katie tried to come too, but she had to quit. She had an attack. I stopped at my house, but as soon as everyone left, I came here."

"I meant what are you doing in my car?" Jonah pressed.

"I don't know where you're going," Oliver said. "But I'm not letting you go alone."

"I don't remember inviting you to come along."

"You didn't," Oliver confirmed. "But there's something wrong, and I'm not letting you leave by yourself. You need help."

Jonah stared at Oliver, then stared at the road. One thing Jonah had learned about those with autism in general and Oliver in particular was that they could be resolute to the point of stubbornness when they had decided on a course of action. Even through his fogged brain, he knew he wouldn't change Oliver's mind. And the longer they lingered on Easley Avenue, the more time he was wasting.

He glanced over at his passenger once again, then over at the Paskiel household. Mrs. Paskiel and Daffodil stood looking out the window, Oliver's mother with a look of dread and the dog barking madly. Jonah looked at his own house and saw Evelyn drift angrily back and forth through the living room. His hands squeezed the steering wheel tightly as he considered his options, then seemed to make up his mind.

"What about your mother?" Jonah asked desperately. "Did she say you should jump in the car with a crazy person?"

"Not exactly," Oliver said. "But she knows she can't stop me."

Jonah looked at his passenger one more time.

"Fine," Jonah finally said. "Come along then."

He turned the key and fired up the Malibu. He pulled out of his parking space and roared down the road faster than needed. He turned several times through the small town streets, and jetted out to the highway running past the town.

"Where are we going?" Oliver asked.

"To hell," Jonah answered.

"Where's that?" Oliver asked.

"Somewhere you don't want to be," Jonah said flatly. "But you insisted on coming along."

"I heard about hell in Church," Oliver said. "I don't think we should go there. It's not a very nice place. And it's very hot."

"I'm already halfway there," Jonah said cryptically as he sped the car up even faster. "I'm just finishing the trip."

The lyrics from the classic AC/DC song rattled through Jonah's head.

Don't need reason, don't need rhyme
Ain't nothing I would rather do
Going down, party time
My friends are gonna be there too
I'm on the highway to hell
No stop signs, speed limit
Nobody's gonna slow me down

As Jonah drove on, he could see Regan aside of him, then in the rear view mirror, and again in the back seat.

"Are you sure you can trust him?" she said menacingly, looking toward Oliver.

Shut up, shut up, shut up," Jonah screamed.

"I'm not saying anything," Oliver said, confused.

'Not you."

Oliver looked over at his friend in utter confusion. He turned and checked the empty back seat. Jonah's face was curled in a look of hysteria and anger. Oliver had never seen anything like this, and wasn't sure what to do.

"Are you OK?" he finally asked.

"No."

"Can I help?"

"No one can help anymore," Jonah said. "I'm beyond redemption."

They drove on in silence. Oliver fidgeted nervously, but Jonah didn't notice. Jonah turned off the main road onto a little-travelled street that led up to the mountains. As the path turned and twisted and climbed higher, the landscape became wilder and more remote. They had passed the last house on the incline shortly after a sharp turn and moved further and further away from any human presence.

"Where do you think you're going?" Regan cackled. "You can't get away. This is insane. This won't prove anything."

And what do you think I am? Jonah thought. *Insane pretty much describes it, don't you think?*

Jonah continued to ignore Regan as best he could, stepping on the gas as emphasis.

"Woah!" Oliver cried. "You're going to drive right off the road! This is a very steep hill."

Jonah didn't answer Oliver either and sped on.

"Don't listen to him," Regan chanted. "Don't listen to anyone. Only listen to me. You can trust me. As I thought about it some more, maybe you should do it and finally get it over with! You'll at least be rid of that pompous monster in the house!"

Regan laughed furiously. Jonah stared at her, then returned his eyes to the road. Jonah turned again, this time off the paved road onto a dirt lane. The Malibu bounced and shook on the rutted passage as it weaved through shabby trees and overgrown weeds. Stones flew as the tires rammed over the hard ground, cracking branches that had strewn across the road along the way. It was all Jonah could do to keep the car on the path.

"What are you doing?" Oliver cried. "Jonah, you're scaring me."

"Exactly what are doing?" Regan hissed. "Do you think you can get rid of me. I will follow you through death and beyond. Do it, I dare you. It's about time you grow some balls!"

The vegetation lessened and the ground turned to a mixture of brown and black – coal mixing with the dirt. Jonah came to a clearing and stopped the car. They had reached the top of the peak. Nothing but an overcast sky appeared above them.

Jonah and Oliver got out of the Malibu. As Oliver look around, he saw they had reached the pinnacle of an old coal strip-mining operation. The mountain dropped off into a precipitous cliff, a man-made scar of rock, coal and dirt that stretched down to the hard surface below.

Oliver hesitated as they approached the edge, but Jonah kept moving forward. He had a purposeful demeanor, as if he had decided on a course of action and would not turn back.

"It's only a little jump," Regan whispered in his ear. "Just one step. If this is what you really want to do, I'll be the only one that comes with you."

As Jonah got closer and closer to the cliff, Oliver became more dismayed.

"What are you doing?" Oliver finally said. "You can't do what I think you're thinking about doing."

"How do you know what I'm thinking?" Jonah asked.

"I don't know," Oliver said. "I'm not sure. But it's not good. I know that."

Jonah stopped and turned toward his friend. He studied him up and down. It appeared for a moment he would move back toward Oliver, but he stopped.

"It's for the best, Oliver," he said. "The house has beaten me. Regan has beaten me. Evelyn has beaten me. Harvey is probably dead – because of me. I should have never come here. There's nothing left for me here."

"I'm here for you," Oliver said, suddenly firm. "I am your friend. Katie is your friend. We are here to help you."

Jonah smirked.

"It's not enough," he concluded. "It was never enough. I should have known better. I'm never going to escape my illness. Both of you will be better off without me. I shouldn't have put either of you through all this."

He turned back toward the edge and began walking toward it once again. He was close enough to see the bottom, a 250-foot drop ending with a winding macadam road punctuated by some unhealthy pine trees. He wondered how long he would be in the air and whether his life would flash before his eyes.

"Just jump," Regan said. "Then your troubles will be over. I'm here with you. I'll help you. I won't let you change your mind and continue your misery."

Jonah took a tentative step forward.

Just a few more steps, Jonah thought, *then all this pain will be gone.*

At that moment, Jonah felt two arms wrap around his stomach, and with strength he could have never expected, watched helplessly as Oliver pulled him backwards and onto the ground. Jonah wrestled to get free, but was unable to pry himself from his friend's iron grip.

"Fight him," Regan implored. "He's ruining everything."

"What the hell are you doing?" Jonah finally said.

"I'm not letting you throw your life away," Oliver said. "You're too important...to me. To Katie. You're my friend. You're my only friend. You're the only real friend I've ever had."

Jonah stopped fighting. Oliver allowed Jonah to sit up, though he still gripped him tightly. Jonah looked at Oliver as if seeing him for the first time all over again. Jonah had a moment of clarity as he forced himself to break through the fog that shrouded his brain. Regan frantically tried to get Jonah's attention, but he used every bit of his will to cast her aside. He stared at Oliver for a long minute, then another. His focus was entirely on the man who had just unexpectedly saved his life. Finally, his shoulders sagged.

"Call 9-1-1," Jonah said. "I need help. Don't let me change my mind. Hang on to me until the ambulance gets here."

"I promise," Oliver said.

CHAPTER 29

Jonah heard the sirens coming closer and closer, saw both an ambulance and a police car reach the precipice, and watched as Oliver frantically tried to explain what had happened. Jonah fought anew, flailing this way and that, as he was being placed on the gurney, until the EMT at the scene came inches from his face.

"Jonah," he said, "it's me. We're trying to help you."

Jonah paused, trying to process the familiar voice. He opened his eyes and looked up. He saw the face of Myles, the customer from Kershaw's.

"Myles," Jonah finally said in recognition. "You run ambulance?"

"Of course," he answered. "Who do you think ran over my flashlight? I still haven't forgiven the driver."

Jonah smiled weakly.

"Don't let me die," he whispered.

"You won't," Myles assured him. "Not today. Not on my watch. But you have to help me."

Jonah calmed down enough to be sedated in order to be safely carried to the ambulance and onto the hospital. He remembered little of the rest of the trip.

In fact, there was little clarity in Jonah's next few days. There were a few moments of consciousness, and fewer still of understanding. He had no idea where he was, what day it was, or why he was there. Sometimes he struggled even to remember his own identity.

He remembered waking in agitation more than once, trying to escape from whatever place he was being held. He tried to get out of bed, but couldn't. He tried again with more force, only to discover he was held by restraints.

Where am I? he thought. *Why am I tied up? Am I being held captive? Someone help me! I've been kidnapped.*

Regan appeared fleetingly, smiled wickedly, then disappeared.

"Son of a bitch," he screamed, then the drugs overwhelmed him again and he relaxed. Blissful sleep ensued.

He woke up again.

How long has it been? Jonah thought to himself. *Hours? Days? Weeks? I have no idea.*

He saw lights above him, figures moving about in his room. They tried to talk to him, ask him how he was feeling. They asked his name, if he knew where he was.

How the fuck do I know where I am? You're the ones holding me captive.

He tried to answer, but couldn't form the words.

Jonah would waken for a few minutes at a time, but had trouble keeping his eyes open. He babbled to the medical staff, telling an incomprehensible story with Regan and Evelyn jumping in and out of the tale, a house gone wild, an attack on his boss. As he talked, he became more emotional and aggressive. Several times, he needed to be sedated. Slowly, Jonah would calm down and go into a fitful sleep.

Where is the end? he thought. *What is happening to me? Am I alive or dead? Am I in hell?*

•   •   •

Jonah opened his eyes. The room slowly came into view. It was white...or cream...or some other maddeningly neutral color. Jonah couldn't be sure, nor did he particularly care.

Suddenly, Regan appeared in front of him.

"I'm here waiting for you," she shrieked. "What do you think you're doing?"

Jonah closed his eyes again.

"I'm not talking to you," Jonah answered calmly. "You're not here. You never were."

His eyes were heavy, his mind addled. He returned to the sanctuary of sleep. A battle was going on inside his brain, between madness and sanity. A new cocktail of medications battled the chemical imbalances that caused his mind to short-circuit. His brain was being re-wired. There were moments of clarity, and moments of fogginess. The war was not yet over.

•   •   •

A few days later, after many fits and turns, Jonah opened his eyes again. For a moment, he thought he saw Regan again. But this time, the image dissolved, and a female nurse in lavender scrubs stood by his bed.

"You're awake, Mr. Frost," she said. "Nice to see you among the living."

"Where am I?" Jonah mumbled, disoriented and struggling to put the pieces of reality back together.

"You're in the hospital," she said. "I'm your nurse. My name is Ann."

Jonah looked slowly about the room. He recognized it as a typical psychiatric room: nearly bare, with nothing that would allow him to hurt himself or others. His bed and a visitor's chair, which sat empty, dominated the space. The nurse had wheeled in a cart with a laptop and several medical devices.

"How long have I been here?" he finally asked.

"This is your sixth day with us," the nurse replied. "How much do you remember?'

Jonah shook his head. He slowly sat up in the bed and tried to orient him better to his surroundings. He looked at the nurse, for the first time recognizing she was a woman of average height and weight, approaching 50 if she hadn't yet reached that milestone. Her auburn hair was flecked with a bit of gray, and she wore little if any make-up. Definitely not Regan or Evelyn.

"Not much," Jonah admitted. "I'm still trying to piece everything together."

"You've been telling us quite a story," Ann said. "We haven't quite gotten down exactly what happened to you."

"Yeah, well," Jonah said, finally cracking a bit of a smirk. "you can't always believe a crazy person."

Ann chuckled. "It's good to hear you're feeling a little more normal," she said. "Your friends will be glad to feel you're starting to feel better."

"Friends?" Jonah asked.

"A young man and a young woman," the nurse said. "Oliver and..." Ann paused to think.

"Katie," Jonah completed her sentence.

"That's it," she said, snapping her finger. "Katie. She seems to be quite fond of you."

Jonah blushed.

"She's put up with a lot," he said, still working to re-assemble the events of the past few weeks. "I owe her a huge apology."

"Well, I'm sure she'll be back soon," Ann assured him. "You'll be able to tell her whatever you need. She'll be thrilled to see you up and about again."

Jonah forced a smile. His mind was still trying to put together what was real and what was imagined over the past several weeks. Regan was his own creation, but Evelyn...what the hell was that? In all of his years battling the beast of mental illness, Jonah had never encountered anything quite like that demon.

"I've still got a lot to sort out," Jonah finally said.

"That's why you're here," the nurse assured him. "We're not letting you leave until you're ready."

The nurse turned toward her cart.

"Now that you're awake," she said. "I'd like to check your vitals. Are you all right with that?"

Jonah nodded his assent, and Ann placed the heart rate monitor on Jonah's finger, then wrapped the blood pressure cuff around his arm.

"Now you just relax," she said. "We're here to help you. And you have friends who will support you down that path. You're in good hands."

In just the nick of time, Jonah thought. *This time, I nearly literally went right off the cliff.*

CHAPTER 30

Jonah opened his eyes. He looked around the hospital room.

Still here, he thought. *Wherever "here" is.*

He hadn't bothered to ask what in what institution he landed. Most of these psychiatric facilities tended to blur one into another after enough visits. Jonah was a veteran of many. He long ago lost track of all the names.

Then, he spotted a woman sitting beside him. Not Regan, certainly not Evelyn, not even Nurse Ann...

"Katie," he whispered. "You're here."

"Of course I'm here, silly" she said. "Where else would I be? I've been waiting for you."

Jonah held out his hand. Katie grasped it and smiled.

"I'm here as long as you need me," she said.

"I'm sorry for the way I treated you," Jonah said. "You shouldn't have had to put up with that."

"I know it wasn't really you."

Jonah gazed lovingly at Katie for the first time in weeks. Then a thought crossed his mind and he became suddenly seriously.

"Harvey?" he asked.

Katie sighed in relief. "He's fine," she said. "Minor heart attack. He'll be back at work in a month or so. Doctor told him he needs to exercise more and eat less fatty foods. He wasn't happy."

"What did he say happened?" Jonah asked.

"He doesn't remember at all," Katie said. "Complete blank."

Jonah thought about that. *Probably for the best*, he surmised. But Katie needed to know.

"It was Evelyn," he told her. "She attacked him. We're lucky she didn't kill him."

Katie looked at Jonah, examining his face, trying to discern what was really inside him.

"I know what you're thinking," Jonah said. "But I am absolutely sure of what I saw. Even in the condition I was in, I swear to you I saw what happened. I was sure at first that Harvey..."

"It's OK," Katie said. "I believe you. And Harvey will be fine. Let's just worry about getting you better. Then we'll worry about Evelyn."

Jonah lay back and relaxed, holding Katie's hand tightly. He felt safe for the first time in weeks. He felt loved. He believed he may have finally begun to find the path forward, with Katie by his side. The two sat there, hand in hand, for a very long time. No words were necessary, though occasionally a few were spoken. Katie's presence helped bring Jonah back, helped him remember, helped his drive to recover. He would not let her go again.

"You want to take a walk?" Katie finally asked after some time.

"Can I?" Jonah said.

"Do your legs work?" Katie asked sarcastically.

"Pretty sure," Jonah said. "I haven't tried them out lately."

"Then as long as you don't go tearing up the nurse's station, I think the exercise will do you good," Katie responded, smiling.

"OK," he agreed. "You're the boss."

Jonah slowly got out of bed. His body had been weakened by the struggle within, and his muscles protested. But as his feet hit solid ground and he stood up, he wrapped his arm around Katie.

"Let's go see the sights," he smiled. "You might have to hold me to make sure I don't fall."

Katie wrapped her arm around Jonah, joyful to have him back.

"I don't think that will be a problem," she said.

Katie led him out of the room and down the hall. In truth, there was little to see. Rows of rooms settled on both sides of the sterile hallway. A busy nurse's station was perched in the middle, with both medical staff and security nearby. Those present smiled as Jonah and Katie passed. Jonah waved, though he didn't specifically recognize anyone present. Still, some had worked with Jonah, and noted the positive effect Katie had on their patient. The was the first time they had seen Jonah leave his room on his own in a sensible state.

A common room was located at the end of the wing, that included a television with a few tables and chairs where patients could relax and socialize. A few people populated the room, but Jonah wasn't ready to meet them. He and Katie peeked inside the open door. Those present made eye contact with the new visitors. The facial expressions ranged from cautious acceptance to wariness to distrust. Jonah pulled back quickly and moved away from the door.

"Not yet," he said.

"That's fine," Katie assured him. "Your pace."

By the time the two of them returned to the room, Jonah was exhausted.

"Wow," he said, "a little out of shape. Don't think I'm quite ready for my Phillies' tryout."

Katie laughed appreciatively.

"That's the Jonah I know and love," she said. "Welcome back."

"I'm not quite all the way back yet," Jonah answered. "But I'm actually getting there. Thank you for waiting for me."

Katie snuggled up to Jonah.

"You're worth it."

"Oh, I doubt that," Jonah said. "But I'm glad you think so."

As the day drew long and visiting hours came to a close, Katie got up to leave.

"How did you get here anyway?" Jonah asked.

"Your car," Katie said, noting the surprise in Jonah's face. "Yes, I can still drive you know. I'd rather not, because you never know when my symptoms will flare up, but I made a deal with the MS gods so I could come and see you."

Jonah looked at Katie in increasing wonder.

"I left my car on the mountain," he said, recalling his last minutes before the ambulance arrived.

"Yes," she agreed. "you did. But did you think they were just going to leave it there? They brought it back a few days afterwards."

"What about Oliver?"

"They brought him back too," Katie said, laughing. "Only the same day."

Jonah smiled, but a clear look of relief creased across his face.

"He saved my life, you know," he said.

"I've heard," Katie said. "I'll bring him along next time so you can thank him yourself."

"There's a lot more to him than you guess," Jonah added.

"Yes, there is," Katie agreed. "No question."

Then she changed the subject.

"Look," Katie said, turning more seriously. "I'm going to figure out what's going on once and for all in your house. I need to find out who Evelyn is and what she is trying to do."

Jonah turned more concerned.

"She's dangerous," he said. "I've seen her at work with my own eyes."

"I know," Katie said. "I'll be careful. But it's time to expose all of her secrets."

CHAPTER 31

With Harvey still recovering and Jonah hospitalized, Katie and Oliver did their best to keep Kershaw's store running, some days better than others. They suspended delivery service, and handled only walk-in customers. They reduced ordering to only the essentials, actually allowing the inventory to work its way down to a manageable level.

At the end of one day, Katie grabbed the keys to the pickup truck and looked at Oliver.

"I'll drive you home today," she said.

Oliver looked at her dubiously.

"Are you sure you can drive that truck?" he asked.

"How hard can it be?" Katie asked. "It's got gas in it now."

Uncomfortable with using Jonah's Malibu on an everyday basis, she had left the car at her apartment. Now she regretted that decision, but she didn't want to take the time to retrieve it. She was afraid she'd lose her nerve with any delay.

"I don't know if this is a good idea," Oliver reiterated.

"Lock the doors and get in the truck," Katie ordered. "I can drive this thing just fine."

Oliver did as he was told. Katie climbed into the driver's seat, pressed tentatively on the clutch, and turned the key. The old truck coughed and sputtered, then died. Katie pressed the clutch down more forcefully, turned the key again, and the vehicle finally came to life. She shifted the truck into reverse, turned her head to see behind her, and left the clutch out just a tad too fast. The truck jumped and stalled.

"Son of a bitch," she muttered.

"Are you sure you know what you're doing?" Oliver asked. "I don't think it's supposed to do that."

Katie looked over at him sternly.

"Don't start with me."

Oliver looked straight ahead and didn't say another word.

After several more tries, Katie finally made peace with the vehicle. It spit and backfired its way through Clayburn, but she finally negotiated the path to Oliver's house and parked.

"What are you doing?" Oliver asked.

"I need something in Jonah's house," she said.

Oliver shook in fear, glancing forebodingly at 225 Easley Avenue.

"Are you sure you should?" he asked. "Do you want me to come with you?"

"No," Katie answered. "Thank you. But I'll only be in there a minute. I'll be right out. You can watch Jonah's door from your house if you want to make sure I leave safely."

"OK," Oliver agreed, finding that solution acceptable. "Please be careful."

"I intend to," Katie assured him.

Oliver walked through his front door and immediately found his mother. As Katie crossed the street, she turned around momentarily and saw Oliver, Mrs. Paskiel and Daffodil all watching her out the side window. Obvious concern creased their faces and Daffodil seemed to be growling. She waved to them, pulled out Jonah's house key to open his front door, turned the knob and disappeared inside.

As she closed the door, Katie gasped and stood frozen as she looked cautiously around the house. This was the first time she had been inside since Jonah had been admitted to the hospital. She had retrieved Jonah's car from the police, but found no reason to go inside his home. In fact, fear kept her far away. Now, however, it was time to find out the real identity of Evelyn and discover if there was any way to combat her. Katie resolved to do what was necessary to save Jonah.

Nothing much had changed since that fateful day that imperiled both the lives of Jonah and Harvey. As Katie finally moved slowly through the house, she picked up a few pieces of still-intact knickknacks and put them back in their place as she cleared a safe path through the rubble. Her head remained on a swivel, looking this way and that, searching for any sign of danger. She walked across the living room and finally reached the door to the basement. She turned the knob ever so slowly and carefully. She opened the door, flicked on the light switch, and peered down into the suddenly illuminated cellar. All was quiet. She crept slowly and tentatively down the steps, one at a time, looking in all directions, every nerve in her body screaming for her to turn around and leave with all possible speed.

She finally reached the landing, and turned toward the nook where the desk was located. As she came closer to the dusty old piece, the lights flickered. Katie froze, but when the bulbs again stabilized, she moved forward. She opened the drawer, pulled out the newspaper clippings and the book on the Molly Maguires, and turned once again to leave. The house rumbled, and Katie felt a clearly angry specter nearby, now fully aware of her presence. She held the clippings and book tightly, and hurried toward the steps to leave.

"Where do you think you're going, you little whore?" a perturbed voice growled. "You don't have permission to take my property."

"Excuse me?" Katie answered valiantly. "Last I checked, you were dead."

Katie felt herself pushed back by some unseen force.

"You think you can find some way to stop me?" the voice growled, and Katie was sure she could see the outline of a woman in the shadows. "What do you think you'll learn?"

"I don't have to answer to you," Katie said, mustering all the courage she could. "This is Jonah's house now."

Katie felt a force circling her body, then pulling back.

"I could swat you like a fly," the voice roared, the image of the malevolent Evelyn becoming more defined. "But you're not worth it. You're nothing but a sickly little girl. You're no use to me. And you're no use to your boyfriend. You can't help him. He will be mine, whether he likes it or not."

Katie straightened her back in defiance. "Go to hell!" she screamed.

The voice laughed a deep guttural howl.

"You don't think I'm already there?" she finally screeched. "Get out of my house. See what you can discover. It will do you no good."

Katie stared angrily at the now fully visible figure, her first clear view of Evelyn. For a moment, she was paralyzed with fear.

Jonah wasn't making this up, a part of Katie thought. *Of course he wasn't making this up. But until now, I could never be really sure.*

Then, she forced herself back to her senses, turned, ran up the steps and out the front door. She burst onto the porch and then the sidewalk, squinting as her eyes adjusted to the bright sunlight. She glanced across the street, gave Oliver, his mother and Daffodil a thumbs up, and headed toward the old truck. Mrs. Paskiel put her hand on her heart in relief and left the window.

"Now comes the really scary part," Katie muttered. "I have to get this damn truck back to the store."

•   •   •

Once Katie returned the balky vehicle back to Kershaw's, she found a shopping bag and stuffed it with the book and newspapers. Then, she walked back to her apartment to examine the relics.

Safely back home, Katie first paged carefully through the remnants of each newspaper, but could find nothing of significance that would relate to Evelyn Donahue or Easley Avenue. Typical small-town news – borough council meetings, local youth sports results, promotions, births and deaths – but not a single story obviously connected to Jonah's home or its former resident.

She then opened her laptop and began to Google the various dates from each newspaper, checking both the day before and that day. She started with September 1961. On the 11th, the Category 5 Hurricane Carla rampaged across Texas. On the 12th, Air France Flight 255 crashed in Morocco, killing 77 passengers. As far as she could tell, however, nothing of note happened in Clayburn or any other neighboring town.

What the hell, Katie thought, *a random date that doesn't seem to have any connection to the area.*

June 13, 1963. The South was in turmoil. Two days earlier, Governor George Wallace stood on the steps of the University of Alabama to protest court-ordered integration. On the 12th, civil rights activist Medgar Evans was shot and killed in Jackson, Mississippi. At the same time, the long-awaited movie epic, *Cleopatra,* starring Richard Burton and Elizabeth Taylor, premiered in New York City after many delays and cost overruns. Finally, on the 13th, two U.S. Representatives were convicted of accepting bribes. Still, nothing that would directly affect Clayburn or Northeast Pennsylvania.

February 11, 1966. The day before, the then controversial novel *Valley of the Dolls* – which eventually became one of the best-selling novels of all time – was released.

Probably still hasn't made it to Clayburn, Katie thought ruefully.

On the 11th, New York City launched a "Crash Clean-Up Campaign" that rehabilitated 40 blocks of the city. In Clayburn, the town council approved bids for several street repairs.

Last time that's ever happened, Katie added, *at least based on the potholes I drove over today.*

March 18, 1969. A tumultuous time in American history. On the day before, Golda Meir became the first woman prime minister of Israel. On the 18th, the covert bombing of Cambodia by the United States, dubbed Operation Breakfast, commenced. Katie noted wryly that on the 20th, John Lennon and Yoko Ono were married.

"Broke up the Beatles," Katie laughed aloud. "God knows what it did in Clayburn."

November 12, 1973. Even the world was quiet. Egypt and Israel signed an U.S.-backed cease-fire the day before. Labor strife hit England. The Clayburn mayor promised to economically revitalize the town by attracting new business, a promise that went unfulfilled even to this day.

April 3, 1977. Palm Sunday. Fleetwood Mac's *Rumours* album charted number one, and remained there for 31 weeks.

"Wasn't country," Katie cracked. "Not number one here."

Overall, a quiet weekend around the world.

"But not here," Katie pondered. "Not for Evelyn. But what happened?"

Katie considered the question, but could come up with no answers. Clearly, why Evelyn kept these specific newspapers, why these dates were so important, was unique to Evelyn, and only to her. No one in Clayburn seemed to be able to shed light on her motivation. And the news of the day – even the local coverage – offered no additional insight.

Katie got up and stretched, walked into the kitchen and retrieved a bottle of water. She picked up Broehl's book on the Molly Maguires and paged through it. Evelyn seemed to have highlighted random passages, most of which justified the group and cast doubt on their fate.

"The Molly incidents, then, did not settle the basic labor-relations dispute, nor have any real effect on the conditions in the coal field which led to so much tension. The atmosphere was still that of the company town, the dangers of coal mining still as frightful, the rewards still as low, and the life of the miner still as depressing and debilitating."

She then read a passage on Franklin P. Gowen, the rail president and attorney who served as the chief ringleader of the Molly Maguire prosecutions. Gowen eventually committed suicide in a hotel room.

"Why he did it remains a complete enigma. Some anti-Gowen, but pro-Molly Maguire writers have attributed the suicide to a guilt complex due to his handling of the Molly cases."

Katie noted again that Evelyn's last name matched one of the Molly Maguires hung in Mauch Chunk: John "Yellow Jack" Donahue. She still thought that was more than random happenstance.

"Let's see what I can find out about Mister Donahue," Katie said. "This looks like the most promising lead."

However, what Katie could discover about Yellow Jack Donahue could be summed up as, "Not much." Historians couldn't even agree where he received his nickname. One argued it came from his reddish-yellow hair. Another said it was from his jaundice-toned skin. Yet others claimed it was a term associated with suspected union organizers.

He had eight children. Katie could trace most of his descendants to the present day. One of his great-great-granddaughters went to court in 2006 in an attempt to get Yellow Jack pardoned and his name cleared. She argued that Donahue had been "punished and murdered for his goal of establishing a civilized, unionized trade" and that generations of her family had "not only endured pain and suffering, but also ethnic racism and prejudice."

Yet, Katie could find no trace of Evelyn in the family tree. So she turned her attention to Evelyn herself. She quickly discovered that Evelyn was a puzzle even in life. As it turned out, Evelyn was not born "Donahue." She was born "Shemanski." But shortly after her parents passed away – her father by undetermined causes, her mother shortly thereafter – she changed her name and began a lifetime of odd and mysterious behavior. As far as Katie could determine, Evelyn never found a husband, so her name change was not due to a marriage.

"So why did you become a Donahue?" Katie wondered, and began digging further back into Evelyn's family genealogy.

The picture slowly formed in Katie's mind as she checked and cross-checked sites and family ancestries. Evelyn's mother's maiden name was Sullivan, a good Irish name if there ever was one. Her grandmother's maiden name was Stewart – as was her great grandmother's. It seemed that Elizabeth Stewart, Evelyn's great-grandmother, never married but birthed a child out of wedlock. And in one genealogical table, an anonymous contributor had added the name of the father.

"John Fucking Yellow Jack Donahue," Katie said incredulously. "You have got to be kidding me. One of the most famous of the Molly Maguires."

Katie thought back to Jonah wondering why everything always came back to the Molly Maguires. The question was more relevant than he even realized.

"It always comes back to the Molly Maguires," Katie said in wonder, "because, somehow, it's about the Molly Maguires. Even after all these years."

A dark, rumbling laugh echoed through Katie's apartment. She shot up from her chair and looked around suspiciously.

"Stay in your own cave," Katie hissed. "You're not welcome here. This is MY home."

CHAPTER 32

Nurse Ann sat in a chair facing her patient. Jonah was slowly returning to his healthy self.

"So what happened that brought on this latest episode?" she asked Jonah. "How did you end up back in a psychiatric hospital?"

Jonah squirmed, recounting in his mind the incidents of the past few weeks.

"I'm going to sound like I'm crazy," he said. "Which, of course, I am."

"Try me," Ann challenged.

Jonah regarded the nurse, then spoke in a tone that was completely serious.

"My house is haunted by the woman who lived there before me," he said. "She tried to kill me."

Jonah paused.

"No, that's not right," he amended. "She doesn't want me dead. She's wants to control me. I don't know why. But she stole my medication. She's a malevolent demon. I have a feeling that whatever evil she committed during her lifetime, she wants me to continue."

Ann looked at him dubiously.

"A devil who took your medications in order to possess you," she said. "You know you sound a little paranoid. Have you told your doctors this?"

"They presume it's part of my hallucinations," Jonah said. "If they thought I believed it was real, they'd lock me up and throw away the key. I know how crazy it sounds. But I'm not hallucinating. This is not my mental illness talking. I know the difference between Regan and

Evelyn. Regan is my madness. Evelyn is – something else entirely. I've never seen anything quite like her."

Jonah could see the skepticism on Ann's face, despite her efforts to hide it.

"I'm being completely serious," Jonah insisted.

Ann had been a psychiatric nurse for many years and had heard any number of stories. Every part of her wanted to dismiss Jonah's tale as a delusion. But he seemed so coherent, so sane, so sure of the difference between reality and psychosis. But sometimes, those with the sickest minds could sound the most normal. She just wasn't sure what to think. Were ghosts real? And if so, could spirits be this evil? Ann had experienced enough personal experiences to not discount out-of-hand the notion of the paranormal. She knew that Northeast Pennsylvania had a reputation of being a grimly haunted region, built on the blood of generations. But still...

I have to think about this more, she thought.

"We'll talk about this more later," Ann finally said. "Why don't you get some rest?"

Jonah shook his head in agreement. He wondered if he had made a serious mistake revealing Evelyn to his nurse.

I guess I'll find out if they don't let me out, he thought.

Was Jonah sentencing himself to a lifetime in a psychiatric facility? If the medical staff concluded that his delusions were that deeply ingrained that he constituted a permanent danger to society, how would they react? He watched Nurse Ann walk out of the room, profoundly conflicted over how he should proceed.

For her part, Ann was pondering exactly what she would write in Jonah's chart.

CHAPTER 33

Mrs. Paskiel had viewed the disturbing occurrences across the street the last few weeks with increasing dismay. She was a devout Catholic, never missing the weekly Sunday Mass and raising Oliver in the faith. Even the scandals the Church had endured over the past years had failed to shake her rock-solid commitment. But whatever was happening at Jonah's house had disturbed her to the core. Seeing things first-hand changed one's perspective.

Over the last two decades, Mrs. Paskiel had learned some innate benefits of Oliver's autism. One of those was that he was virtually unable to exaggerate or embellish. His descriptions were inevitably unvarnished and matter-of-fact. He was very specific in detailing what had occurred. So when Oliver described the ghostly happenings in Jonah's house, Mrs. Paskiel had no idea what to make of it. She spoke to the parish priest about it, who dismissed it as the overactive imagination of a malleable mind.

"Oliver doesn't have an imagination," Mrs. Paskiel responded, "much less an overactive one. He's very literal."

The priest, an older man years beyond normal retirement age, lacked any perceptiveness into autism and was skeptical of ghost stories. He viewed the public's fascination with exorcism and demonic possession over the years with dismay. The elderly priest had no interest in bringing such sensationalistic headlines to Clayburn and his quiet church. He was as kind as he could be to his parishioner, but essentially sent Mrs. Paskiel away with nothing more than soft assurances and promises of prayers.

Helen Paskiel left the Church deeply unsatisfied, but filled a flask with Holy Water on the way out.

"If he's not going to do anything about it," she muttered, "I will."

That afternoon, Mrs. Paskiel, took her trusty weed trimmers next door and tidied up the outside of Jonah's house. Then she pulled out her lawn mower and cut the grass.

"We can't have this looking like it's abandoned," she said to herself. "The town looks bad enough as it is. We have to maintain our respect."

By the time she was done, Mrs. Paskiel had worked up a good sweat. She went back into the house to cool off and drank a sizable glass of water. After she patted off the worst of her accumulated sweat with a towel, she pulled the flask of Holy Water out of her purse and looked back toward the house across the street.

"Now comes the most difficult part," she said resolutely. "But good Catholics have an obligation to confront and stop evil where they find it. We certainly have some sort of devilry across the street, the likes of which I have never seen in my life. Who knew my calling was to serve as a Christian solder?"

Mrs. Paskiel made the sign of the cross, walked out of the house and strode diagonally across Easley Avenue. She heard Daffodil barking loudly at the window, as if sounding an alarm. As she approached the front door of Jonah's home, she again blessed herself and began to chant, "In the name of the Father, the Son and the Holy Spirit..." as she sprinkled a good amount of the sacred liquid on the outside of the building.

As soon as the water hit the wall, it sizzled and popped, with such ferocity that Mrs. Paskiel jumped backwards in shock and surprise.

"Oh my Lord," she said. "What kind of wickedness is this?"

"LEAVE THIS HOUSE!!!!" a voice screeched from inside the building in a deafening growl. "And take your foul fluid along with you."

When it came to Satan and his minions, Mrs. Paskiel was not so easily scared away.

It's my sacred duty to face evil where I find it, she thought. *I am part of the army of the Lord.*

"Our Father, who art in Heaven," she began to recite *The Lord's*

Prayer, "hallowed by thy name. Thy kingdom come, they will be done, on Earth as it is in Heaven. Give us this day our daily bread, and forgive us our trespasses, as we forgive those who have trespassed against us. And lead us not into temptation, but deliver us from evil. Amen."

As she prayed, Mrs. Paskiel again sprayed the house with Holy Water, this time with even greater determination. Daffodil's barking became more frantic in the background.

Once more, as soon as the liquid hit the wall, it crackled and boiled with an even more horrific cry than before.

"Your pitiful God cannot do me harm," a dark, sinister voice boomed. "You think you can defeat me with water blessed by some profane and damaged priest? Ha! He's probably screwing an altar boy as we speak."

Mrs. Paskiel's face twisted into a look of disgust and determination.

"Satan!" she reproached the demon. "How dare you demean the vessels of the Lord."

Suddenly, Evelyn's face, grim and menacing, appeared at the window by the door. She flicked her tongue, long and forked, at Helen Paskiel, who jumped backward as the tongue appeared for an instant to come through the window and bear down on her.

Mrs. Paskiel remembered Psalms 140:3.

"They sharpen their tongues as a serpant; Poison of a viper is under their lips."

"My Lord, Jesus Christ Almighty, I beseech you to protect me," Mrs. Paskiel yelled, blessing herself over and over, "save me from this abomination."

She again shook the bottle of Holy Water at the house. Again it sizzled, this time flying back at her at a near scalding temperature.

"Get off this property," Evelyn said resolutely, "or I will strike you dead where you stand. God has abandoned this place. He cannot protect you here."

Mrs. Paskiel stood defiantly for a moment, then grimaced as Evelyn thrust out her hand. The hand burst through the window and a wave of searing heat enveloped Mrs. Paskiel. She turned and tried to hurry off the lawn as quickly as she could. She stumbled and fell, turned back around and saw Evelyn's forked tongue once more approaching her. It too had pierced the window and was now crossing the space between the specter and Oliver's mother.

Suddenly, Daffodil burst through the doggy door, jumped the fence in the backyard and ran to Mrs. Paskiel. The dog barked viciously at Evelyn and the protruding tongue, snapping at the approaching appendage. Daffodil then tugged on Mrs. Paskiel's dress, urging her to stand. Back and forth, Daffodil alternately barked madly at Evelyn, cried for Mrs. Paskiel to move while nudging her to stand, and growled when she spotted Evelyn suddenly fully materialize menacingly on the porch, threatening to come forward.

Mrs. Paskiel finally responded to Daffodil's entreaties and mentally returned to some sense of order. She put one hand on the dog and she forced herself to stand and turn toward her house. She continued to make the Sign of the Cross, praying incessantly as she crossed the street and climbed up her own steps. She left Daffodil into the house and followed her inside, slamming the door shut and locking and chaining it as fast as she could. She huffed from the exertion and worked to catch her breath, sweat once again pouring from her body.

"Hail Mary, full of grace, the Lord is with thee," she began to pray once again, grabbing a Crucifix from the wall. "Blessed are thou among women and blessed is the fruit of thy womb, Jesus. Holy Mary, Mother of God, pray for us sinners, now and at the hour of our death. Amen."

As she continued jumping from one prayer to the next, Mrs. Paskiel stared suspiciously out the window to the house across the street. Once again, she saw the old, haggard, inhuman woman staring malevolently back at her. Mrs. Paskiel thrust the Crucifix forward toward the window to face her oppressor. Evelyn scowled, then disappeared back into the house.

"Lord in Heaven," Mrs. Paskiel cried, finally pulling down the blinds and closing the curtains tightly. "The devil has indeed come to Clayburn. What is this world coming to? I never thought I'd see the day. Who knew I'd have to come face-to-face with Lucifer himself?

Thank goodness my faith in the Lord is strong."

Mrs. Paskiel pulled open a drawer in a nearby cabinet and snatched a rosary from its contents.

"I need to call the parish prayer group," she said to herself, and hurried toward the phone. "This is beyond the power of any one of us."

CHAPTER 34

Jonah followed several other patients into the common room for his daily group therapy session. Nine chairs were arranged on one side of the room in a ragged circle, and one by one, the group members took their seats. On one of the chairs sat Erin, a hospital counselor, who served as the facilitator for the group.

Over the past week, Jonah had become more accepting of the group interaction. The first several days, he had sat in his seat, arms crossed, without participating. His facial expression was a mix between a scowl and disinterest. When the facilitator asked if he would like to add to the discussion, he turned away and ignored the question. But as Jonah's mind cleared and his footing in reality became more grounded, he took the first tentative steps toward becoming part of his small community. Now as he approached something close to normalcy, he had accepted himself into this collection of unique souls. His participation aided his own recovery, and he hoped, those of others.

The other seven members of the group were a mixed bunch.

Mixed nuts, Jonah thought. *Appropriate. I'm the macadamia nut.*

Jonah smiled at his own joke.

Two men, clearly senior citizens, appeared to be long-time members. Conrad and Adam apparently had seen the inside of any number of psychiatric institutions, and knew – though didn't much care – for each other. They seemed to have already begun their most recent squabble before they even entered the room. From what Jonah could tell, it didn't really matter the tenor of the opinion of one, the other would find a way to argue.

There were several middle-aged men and women. Alfred, an

African-American with thick glasses and a two-day stubble, suffered from clinical depression, worsened by the loss of his wife and youngest child in a car accident several years back. He has already survived two suicide attempts. Alfred was the only person of color in the group.

Alice was bipolar, and Janet was a paranoid schizophrenic. Jake was a raging alcoholic whose brain was hopelessly addled from years of substance abuse. All appeared to be somewhere in their late 30s or 40s, though Jake had aged beyond his years.

Finally, there was a woman barely out of her teens, if that. Kristin had come from a violent household and had been sexually abused as a young teenager. She suffered from symptoms of PTSD, but Jonah was sure there was more than that torturing her troubled mind. Of all the members of the group, Kristin was the one with whom Jonah felt the most empathy. Jonah found a seat next to her, turned his head and nodded hello. Kristin was reserved and quiet, and suffered from severe trust issues, but she smiled back in return before turning away.

Erin was a petite redhead in her mid-30s. She began the group session with mixed success. Few if any of the participants typically began sharing in these sessions without some prompting, some days more than others. After some urging, however, the participants began to talk, becoming more animated as they became more comfortable and settled into their stories.

Alfred reflected on how difficult it was for him to get out of bed each morning when severely depressed, how hard it was simply to get dressed and go about life. It would be so much easier if he fell asleep and never awoke. Many nights, he prayed fervently for that to happen.

"But today is a good day," he concluded. "I'm up, I'm dressed, and I'm happy to be here."

Jake was hardly coherent, while Alice struggled controlling her emotions as her wish to leave the institution was overwhelming. She broke into tears and was nearly inconsolable. Janet was sure her room was being watched, that someone had installed devices in her walls that kept her awake all night, and that same person was somehow making train noises outside her window. Even Erin reminding Janet that her room was on the third floor seemed to have little impact on

213

her resolve. She was convinced, and no factual evidence to the contrary would change her mind. Reasoning with her proved fruitless.

There's a lot of sick people here, Jonah thought. *There's a lot of sick people everywhere.*

The counselor then turned toward Jonah. It took a second for him to remember Erin's name. So many counselors, therapists, nurses, and doctors, added to the list of other medical professionals who had treated his madness for years. By now, they all ran together in a blur.

"So how are you feeling, Jonah?" the counselor asked.

"I'm doing fine," he said.

"Now, we know what FINE stands for," Erin retorted.

Yep, Jonah thought, *fucked up, insecure, neurotic and emotional.*

"I'm actually doing much better than that," Jonah said. "I'm feeling much more myself. It's nice to feel part of this Earth again."

"That's good to hear," the counselor opined. "What will you do when you're discharged?"

"I'm pretty sure it's time for me to find a new place to live," Jonah answered honestly. "Where I recently moved definitely played a role in me being here. I'm very sure it's time for a fresh start."

"Do you think moving will help resolve those issues?" Erin asked.

Jonah chuckled.

"Without a doubt," he said "You have no idea. I need to leave Clayburn as fast as my car will take me."

Erin seemed satisfied with Jonah's responses and didn't push him any further. She then turned to Kristin, but despite repeated prodding from the counselor, Kristin was virtually non-responsive.

"We'll talk later," Erin assured her.

The counselor surveyed the group, settling on Conrad and Adam, who had continued their dispute throughout the session and were still bickering between themselves.

"Are we having a problem over here?" Erin asked, vocally attempting to take back command of the group.

"This son of a bitch," Conrad said, pointing toward his recent adversary, "is descended from the Molly Maguires. They shot my great-great grandfather in the back."

Jonah suddenly paid more attention to the conversation.

The Molly Maguires again? Jonah thought. *They follow me wherever I go. They seem to be the ghosts from whom I can't escape.*

"Those damn Mollies have put a scar on the whole history of this area," Conrad stated further. "They should have never left them get off the boat from Ireland. They're lying, murderous vermin."

"That is such bullshit," Adam responded. "All the Molly Maguires did was stand up for the rights of the miners, who were used and abused by the rich coal barons. The Molly Maguires were set up and slaughtered for standing up for worker's rights. This idiot is just a prejudiced English bastard. And dumb as a stump."

"You are full of shit," Conrad said. "Were you there?"

"No, I wasn't, but maybe you were," Adam said. "You're goddam old enough."

"OK, OK," Erin interjected. "We're not here to try to argue history all over again. What you two are talking about happened 150 years ago. No one knows exactly what happened. Can we move on to what's affecting you today?'

After a bit more negotiation, Conrad and Adam calmed down and turned to more mundane topics. Jonah eventually lost interest in the tales of the two crotchety old men. He looked away, toward one of the iron-barred windows in the community room.

Can't give anyone an easy escape route – or a way to kill themselves, he thought.

He let the conversation from the group drift from one topic to the other as he pondered life once again outside this institution and his course of action once he left. His eyes crossed the room, going from one window to the next. Suddenly, he jumped back in his chair. The menacing figure of Evelyn stared back at him through one of the sets of bars, a look of fury etched across her face.

"I'm waiting for you," she said, Jonah reading her lips and hearing her voice in his head. "Don't think for a minute that you've gotten away from me."

Evelyn's mouth formed a decadent grin.

Erin noticed Jonah was in some type of distress and put her hand up to pause Alice, who was speaking. She stopped immediately. The rest of the group was already staring at Jonah.

"Is everything all right, Jonah?" she asked.

Jonah didn't answer, paralyzed as he watched Evelyn's visage fade away.

"Jonah?" Erin prompted, this time a bit more forcefully.

He pulled himself to attention, forced the image of Evelyn out of his skull, and looked back at the counselor.

"I'm OK," he said. "Just had a moment. I'm good now."

Erin peered thoughtfully at her patient for a few more seconds. Jonah worked hard to appear as though nothing had happened. The counselor, seemingly satisfied whatever crisis was now over, shook her head approvingly. She turned back to Alice.

"I'm sorry that I interrupted you," Erin said. "Please continue."

The counselor glanced back at Jonah, who sat stone-faced on his chair.

Once Erin turned away, Kristin leaned over from the seat next to Jonah.

"I saw her too," Kristin whispered. "I believe in ghosts. I've seen them all my life."

Jonah turned toward the fragile, broken young woman and smiled. He appreciated the comfort and reinforcement Kristin had provided.

"Thank you," he said softly.

•   •   •

Sometime after the therapy session, Nurse Ann came into Jonah's room to dispense medication and check his well-being. The day was relatively quiet – a rare occurrence – and the nurse had a few minutes.

"So tell me about your house once more," she said to her patient. "I'd like to hear more."

"You're going to think I'm delusional again," Jonah protested.

"How about I give you the benefit of the doubt?" Ann asked. "I want to hear your story without you worrying what I'm thinking. I promise I will suspend my disbelief."

"Fair enough," Jonah said. "But I have to tell you, While I'm sure of what's real and what's not, I know how this is going to sound."

Overcoming his initial hesitation, Jonah related to the nurse the entire story of his time in Clayburn: the odd happenings in the house; Oliver's stories of the occurrences before he moved; his medications suddenly disappearing; the emergence of Evelyn and the battles between Evelyn and his own demon, Regan; and now, the link between Evelyn and the legacy of the Molly Maguires. The entire sequence of events seemed so unbelievable, but Jonah finally was able to own them with perfect clarity. The nurse listened intently as Jonah completed his story, finishing at the top of the old strip mine having Oliver call for help, and the vision of Evelyn in the window even today.

Ann stayed silent for a minute, processing what she just heard. She had never heard anything quite like this in all her years as a psychiatric nurse.

"How do you know Evelyn isn't just part of your delusions?" she finally asked.

"Like I told you before, I know the difference," Jonah asserted. "I know Regan is a creation of my own mind. Evelyn and everything that happened in that house is a whole other story. And besides, Oliver, Katie and even Mr. Kershaw have seen her too. And today, Kristin saw Evelyn in the window. It was the only time she showed any life during the entire group."

The nurse studied him thoughtfully, still sorting out in her mind the complete chain of events.

"I understand that you can't possibly believe me," Jonah said. "If I were you, I wouldn't believe me either. I'm here because I'm crazy, after all. But everything I've said is true."

"OK," Ann said. "For now, let's assume it is. Now what?'

"That's why I have to leave town as soon as I'm out of here," Jonah said. "Pick up a few things and get out of Dodge."

"Why do you even have to go back?"

"There's something I left that can't be replaced," Jonah said. "Family memorabilia. All that I have left, really, of my parents. It won't take more than a few minutes. And besides, I'm back on my meds.

Evelyn had to trick me to stop taking them to take advantage of me. She's not as strong when I'm thinking straight. I can hold her off for a few minutes."

Ann still looked dubious.

"And I'll take my friends with me," Jonah promised. "I won't face her alone."

"If that's what's best for you," Ann said, "then I think you should do it as soon as you're discharged."

"How much longer will that be?" Jonah asked.

"I believe you're making remarkable progress," Ann said honestly. "Let's see what the doctor says and we'll go from there."

Nurse Ann left the room. Jonah looked out the window. Evelyn wasn't to be found. He was starting to feel strong enough to face the world once again. And to face Evelyn one final time.

CHAPTER 35

Dr. Sheffield looked across the room at her patient, examining him closely. Jonah had been through a severe psychological trauma over the past several months, and she was trying to assess exactly where he was, both mentally and physically. He had not exactly been forthright with her during their regular sessions, and Dr. Sheffield now had to determine if Jonah was being more honest now.

No doubt, the young man who faced her now looked far healthier than the one that caused her such concern after their last few meetings. He was more lucid, more open, and more engaging. He did not appear to be holding back secrets. Was this the "healthy" Jonah that could again become a productive member of society?

It was time to find out.

"So are you ready to tell me the truth now?" the psychiatrist asked, not trying to sound too judgmental but clearly voicing her displeasure. "We've been in quite a wrestling match the last few sessions. I'm not sure that did either one of us any good."

"I was in a bad spot," Jonah admitted. "I'm sorry. I promise I'm doing better now."

"You know," Dr. Sheffield reminded her patient, "that's why I'm here. My job is to help you stay healthy. I am not your enemy, no matter what you may think. Do you have a plan going forward?"

"I do," Jonah said. "You were right. I think maybe I took on too much too soon. It's time to leave Clayburn behind."

Dr. Sheffield showed only a moment of mild surprise, then jotted down a few words.

"What will you do?" she asked.

"I think I'll find a small apartment somewhere," Jonah said. "Home ownership doesn't seem to agree with me. I'll find a place closer to support networks where I can get help if I need it. Clayburn was a little too isolated for my own well-being."

His psychiatrist seemed pleased. She again wrote a short note on her pad.

"How soon do you plan on leaving?" Dr. Sheffield persisted.

Jonah chuckled.

"As soon as my doctor lets me out of this place," he cracked.

The psychiatrist smiled in spite of herself.

"And what about Evelyn?" she asked.

Jonah waved his arm dismissively.

"Whatever ghosts exist," he answered, "I think I'm going to leave them to Clayburn. They seem very happy to stay there. I'm pretty sure that's where they belong."

CHAPTER 36

Katie sat on Jonah's bed and Oliver settled in the lone guest chair in the room. Katie and Jonah held hands comfortably. Jonah was in a particularly good mood, lightening the spirits to a level unknown for many weeks. His head was clear, his medications were working, and he was ready to move on with his life.

He glanced over at Oliver, who smiled happily and bounded back and forth seeing the condition of his friend.

"I still can't believe you saved my life," Jonah said. "I owe you big time, buddy."

"I had to," Oliver said. "You had your phone in your pocket. I lost mine as I ran home that day. If you jumped, I didn't know how I would have been able to call anyone to get a ride home."

Jonah and Katie looked at Oliver incredulously. Oliver kept a matter-of-fact demeanor for as long as he could, then broke into a big smile. He finally brought both of his hands up and covered his face.

"It was a joke," he squealed.

Jonah and Katie both laughed hysterically. There were times that Oliver delivered the unexpected.

The three sat quietly for a few minutes until Katie changed the subject.

"So you're sure about moving?" Katie asked.

"Are you kidding me?" Jonah said. "After all that's happened? I can't wait to get out of there and start again. I didn't count on the house already being inhabited when I bought it."

"Then why go back at all?" Katie asked. "Why not just walk out of here and drive to your new life?"

Jonah thought back to the box of family heirlooms sitting in his bedroom night stand. It was all he had left of his family. The words in that Bible were the first words he had read to him, even before he left the womb.

"There's something I have to get that's very special to me," he said. "I can't let Evelyn take even that away from me. Five minutes to grab what I need, then off we go."

"What about that witch?" Katie persisted. "I've seen her with my own eyes. She's very dangerous."

"I know," Jonah said. "But listen, she had to screw with my meds to get the best of me. I'm back on them now. She's not as strong as she thinks when I can face her with a clear mind."

Katie thought about that, wondered if Evelyn had grown more powerful while Jonah was gone. She certainly didn't seem harmless when she went into the house. But then again, she rationalized, she had gotten back out. No reason to believe Jonah couldn't go in, get what he needed, and leave again.

"So where are you going after that?" Katie asked.

"Not sure yet," Jonah said. "I'll keep going until I'm there. I'll know it when I see it."

"I hope your vision is 20/20," Katie said.

Jonah chuckled. "One thing I can tell you. It won't be in the Coal Region," he said. "Too much history. Way too haunted. Too many skeletons in the closet."

"I don't have any skeletons in my closet!" Oliver objected.

"None that you can see," Jonah cracked, leaving Oliver to ponder what he meant.

No doubt he's going to look again, Jonah thought. *This time in the back of the closet.*

Jonah then gazed at Katie, studying her face carefully.

"Are you coming with me?" he asked earnestly.

Katie hesitated, then smiled.

"If you want me to," she said timidly.

Jonah grinned broadly and pulled Katie toward him.

"Of course I want you to," he said. "I'm not leaving town without you. I love you."

Katie smiled and snuggled up to Jonah.

"I love you, too," Katie whispered.

Oliver squirmed excitedly in his seat.

"What about me?' Oliver finally chimed in.

Jonah looked at his friend, somewhat surprised. He chuckled at the thought.

"I don't think your mom will let me take you," he finally said. "But I promise I will come back and visit."

"OK," Oliver said. "I guess Mom can't do without me. Somebody has to keep her company."

•   •   •

Two days later, Jonah was discharged, but only after several hours of paperwork, multiple prescriptions and instructions for aftercare. Katie and Oliver waited through the long process. Jonah shrugged; he had been through this routine many times previously and knew what to expect. Jonah hugged Nurse Ann on his way out.

"I don't want to see you back here again," she told him.

"Neither do I," Jonah said honestly. "Thank you for believing me."

He left the hospital, arm and arm with Katie. He climbed into his Malibu that she had brought to the facility, turned the key, and heard the familiar rev of the engine. Oliver settled himself into the back seat. Jonah glanced over to Katie with an easy smile.

"We're all set to go," he said. "Ain'a?"

Katie doubled-over in laughter.

"I knew you'd eventually use it," she howled. "Let's get out of here."

Jonah shifted into drive, stepped on the gas and pulled onto the road toward Clayburn.

Jonah turned on the radio and somehow found a classic rock station playing Steppenwolf, to which he and Katie were soon singing:

Get your motor runnin'
Head out on the highway

Lookin' for adventure
And whatever comes our way
Yeah Darlin' gonna make it happen
Take the world in a love embrace
Fire all of your guns at once
And explode into space

Oliver cringed at Jonah and Katie's howling as the song went on, but to no avail. He clapped his hands over his ears to block out the off-key notes, finally resorting to singing "Lalalalalalalalala" softly to himself. No use. The singing continued until the song concluded.

Like a true nature's child
We were born, born to be wild
We can climb so high
I never wanna die
Born to be wild
Born to be wild

Not exactly located in the hotbed of civilization, Clayburn was a good 45-minute drive from the institution. In that time, Katie saw the real Jonah again – not haunted by demons, real or created. Happy, content, living in the moment. This was the man with whom she had fallen in love, despite all the reasons to avoid it. Jonah glanced over and caught Katie's eye, and she saw the pure soul within. Maybe now, after all they had been through, they had a future.

CHAPTER 37

Jonah pulled into Leiby's Ice Cream House Restaurant for lunch since both he and his passengers were starved from the long wait at the hospital. Located outside Tamaqua on the corner of Routes 309 and 443, Leiby's is a local tradition, a family restaurant famed for its elaborate dessert menu of pies and seemingly endless flavors of Leiby's Premium Ice Cream.

"I always wanted to try this place," Jonah said as they hopped out of the car.

Jonah, Katie and Oliver devoured their burgers and still had plenty of room for dessert – peanut butter pie for Jonah, banana cream pie for Katie and chocolate marshmallow ice cream for Oliver.

All of them overstuffed, Jonah and his friends slowly walked to his car, he and Katie hand-in-hand. He finally pulled his Malibu out of the parking lot, and fifteen minutes later was parking his car in front of his house in Clayburn. By now, it was mid-afternoon. The sun shone brightly in the cloudless sky, though it had begun its downward descent. Jonah looked at Katie and Oliver, who peered at the home fearfully. He was ready to say goodbye to this haunted mansion, though at the moment, the place seemed peaceful enough.

"Are you ready to do this?' Jonah asked.

"Do we have to?" Katie asked, hoping one last time that Jonah would change his mind.

"I only need a couple of things," Jonah said. "We'll be in and out. I promise. Evelyn won't even have time to wake up. Remember, she's not as strong as you think, and I'm stronger than I was."

"If you say so," Katie said dubiously.

"Trust me," Jonah assured her. Katie nodded in agreement.

"Do I have to come in?" Oliver now interjected.

"Not if you don't want to," Jonah said, then looked back and forth at his two friends. "Look, I can do this alone. Neither of you have to come into the house. I'm not asking you to do anything that makes you uncomfortable. I'm going to be inside for less than five minutes."

"You're not going in there alone," Katie said firmly. "I'm coming with you."

"Me too," Oliver said, though less convincingly.

"All right," Jonah finally concluded. "Then let's do what we came to do and leave."

The three walked toward the door. The house was quiet. Too quiet. At some level, they could all sense it. Evelyn was lying in wait, luring them into her trap. Every fiber of Katie's being wanted to beg Jonah to turn around and leave Evelyn and the house at rest. But she knew her entreaties would be useless. An important part of Jonah's past still lay in his bedroom night table.

Jonah pulled out the key, slowly inserted it into the lock, and deliberately turned the mechanism. He gave the door a slight push, and it squeaked slightly as it cracked inward. Jonah pushed the door completely open. He stepped into the building first, one foot then the other, and flicked the switch on the wall turning on the ceiling light. He stopped and looked around.

Even Jonah was in shock at the condition of the house. The place remained the disaster it had become during Jonah's last episodes with Evelyn and Regan, and it was the first time Jonah surveyed the damage with a clear mind. Furniture was overturned and torn, glass broken across the floor. Seeing his house with renewed sanity, Jonah could see the destruction that inevitably lay in his previous path.

"Holy crap, was I crazy," Jonah said. It wasn't a question. "How the hell did I live through this?"

After he overcame his initial reaction, Jonah became more optimistic.

Nothing, he thought. *Not a sound. Maybe she's busy elsewhere. Or maybe she's given up. I can only hope.*

Katie and Oliver followed him into the house. They looked around apprehensively. The house remained silent as the grave. They moved stealthily further into the living room, their eyes darting to every corner of the home.

"See?" Jonah whispered. "She doesn't even know we're here. I'll get my stuff, and then we're gone."

"Let's not wake her up," Katie said. "I've met her. She's nasty. Let's grab what you need and get out of here."

Jonah walked across the room and headed toward the hallway leading to his bedroom. The one thing he wanted the most – his small box of family mementos – would take only a minute to retrieve. The rest of his belongings, he decided, could remain. Nothing stopped him from buying new clothes or other essentials. He had nearly reached is destination when a frying pan flew off the kitchen counter onto the floor.

"Aww shit," Jonah screamed, "she's here!"

He broke into a sprint. With each step, he felt the house begin to awaken under his feet. Walls shook. The sounds of far-off screams of children and adults jolted closer. Evelyn's hellish screech joined the chorus.

Jonah rushed into the bedroom, tore open the drawer on the nightstand and grabbed the box. The drawer slammed shut, nearly trapping his fingers. Some power kept him from leaving the room, despite his best efforts. He was about to be thrown backwards, when Katie and Oliver forced themselves through the door and pulled Jonah into the hallway. The door splintered shut behind them as it broke from its hinges.

"Let's get the hell out of here," Katie cried. Jonah nodded in agreement.

"Follow me," Oliver said, and summoning all of his courage, led the three down the hall and back into the living room. They were halfway across the expanse when the front door slammed shut in front of them.

"Did you honestly think you could get away from me?" a demonic voice roared angrily. "You can't escape."

Suddenly, Evelyn appeared, larger and more ominous than before, in the middle of the room.

"You bitch!" Jonah cursed. "We're leaving here and you will be left all alone!"

"I am never alone," Evelyn said ominously. "And you're not going anywhere."

Doors and windows slammed shut and locked throughout the house. An ear-piercing cry reverberated through the building, shaking the walls. Jonah and his friends covered their ears at the sudden bombardment of sound and fury.

She's much stronger than when I left, Jonah realized. *She's grown in power. And in purpose.*

"Leave us alone," Katie screamed. "We just want to get out of here."

"No one asked you, slut," Evelyn sneered. "I don't need your pitiful interference."

Evelyn waved her hand violently. An unseen force sent Katie flying against the back wall. Katie felt dizzy and her vision blurred. She fell to the floor, muscle spasms streaking like lightning bolts through her legs. She couldn't see, she couldn't move.

Damn MS, she thought. *How did she trigger that?*

"Leave her alone, you son of a bitch," Jonah howled and forced himself toward the specter. "I'll send you to hell where you belong."

Evelyn cackled.

"Really?" the ghost demon said mockingly. "How do you think you're going to do that? You've tried over and over again, and you've done nothing but fail."

She waved her arm casually to swat Jonah away, but Jonah surprisingly resisted and kept advancing. The slightest hint of doubt cascaded over Evelyn's face, then she flushed with renewed anger.

"You're getting more forceful yourself, I see," she hissed. "So much the better. I can use that ferocity so I can channel it to my needs. But you still can't resist me. I've grown more powerful as well."

Evelyn stepped forward, physically pushing Jonah and sending him through the air. His box of heirlooms dropped on the floor next to him as he slid hard against the wall.

"Why me?" Jonah said. "Why am I so important to you?"

Evelyn paused. She looked at Jonah more closely, a sneer of derisive surprise on her face.

"Don't you know?" she asked. "Haven't you figured it out yet?"

"I have no idea what you're talking about?" Jonah answered.

"You and I are more alike than you think!" Evelyn said slyly. "Think about it."

Jonah shook his head.

"We are nothing alike," Jonah objected. "We have absolutely nothing in common."

"Really?" Evelyn persisted. "What did your girlfriend find out about me when she did her so-called research?"

Evelyn hissed in disgust, glaring for a second at Katie.

Jonah cast his eyes toward Katie, who was crouching and writhing in pain. Jonah forced himself over to her inch by inch and held her tightly.

"Katie has nothing to do with this," he screamed angrily at his oppressor.

"What did she discover?" Evelyn demanded.

"She found out you were descended from Yellow Jack Donahue, one of the Molly Maguires hung in Jim Thorpe," Jonah answered. "Explains why you're so fucking crazy. So what?"

Evelyn cackled gloriously.

"I had to get revenge on those who murdered him in cold blood," Evelyn said bitterly. "He was innocent, you know. All he ever did was try to get better working conditions for the abused coal miners. The millionaires who owned the company, the superintendents who ran the mines, the people who framed him and killed him – none of them cared. Those poor Irish miners – if one died, there would be another to replace him."

Evelyn paused, a glorious smile crossing his malformed lips.

"So I followed others in what has become a long and proud tradition," she continued. "We started with that bastard Franklin Gowen – made it looked like he committed suicide in his hotel room. Others have continued that work throughout the years. But I took it one step further. I sought out the great, great grandsons of those who killed my ancestor. Fucked them, conceived their children, and then... "

Evelyn laughed a deep, evil guffaw. She glared at Jonah, then at Katie, and back again at Jonah.

"Killed both them and their offspring," Evelyn finished. "Sons of bitches deserved it."

Jonah and Katie stared at each other in horror as they began to put the pieces together.

The newspapers...the uneven concrete...the cries of infants and the adults in the house, Jonah thought. *Oh my God. She couldn't have. But she did. She's more psychotic than I thought.*

"The children were easy to hide in the basement," Evelyn said. "But the fathers, they perished, according to the coroner of 'natural causes.' He didn't know very much about poison. The dumb bastard couldn't figure out why perfectly healthy men were falling over dead of heart attacks."

Evelyn laughed heartily.

"It was glorious while it lasted." Evelyn continued, then her voice betrayed a glimmer of lament. "But I got too old. I couldn't have children anymore. I managed to pick off a few more descendants, men who slunk into my web. But after a while, even they stopped coming around. I needed someone to continue my work. So I had to lure someone here. Just the right person. You have no idea how many people I had to scare away. It took considerable effort and energy, exertion I could barely muster because I was only gathering my strength. But I did, because I had to continue my quest. I needed just the right person. And then you came along..."

She glared at Jonah, as though her gaze would penetrate into his soul.

"Mentally defective," she said, "easy to control, and with just the right background. The perfect successor."

"What the hell are you talking about?" Jonah hissed. "What kind of freaking background are you talking about?"

Evelyn nodded over to Katie.

"Your girlfriend didn't do quite enough homework," Evelyn said, then bore her complete focus upon Katie. "Did you girlie?"

"I don't understand," Katie started, then turned to Jonah. "What is she talking about?"

Jonah felt an emptiness in the pit of his stomach.

She can't be right, Jonah thought. *It can't be true. She's lying. Don't believe her.*

Evelyn laughed deeply and heartily.

"The boy is starting to figure it out," the ghost said triumphantly. "Aren't you? You aren't as dense as I thought."

Jonah remained silent. Evelyn turned back and glared wickedly at Katie.

"You weak sniveling little thing," she said. "Don't you know you've been sleeping with the great, great, great grandson of the legendary Black Jack Kehoe?"

Katie turned disbelievingly at Jonah. Jonah sat unmoving and shell-shocked. Evelyn laughed victoriously, her bellowing filling and echoing across the room.

"Isn't that just PERFECT?" she cackled. "Who better to continue exacting my revenge on those people who tortured our ancestors than recruit the descendant of the King of the Mollies?"

"Jonah?" Katie asked pleadingly. "Is that true?"

"I have no idea," Jonah said. "It might be. It feels like it's true. But..."

Jonah shook his head defiantly. He was not going to let Evelyn get inside his skull.

"But it doesn't matter," he said with new resolution. "I don't have her blood lust. I don't need revenge for an ancestor I never knew. I have no idea if he was good or bad, if he murdered anyone or not. I don't even know if she's telling the truth. Evelyn didn't put that into her calculations."

Jonah forced himself to stand up. With considerable effort, he pulled himself upright and faced his antagonist.

"I have no desire to follow in your foul murderous footsteps," he said commandingly to Evelyn. "I'd kill you if you weren't already dead."

"You don't have the guts," Evelyn taunted.

"You son of a bitch," Jonah said. "You underestimate me."

"And what are you going to do about it?" the demon said.

"I'm going to finish this for good," Jonah said. He pushed himself to the kitchen, opened a drawer, and pulled out a lighter.

"Oliver," he said, turning his attention to his neighbor, "Help Katie get out of here."

"What are you going to do?" Oliver asked.

"I'm going to do what I should have done in the first place," he said decisively. "I'm going to burn this place to the ground. See who this old bat can haunt then."

Evelyn's lips curled. For a moment, Jonah thought he could hear the screams of both children and men in the distance. He opened the lighter, and put his thumb on the ignitor. He stared back at Evelyn.

"If you won't burn in hell," he said. "You can burn here."

"You think you can get rid of me that easily?" Evelyn laughed. "I'll show you how to kill someone."

Evelyn strode forward with lightning quickness and swatted the lighter from Jonah's hand, grabbing him by the arm. She held Jonah with unbridled ferocity. She turned, and with a nod of her head, the basement door flung open, nearly splintering into pieces. Then, she stared at Oliver, and with steely resolve, used her power to force Oliver closer and closer to the basement steps.

"Do you think he'll bounce?" Evelyn laughed. "Let's find out."

Jonah used all his strength plus some supernatural power that came from an unknown source to free himself from Evelyn's icy grip.

Was that my mother's voice telling me to fight? Jonah wondered fleetingly. *Aadya was right. She was here all along.*

Evelyn turned momentarily toward him in surprise as Jonah resisted Evelyn's might and drove himself toward Oliver. Oliver looked fearfully at the steps as his body inched closer and closer to the stairway against his will. He tried to stop his progress, to no avail. He tried to scream, but no sound came from his mouth. He wordlessly cried for help.

Oliver was now teetering at the top of the steps, fighting to not fall. He felt himself losing his balance and start hurtling toward the darkness below him. Suddenly, he felt a hand grab his arm and pull him back. With all of his strength, Oliver did the most difficult thing he could – he looked up and met Jonah's eyes with his own. Pure gratitude enveloped his face.

"Gotcha, buddy," Jonah said.

"You bastard!" Evelyn screamed, and sent a tidal force of energy toward the two men. "How dare you interfere with my plans!"

Jonah looked back at his nemesis, then pushed Oliver away from the steps. Oliver fell to the floor and he watched as the full fury of Evelyn's power hit Jonah in the chest, pushing him backwards.

Though he fought as best he could, he was no match for the entire might of Evelyn's angry demonic turbulence. Jonah fell backwards, and felt himself tumbling down the steps, though the action seemed as if it occurred in slow motion. He tumbled out of control, feeling bones breaking and organs slicing open on the ragged, steep stairway. His mind heard screaming, disembodied from the pain he was enduring.

"Noooooo!!!!!!!!"

Jonah couldn't be sure if it was Evelyn...or Regan...or Katie. Maybe all three. The voices faded away. Katie's face appeared in front of him.

"I will always love you," she said.

"I love you," Jonah responded.

Then Katie disappeared and he saw Regan or Evelyn – or both – trying to push through. Jonah swatted them from his mind.

Jonah thumped down on his head on the concrete landing at the bottom of the steps. He felt his neck snap. For a few moments, as his eyes gazed into his basement, he saw the shadows of six children floating above the patches of concrete he had discovered when he first moved into this cursed house.

In the depths of his mind, Jonah could hear the words of The Doors, and knew their message rang true.

This is the end, beautiful friend
This is the end, my only friend, the end
Of our elaborate plans, the end

Of everything that stands, the end
No safety or surprise, the end
I'll never look into your eyes, again

Then, his eyes closed, and everything went black.

•   •   •

"Dammit all to hell," Evelyn ranted. "He wasn't supposed to die. I needed him. This ruins everything."

Katie and Oliver watched as they lay on the floor. Evelyn began to discernibly shrink and weaken as though she had drawn much of her earthly energy from Jonah's presence. With her designated successor gone, Evelyn was far less threatening and powerful. A look of confusion and even fear crossed the spirit's face for the first time.

She looked over at Katie and Oliver. As Evelyn lost power in this world, the two began to regain their own strength. Oliver got up first, and helped Katie to her feet. Katie took several seconds to compose herself. Part of her cried to go to Jonah. But she knew she couldn't turn her back on Evelyn, even in her weakened state.

"It's you and me, you monster," Katie finally said. "What is it going to be?"

Katie could feel the sudden hesitation in Evelyn's demeanor.

"You're worthless to me without him," Evelyn finally said, trying to sound menacing but with an undertone of defeat. "But you'll suffer knowing you can't have him either. That will give me solace."

With that, the demonic spirit disappeared.

CHAPTER 38

After Evelyn vanished into the ether, Katie stumbled down into the cellar, Oliver supporting her as best he could. As soon as she saw Jonah's twisted, mangled body laying at the foot of the basement steps, intellectually, she knew he was gone. But she hurried to him anyway in a futile effort to try to save him.

It was too late. Jonah lay still, eyes fixed. Tears filled Katie's eyes, and she threw herself over his body. Oliver stood there, not quite knowing what to do.

"Call for help," Katie finally said. "Hurry."

Oliver ran upstairs, found his cell phone and dialed 9-1-1. The phone rang once and was quickly answered.

"9-1-1 operator, what's your emergency?" the voice over the phone asked.

"Jonah is dead," Oliver said. "We need help. We've been attacked."

The 9-1-1 operator paused for only a second.

"What's the address?"

"225 Easley Avenue," Oliver responded desperately.

"Is the attacker still in the house?" the operator asked, searching for additional information.

Oliver looked frantically around the room.

"I don't think so," he finally answered. "I think she left."

"Is anyone else hurt?"

"Yes," Oliver said. "Katie and I need help."

The 9-1-1 operator continued to press for additional information, but soon realized she was reaching the point of diminishing returns.

Shock, she thought. *Or worse.*

She dispatched both police and ambulances to the scene even as she spoke to Oliver calmly, trying to assess and control the situation as best she could.

A few minutes later, Oliver heard sirens, starting in the distance and coming closer and closer. Finally, red lights flashed through the windows, and seconds later, two police officers – Officers Normann and Fanelli – crashed through the front door, guns drawn. They saw the carnage, spotted Oliver crouching near the phone. He pointed toward the basement. The two officers slowly went down the stairs, their eyes constantly moving to identify any threat. They found Katie draped over Jonah's body. They searched the basement thoroughly, making sure there were no hidden threats. In addition to the ambulance, the officers called for the coroner.

This is going to be a long day, Officer Normann thought.

•   •   •

Ambulances arrived several minutes later, first from Clayburn then another from a neighboring town. The street quickly turned into a cascade of emergency vehicles, flashing lights calling attention to anyone with a view. Medical personnel rushed into the house, checking the three victims. Myles was the first to reach Jonah. He checked desperately for a heartbeat or a pulse. He found none. Medically, he knew quickly that Jonah was dead and gone. Emotionally, it took longer to accept.

"Sorry, buddy," Myles finally whispered to the body. "I can't save you this time. I am sorry."

The others in the vicinity slowly urged Katie to come back upstairs. Eventually, she reluctantly agreed.

Emergency officials tried to balance the need for medical care with an attempt to re-construct what had happened in the house and determine if the community faced any additional danger. While Katie and Oliver were being checked by the ambulance personnel, they simultaneously gave the police officers a narrative of the events that had occurred. Even though Katie and Oliver corroborated each other's version of events in a near hysterical, broken fashion, the officers looked skeptical. Normann pulled Fanelli to the other side of the room.

"The girl had a thing for him and Oliver has never been right," he said. "This looks like a suicide to me. Or an accident at best."

Despite the hushed tones, Oliver overheard the officer's conclusion and jumped up in dismay.

"Jonah did not kill himself," he said defiantly. "It was Miss Donahue. I'm telling you. I know what happened. Jonah saved my life."

"Oliver," the officer said. "Miss Donahue has been dead for more than a year."

"She might be dead," Oliver answered. "But she's still here."

Myles finally broke into the conversation.

"We need to get this girl to the hospital and have her checked," he said. "She's had quite the trauma."

The officers nodded in agreement. Despite her verbal protestations, Katie allowed Myles and the rest of the ambulance workers to place her on a stretcher and remove her from the house. As the weight of events set in, Katie could not do much more than sob and cry "No" in protest.

Mrs. Paskiel had come home from her knitting group a few minutes earlier only to see police cars and ambulances throughout the block. She had to park up the street since her usual parking space was cordoned off by barricades and emergency personnel. As soon as she could get out of the car, Mrs. Paskiel rushed over to Jonah's house, in time to see Katie being carried out. She pushed herself past the police officers and blasted through the front door.

"Is my boy all right?" she screamed. "Where's Oliver?"

"He's right here," Officer Fanelli said. "He's fine."

"What happened?" she demanded as she rushed to her son and draped her arms around him.

"Jonah is dead," Oliver said without emotion. "Miss Donahue killed him."

Mrs. Paskiel looked at the officers with a mix of fear and confusion.

"He's upset," the officer said. "The victim fell down the steps.

Whether it was an accident or on purpose, we can't say for sure."

Mrs. Paskiel stiffened her back.

"If Oliver says Jonah was murdered, I believe him," she said. "Oliver does not make things up."

The police officer relented, physically taking a step backwards.

"Yes, ma'am," Officer Normann. "I understand. We need to continue our investigation here. We will keep all options open."

"Can I take Oliver home?" Mrs. Paskiel persisted.

The officer looked over at the paramedic.

"He doesn't seem to be injured," he said.

"Yes, ma'am," Officer Normann affirmed. "We will want to talk to him later."

Mrs. Paskiel nodded.

"That fine," she said curtly. "We live right across the street."

She then abruptly turned toward the door, pulling her son along with her as she draped her arm around him protectively. She led an unwilling Oliver back to her house.

•   •   •

The coroner's van arrived about thirty minutes later. The assistant coroner walked carefully through the house and reviewed the scene. He took any number of photos, carefully surveyed the crumpled body and cocked his head toward the stairs.

"Looks like he broke his neck," he said. "Jump or fall?"

"According to eyewitnesses, he got pushed down the steps," Officer Normann relayed. "Fighting ghosts."

"Really?" the coroner said. "Well, that will be an interesting detail for the report. I'll let the medical examiner know to look for paranormal ectoplasm during the autopsy."

He took one more look at Jonah.

Can one of you help me with the body?" he asked.

Jonah's body was carried up the stairs and into the coroner's van. Once the corpse was properly secured, the van drove away. The medical examiner would conduct an autopsy the next morning. He would determine that Jonah suffered a fatal fracture of the C1 and C2 vertebrae, which severed the spinal cord and cut off blood to the brain. The cause was listed as "fall." The question of accidental or on purpose was left unanswered. Murder was never considered.

The next day, the officers were filing their report on the incident when the phone rang. "This is Officer Lawrence Normann," he answered.

"Officer, my name is Ann Barkley," the caller said. "I'm a nurse at The Terraces where Jonah Frost recently spent some time. I know this is an unusual request, but I wonder if you could hear me out."

Officer Normann put the nurse on speakerphone and motioned his partner over to his desk.

Normann and Fanelli looked at each other skeptically as Ann relayed her story, but they finally agreed to inspect the basement more closely. It took more than a little justification with the chief, and Officer Normann assumed the only reason he finally relented was that the town was otherwise quiet. When he and Fanelli reached the home on Easley Avenue, they took down the yellow police tape and walked carefully down the stairs.

The two moved their flashlights across the basement, their curiosity growing more acute as they analyzed the scene before them. The basement floor was not a detail they took into account during the chaos of the day before.

"Well," Officer Normann said. "I have to admit, I've never seen a concrete floor poured in sections quite like this. Why would you keep pouring blocks haphazardly all over the place?"

"Do you think the Chief will let us call in a tech?" Officer Fanelli asked.

"All we can do is ask," Normann answered dubiously.

The Chief reluctantly agreed to the officers' request, wondering exactly how much more time and money they would waste on this case. Later that day, a technician with ground-penetrating radar arrived at Easley Avenue to check Jonah's home. He set up the equipment, took some baseline readings, then focused on the unusual pattern.

"You don't really expect to find anything here, outside of some bad concrete work, do you?" the technician asked.

"Probably not," Fanelli said. "But we want to cover all our bases."

The technician proceeded, working his way across the basement. A few minutes later, his demeanor changed dramatically.

"Holy shit," he finally said after ten minutes. "What the hell is that?"

"What?" a startled Officer Normann asked.

"There's definitely something down there," the technician said. "Let me check these other patches."

By the time the technician completed his survey, the radar located six anomalies underground that called for further investigation.

"This is very strange," the technician said. "I've never seen anything like this."

"The Chief is going to love this," Normann muttered. "Now we're going to have to get an excavation crew down here."

"I'm not calling," Fanelli said. "Let him chew on your ass for a change."

"Pretty sure he's going to have us both on a buffet," Normann cracked. "Just a question of who's the dessert."

The next day, much to the chagrin of the Clayburn police chief, a work crew with a jackhammer and shovels arrived on the scene. They were instructed by Normann and Fanelli to only use the power equipment to break through the concrete. They would need to hand shovel after that, in order to disturb the scene as little as possible. The officers were intent on preserving whatever evidence they would discover, if only in the hope of justifying the time and expense with their boss.

Mrs. Paskiel, Oliver and Daffodil watched out the window incredulously as the crews descended on the home across the street. While Oliver had overheard the discussion between Evelyn, Jonah and Katie, he was keeping that secret to himself. His mother was already hyperventilating and didn't need him pouring gasoline on her internal fire.

It took some time and a significant amount of noise to break through the concrete, but the dirt beneath it was relatively easy to move. It was clear the earth had been disturbed at some earlier point. The crew had only gone down a little more than a foot and a half when one of the workers hit something hard with his shovel.

"Hold on," he said. "I think I have something."

The crewman put down his shovel and slowly uncovered the object with his hands. It was painstaking work, but ten minutes later, he had seen enough.

"Jesus Christ!" he proclaimed. "It's a goddam skull."

"What?" Officer Normann asked in surprise. "Let me down there."

The policeman clambered down into the excavation and carefully cleared more of the object. In just a few minutes, the officer had verified the discovery.

"Holy shit, it's human," he said. "Looks like an infant."

Normann looked up at his partner, who stood over the scene with his arms crossed.

"Wait until the chief hears this," Fanelli said, shaking his head.

The discovery prompted a whole new level of attention and investigation. The Chief called in the Pennsylvania State Police, because this case had suddenly become much bigger than the resources a small borough police force could offer. The State Police brought in their Forensics team. The media soon followed. TV trucks with satellite uplinks arrived, with reporters and camera operators prowling the street as close as they could get to the scene.

Oliver and Helen Paskiel watched the event unfold from their home across the street with increasing astonishment. Daffodil barked incessantly at the constant parade of strangers.

"Oh my goodness," Helen said over and over, shocked beyond belief. "What in heaven's name is going on? Who would have ever thought something like this could happen right next door and no one was the wiser?"

Mrs. Paskiel made the sign of the cross, then for good measure, repeated the action.

"Jonah was right," Oliver said. "He knew all along. He always knew there was something strange about that basement."

It wasn't long before reporters started knocking on Mrs. Paskiel's door looking for an interview. She looked out the window next to the door, gave each reporter a stern look, and turned out the lights. She pulled the curtains closed and yanked down the shades.

"That's all I need," she huffed. "All the neighbors watching me and Oliver on the evening news. Let those fancy reporters with their six hundred dollar suits find someone else to talk to."

Mrs. Paskiel was resolute until a local telephone call she cavalierly answered turned out to be a reporter from WNEP-TV. An ABC affiliate that primarily serves the Scranton and Wilkes-Barre market, WNEP in actuality has a much great coverage area than at first appears. It has, for years, served as the dominant TV news station throughout Northeastern Pennsylvania. Mrs. Paskiel wouldn't talk to the reporter, but she agreed to an interview if the station met her unusual demand: that the interview be conducted by WNEP's morning weather man.

Jack Kowalchek was long-term fixture at the station, mixing a quirky personality with oddball stunts and the occasional weather forecast. Despite the station's multiple newscasts and well-staffed news department, Kowalchek remained by far the most easily identifiable and popular personality.

Mrs. Paskiel, like many residents, had a love-hate relationship with any local weather forecaster, especially when an unexpected winter storm slipped by the Doppler.

"I've shoveled his sunshine many times," Mrs. Paskiel said often, a statement that left Oliver wondering how such a feat would be accomplished. Nevertheless, the opportunity to meet the regionally famous personality was enough to overcome her reticence of appearing on camera.

Jack showed up that afternoon with a videographer and a list of questions. Mrs. Paskiel wore a dark blue dress usually reserved for Mass and had applied lipstick and blush – a decision that even made Oliver take notice. As the videographer set up the camera and microphone, Mrs. Paskiel sat demurely on her sofa chatting with Jack. Finally, the interview was set to begin.

"What can you tell me about Evelyn Donahue, who is suspected of killing these innocent children?" Jack asked, reading from his script.

"She was always an odd duck," Helen Paskiel said matter-of-factly. "I hardly ever saw her come out the house the last years of her life, but when she did, she was never pleasant. Didn't say hello or even acknowledge me or my son, like you would expect of a normal neighbor. I tried to be as civil as I could, but she was having none of that!"

"Did you ever suspect she would be capable of such a crime?" Jack continued.

"Oh, heaven's no," Mrs. Paskiel answered with more emotion. "Lord knows I would have never expected such a thing to ever happen in Clayburn. Evelyn Donahue was a surly woman, but I NEVER would have taken her for a murderer. I've prayed and prayed to understand why such evil has come to our quiet, God-fearing town."

"And what have you concluded?" Jack pressed, going off script.

"The Lord works in mysterious ways, Mr. Kowalchek," she concluded. "I'm sure this is a test of our faith, and it's a test I intend to pass."

Mrs. Paskiel made the sign of the cross, and after a few more questions, refused to provide any additional answers. It was the only interview she ever granted.

•   •   •

The crews continued to work across the street from Mrs. Paskiel's household. Ultimately, six graves with skeletal remains were unearthed. All were infants of no more than a few days old. Forensic testing dated the graves to between 50 and 60 years old – dates that corresponded to the newspapers Katie had found months before in the desk in the basement. DNA results confirmed all were children of Evelyn Donahue. All six had different fathers. There were four girls and two boys.

Police put together a grisly scenario: Evelyn Donahue had taken on a series of lovers from her late teens through her 40s that resulted in at least six pregnancies. Soon after giving birth – presumably at home since no birth records were found in the archives of any local hospitals, the county or the state – she suffocated and buried each child in the basement. Then, she purchased a bag of concrete, possibly at Kershaw's, and sealed the unmarked graves under her home. Afterward, she went about her business, conducting her life as if nothing had happened, until she repeated the scenario again.

Many years later, she died, presumably taking her secret to the grave. But her work was not yet completed, and she had more revenge to exact.

CHAPTER 39

While one grisly discovery after another occurred at 225 Easley Avenue and drew sensationalistic headlines, the sadder work of laying Jonah to rest fell upon those few who knew him. He had no remaining family. The few cousins, nephews and nieces who might have qualified had disowned him years ago, despite the protestations of his parents. Jonah's final arrangements were left to Harvey Kershaw, Katie, and Helen Paskiel.

Jonah had enough money in his account to pay for a decent funeral. In addition, while in the psychiatric hospital, Jonah had contacted an attorney, drew up a new will, and made Katie the heir to his estate. Katie was as surprised as anyone, but secretly, she wondered if this demonstrated that Jonah knew his conflict with Evelyn held more danger than he admitted.

Mrs. Paskiel insisted on a church service and berated the parish priest to accommodate her. It was a small but heartfelt Mass, attended by Jonah's small circle of friends. In Northeast Pennsylvania tradition, Mrs. Paskiel insisted all the guests attend a bountiful feast at Albert's, the only restaurant in Clayburn with a formal dinner menu and private event rooms. The meal included every Slovak and Polish dish ever created, with a few Italian delicacies thrown in for good measure.

As the guest party commiserated after the meal, the owner of the restaurant – not surprisingly a man named Albert, a spry gentleman in his late 70s – came into the event room with his accordion and began to play a variety of music that spanned most of the past 100 years. Albert was neatly attired in a dress shirt, pants and bowtie, and regaled his guests the best way he knew how. At first, Katie found the development ridiculous – then thought otherwise.

What better way to honor Jonah, she said to herself, *than through music? I wonder if the old man can play the Rolling Stones on that thing.*

Following the solemn service, Oliver and Katie began to return to their previous lives and tried to re-introduce some level of normalcy back into their lives. But a few days after Jonah's funeral, the two survivors of the trauma at 225 Easley Avenue had a dream – indeed, very much the same dream.

Jonah appeared to them, perfectly healthy and alive.

Oliver saw him and immediately felt himself sit up in the bed.

"Jonah," Oliver said. "You're alive."

Oliver paused. "But you're dead."

Jonah smiled.

"Yes, I am," he affirmed. "I haven't risen from the dead. Don't give your Mom any ideas."

"Are you OK?" Oliver asked.

"I'm fine," he said. "No more demons. My mind is clear. No more meds. I'm at peace."

Oliver wanted to ask any number of questions, but Jonah stopped him and changed the subject.

"Listen," he said, turning very serious. "I need you and Katie to do something for me."

"What's that?" Oliver asked. "I'll do anything you need."

"You have to burn it down."

"What?" Oliver asked. "Burn what down?"

"The house," Jonah said more emphatically. "My house. The one across the street from you. You have to burn it down. I tried but failed. Now you have to finish what I started."

"But why?"

"Evelyn is never going to leave," Jonah said. "She has incredible power. She's weakened now, but she will grow strong again. You have to strike while she can't fight back. You can't leave anyone else live in that house."

"Burn it down?" Oliver and Katie repeated in unison. They could hear the echoes of each other's voice through the haze of the dream.

"To the ground," Jonah concluded. "Torch it. Turn it to cinders. Leave nothing left. Do it for me."

Oliver nodded. In a different bedroom several blocks away, Katie did also.

"What about Evelyn?" Katie asked. "Are you sure she won't try to stop us?"

"She will," Jonah said. "But now, she has to deal with me. I'll take care of Evelyn. She won't bother you, because she won't be expecting me to interfere. I will keep you safe while you're doing what you need to do."

"I love you," Katie said.

"I love you too," Jonah said. "You are the love of my life. I'll be here waiting for you."

"You won't have to wait long," Katie said. "I can't fight this MS forever."

"I know," Jonah said. "You won't have to. When it's time, I'll bring you over to this side. I won't let you suffer."

Katie smiled. Slowly, Jonah faded away, then disappeared.

The next morning, Oliver and Katie met at Kershaw's for work. They looked at each other knowingly.

"I had a dream last night," Katie said.

"So did I," Oliver affirmed.

"Then we know what we have to do."

Oliver nodded.

"Isn't this against the law," he asked.

"Yes," Katie answered. "But sometimes you have to break the law to accomplish a greater good."

Oliver processed the answer.

"OK," he agreed.

"Tonight," Katie said. "After work, when it gets dark. Can you get out of the house?"

Oliver nodded.

"I'll slip some schnapps into Mom's tea," Oliver said. "She'll be out in no time. She doesn't handle her alcohol well."

"Oliver!" Katie said in genuine surprise.

The young man smiled.

"Sometimes Mom gets a little overbearing," Oliver admitted. "I've learned a few tricks along the way to calm her down."

Katie smiled and mussed up Oliver's already half-mussed hair.

"There's much more to you than you let on," she said.

"I don't think there's more of me than what's here," Oliver answered.

Katie started to respond, then thought better of it.

Katie purchased a gasoline container later that day, much to Harvey's curiosity. Mr. Kershaw wasn't yet up to putting in full days at the shop, but he did try to get down for a few hours.

"Wasn't aware you had any yard equipment that needed gasoline," he said.

"It's for a friend," she said. "He asked me to pick it up."

"Well, OK," he said, unconvinced of Katie's explanation. "You still get your 15 percent employee discount."

Katie walked home with Oliver, a tough trip for her, but one she forced herself to make. The two took several breaks to make the distance bearable. Katie wished she had Jonah's car, but it was still parked in front of his house. Katie wasn't even sure what happened to the key for the Malibu after Jonah's death.

When they finally reached the Paskiel home, Katie and Oliver hid the gas container under the front steps of the house and walked through the door to the aromatic scent of Mrs. Paskiel cooking a full dinner.

Mrs. Paskiel was delighted with Katie's presence, and gave her the full once-over when she got through the door.

"Oh, how are you doing, dear?" she said. "Look at you, there's nothing to you. Skin and bones. We have to get some food in you. You have to eat to keep up your strength."

Katie tried to protest, but she knew it was in vain.

"This has been a tough time, ain'a?' Mrs. Paskiel said. "And for you especially. We're all praying for you. Are you all healed up?"

"I'm about as good as I'm going to get," Katie said, forcing a smile.

"Yes, you poor dear," Oliver's mother continued. "Such a terrible disease on top of everything. You'd think they would come up with a cure for these things. Well, let's get you to sit down at the dinner table. I've made a nice big pot of halupki that should help put some meat back on you."

Mrs. Paskiel continued her monologue all the way through dinner, rarely allowing Oliver or Katie to get a word in edge-wise. Katie noticed that Mrs. Paskiel never brought up Jonah or his house across the street. Indeed, she barely even looked that way. Once, when Katie caught her glancing out the window in that direction for a moment, she saw Mrs. Paskiel making the sign of the cross as she turned away. She has clearly been shaken to her soul by the recent events, and she was dealing with them the best way she knew how – by creating as much normalcy as possible.

Mrs. Paskiel forced as much of her combination of cabbage, ground beef, rice and tomato sauce as possible into her son and her guest, then magically appeared with a tray of palacinky, a Slovak dessert consisting of a sweetened, crushed walnut-filled crepe sprinkled generously with powdered sugar. After she encouraged Katie and Oliver to indulge in at least several pieces each, Mrs. Paskiel then busied herself cleaning up the dinner plates.

Katie noted that Daffodil, who had hovered around the dinner table, did well with leftovers. *Jeopardy* followed by *Wheel of Fortune* played on the TV, but Mrs. Paskiel rarely paid attention. She had an audience and plenty of town news to share, and Katie had nowhere to hide.

Hopefully, she'll talk herself into exhaustion, Katie thought, though she doubted that was possible.

After dinner, Mrs. Paskiel cleaned the table and began the dishes. Despite Katie's protestations, she wouldn't allow her guest to help. In the meantime, Katie and Oliver sat in the living room watching TV, Katie half listening to the broadcast while trying to follow Mrs. Paskiel's ongoing litany of gossip. Katie allowed her eyes to wander about the room and the adjoining dining area. Every square inch of table top, hutch, cabinet or china closet was filled with various baubles and mementos. They ranged from antique vases and glass sets handed down through Mrs. Paskiel's family to an eclectic collection of salt-and-pepper shakers Helen had collected from various vacation spots. A crucifix hung on the wall, a statue of the Virgin Mary stood on a small shelf in the corner of the room. Various photos of Oliver from childhood to adult hung on the wall. In many ways, Mrs. Paskiel's home told the story of her life.

As they waited, Oliver pulled out a drawing pad from the bottom shelf of an end table, and quietly started sketching with a charcoal pencil. After a few minutes, Katie walked over to him quietly and peered over his shoulder. Oliver stopped, and angled the pad so Katie could get a better view. It was an illustration of Jonah and Katie, remarkable for its accuracy.

"Aww, Oliver," Katie said, a tear coming to her eye. "I had no idea you were an artist. That's beautiful."

"Thank you," Oliver answered. "You can have it once I'm finished."

Katie leaned over and gave Oliver a soft hug. He began to flinch, then relaxed and leaned into Katie's arms.

It took some time, but Mrs. Paskiel finally finished straightening up her kitchen. She removed her apron and laid it over the back of a chair, heaved a fatigued sigh, and declared her day done.

"I am exhausted," she proclaimed.

I guess I was wrong, Katie thought. *She did tire herself out.*

Mrs. Paskiel walked back into her living room, planted herself on her reclining chair and relaxed in front of the television. A few seconds later, Daffodil jumped on the chair and snuggled herself tightly against Mrs. Paskiel, who didn't seem to object.

Oliver, who had successfully ignored most of his mother's verbal onslaught, put down his drawing pad when he had determined they had entered safer ground.

"Can you I get you your tea, Mom?" he asked.

Mrs. Paskiel looked over at her son.

"Oh my, I forgot to get it myself with everything going on," she said. "That would be wonderful, Oliver."

Oliver nodded and walked into the kitchen. He returned a few minutes later, steam coming off the hot liquid. He placed the cup and saucer on the table next to his mother's chair. As he turned and spotted Katie out of the corner of his eye, he winked. Katie held back a giggle.

"Thank you, Oliver," Mrs. Paskiel said, then turned to Katie. "He's a good boy, ain'a?"

"The best," Katie agreed. "You're very lucky."

"Yes, I am," Mrs. Paskiel said, and took a long sip of her drink. "Oh my, this tastes extra good tonight."

Oliver and Katie exchanged knowing grins with each other.

It wasn't long before Mrs. Paskiel's eyelids grew heavy. Oliver found a throw blanket and covered her, and a few minutes later, soft snoring from both Mrs. Paskiel and Daffodil could be heard throughout the room. Katie and Oliver gave Mrs. Paskiel a good half-hour to fall into a sound slumber. Once they were sure she would not disturb them, they walked outside, retrieved their gas container, and headed to the gas station, just down a block and across the one road that led in and out of Clayburn. They filled the container and purchased a lighter and a newspaper.

Katie still had a key to the house, retrieved from Mr. Kershaw when he returned to the shop. She slipped through the police tape and slowly opened the door. She fully expected the hell and fury of Evelyn to greet her when she walked inside, but instead, the house was quiet. Oliver went to turn on a light switch, but Katie stopped his hand and shook her head no.

"We can't draw attention to anyone that we're here," she whispered.

As they moved through the house, Katie and Oliver heard a few rumbles and some distant cries but no imminent threats. Oliver took the gas container and poured the pungent liquid throughout the house. As he did so, the clear sounds of a struggle emanated, moving from one room to the next. Katie was sure she heard Jonah's voice, but Oliver could only hear Evelyn. Evelyn sounded both shocked and furious by the surprise intrusion, but appeared to have little recourse, fighting off the unexpected interference from Jonah. Whatever was happening, the struggle never reached into the realm of the living world.

After the gas can was emptied, Katie and Oliver slowly backed toward the front door. Oliver brought the empty container along with him.

"Time to finally finish this," Katie said, taking the gas container from Oliver and throwing it back into the center of the house.

"Wait!" Oliver said. He ran back into the living room, and picked up Jonah's box of family memorabilia from the floor, where it had dropped on that fateful night.

"If this was important enough to Jonah to die for," he said. "It's important to me."

Katie nodded and pulled out the lighter, lit the newspaper and let it collect a healthy burn. She then threw it into the path of gasoline. It immediately erupted violently and spread throughout the house.

"Let's get out of here," Katie said as she felt the heat from the flames on her face.

Oliver and Katie ran out of the building, across the street and into the back door of the Paskiel home. They positioned themselves on the sofa next to Mrs. Paskiel's chair as if they had never left. Oliver's mother continued to sleep peacefully next to her dog.

In a few minutes, Jonah's home was engulfed in flames. Windows burst open as the blaze spread throughout the building. The fire spread up the stairs and then into the attic. The entire block glowed, which shone through the windows in the Paskiel household. Oliver and Katie could feel the heat from the inferno across the street.

The two stood up and watched out the window as the hungry fire continued to devour the structure across the street. Finally, the brightness and the heat emanating from the blaze into the Paskiel household awoke both Helen and Daffodil. In unison, they jumped with a start and leapt out of the chair to look out the window. Daffodil began to bark in distress.

"Oh my goodness," Mrs. Paskiel screamed. "Jonah's house is on fire! Why aren't either of you calling the fire department?"

Helen immediately dialed 9-1-1 and shrieked into the phone. Katie and Oliver never moved. A few minutes later, a police siren blared down the street, blocking the road to traffic. However, by the time the volunteer firefighters arrived at the firehouse, put on their gear and pulled out the equipment, another 15 minutes had elapsed until the trucks rolled onto Easley Avenue.

When the engines finally arrived, the building was fully engaged, flames shooting out of every window and poking holes in the roof. The firefighters laid down a perimeter of water and concentrated on not allowing the blaze to spread. It was clear the house would be a total loss.

It took several hours for the fire to burn itself out. By then, the building had been reduced to near rubble. A foul burning stench filled the air. The fire department stayed most of the night, putting out spot fires and ensuring the safety of the rest of the community. By morning, wisps of smoke strayed from the ruins. Little or nothing was left of Jonah's house. Katie and Oliver had accomplished their task.

With all the activity, Katie stayed the night in the Paskiel home. She finally retired to the spare bedroom well into the night, but truthfully, no one in the household got much sleep that evening. When Helen finally forced herself downstairs in her housecoat too early that morning – since this was breaking news she couldn't miss – she looked little like her normal ebullient and overbearing self. The coffee pot would be put to good use that day.

"Extra strong this morning, Daffodil," Mrs. Paskiel said.

Over the next several days, a cursory investigation was done. The fire investigator was confident of the probable cause and the most likely perpetrators. But after internal discussions between the fire and police departments, no charges were ever filed. All agreed there had already been enough victims in this tragedy. Perhaps the old Donahue house being reduced to cinders was the most fitting end for the building.

"Good riddance," the police chief finally said. "We didn't need that place turned into a tourist attraction."

Indeed, Mrs. Paskiel also had a good idea what happened the night before while she was asleep. More than once, she looked at her son and Katie and wondered if they had the gumption to actually go through with such a feat. But, fighting every urge in her body, she never asked.

They knew what they were doing, she thought, *and they knew why. I've always said the Lord works in mysterious ways. Better not to know. If we can cast the devil out of town through its own fire, Praise be to God.*

The remnants of Jonah's house smoldered for a few days, and the acrid odor of burned lumber, siding, insulation and electrical wiring lingered longer than that. But a few weeks later, a construction crew arrived with a backhoe, a dump truck, and other equipment. The crew hauled away the rubble, brought in soil to fill in the basement, and leveled the lot. Grass was planted and watered, and the crew packed up and drove away. In two days, all evidence of the home had disappeared.

Before the winter arrived, 225 Easley Avenue joined the other abandoned and empty lots on the sparsely inhabited street. For those unaware of what happened, the plot of land marked another piece of the town's history that had succumbed to the mists of time.

CHAPTER 40
TEN YEARS LATER...

Oliver was awakened one morning by the sound of a hammer. He climbed out of bed, and looked out his window toward the offending sound. He still was in the same room, in the same house where he was raised. As Oliver looked across the street, he saw a middle-aged man in a polo shirt and khakis banging a sign into the ground in front of the former location of Jonah's house.

"What is he doing?" Oliver said to himself. "This is very strange."

He dressed meticulously, walked down the steps, and stopped in the kitchen. There was a note scrawled hurriedly from his mother: "Gone shopping. Be back shortly."

Oliver poured himself a glass of orange juice, drank it slowly as he sat at the kitchen table, and noticed that the banging had stopped. A few minutes later, he heard a car pull away. Oliver got up, put his glass in the sink, then headed outside to check the sign.

Much had changed in Clayburn over the past 10 years.

Harvey Kershaw had passed away two years earlier, and with it, his store – much like other parts of the Coal Region – became a part of history. Harvey had staved off the influx of the big chains longer than most, but there was no one to continue his legacy. The Walmarts and Home Depots of the land eventually overran even the smallest of towns, and the continued growth of online shopping threatened even the big box stores.

Katie's MS took a dramatic turn for the worse shortly after Jonah's death and the fire that had burned down the house. What Katie hadn't told most people was that she suffered from one of the most aggressive forms of Multiple Sclerosis. Primary Progressive MS worsens from the onset with few if any relapses. Only 15 percent of those with MS are diagnosed with PPMS. Undoubtedly, her overall physical condition was negatively impacted and exacerbated by the terror at 225 Easley Avenue and the loss of Jonah. It wasn't long before Katie was unable to work, and she moved from Clayburn. She sent Oliver a message intermittently for a few years, then the communication stopped. The last Oliver heard, Katie was hospitalized as often as she was home, and was now in an assisted living facility. Her prognosis was grim.

Helen Paskiel was a little grayer and a little plumper, but otherwise, continued to live her life to care for her precious son. She still went to Mass every week, and still made the sign of the cross each time she peered across the street to the site of Jonah's old home. She never considered leaving her home town of Clayburn, nor the house where she had lived her entire adult life.

Daffodil has passed away from old age and had been replaced by yet another Heinz 57 from the shelter. This time, Mrs. Paskiel had named her pet Magnolia. She did love her flowers.

For Oliver, life went on. There were few jobs in Clayburn, and he had never learned to drive. After Kershaw's closed, Oliver started working part-time at the gas station down the street, where he was always punctual and reliable. He missed Jonah and Katie, but his bedroom served as his haven from the world. Occasionally, he would walk to the Saint Cyril's Cemetery and visit Jonah's grave. He would sit there and catch Jonah up on the news with a long monologue. Jonah didn't usually answer, though every so often, Oliver was sure he heard his laughter in the wind when he relayed a particularly funny incident.

After completing his morning ritual, Oliver finally walked down the front steps of his house and headed across the street. The few homes remaining were ten years worse for wear than they were a decade ago. So were the residents. Few new people moved into town.

Oliver reached the sign the stranger had hammered into the ground. He looked at the empty lot where so much had happened and he had lost his best friend. Though no building remained standing, his proximity to the parcel still felt disconcerting. Oliver finally looked up at the sign and read it carefully. A feeling of dread enveloped him as he read, then re-read the announcement.

"Oh no!" he cried in despair. "This can't be true."

The sign read:

Coming soon! Deluxe Senior Residential Apartments. Opening in the Spring. Call 570-666-7777 or visit www.GardenEstatesVillageClayburn.com to Reserve your Space Now!

CHAPTER 41
FIFTEEN YEARS MORE...

Ann Barkley wasn't a nurse anymore. She had given up the stress and the daily grind and had retired a few years ago, only to lose her husband to a severe stroke six months later. Now she was getting on in years. Her children were married and had moved away, and she wasn't as spry as she used to be. Not only that, most of her friends had either passed on or moved away. Ann decided that she no longer could care for the big house where she had raised her family and decided to live out her later years in a more convenient setting.

A brochure arrived in her mail one afternoon advertising Garden Estates Retirement Village, located in Clayburn.

Clayburn, Ann thought. *What was it about Clayburn?*

A thought floated through her head, but at that instant, the phone rang, distracting her attention. She answered, but no one was on the line. She looked at the phone curiously, then hung up.

What was I thinking? She asked herself. *Oh well, if it's important it will come back to me.*

"Old age," she muttered. She picked up the brochure and read through it. Then she went online and did some additional research. The facility received good reviews: caring staff, good food, nicely appointed apartments.

Why not? Ann thought. *It's worth at least checking out.*

She picked up her phone and dialed the number. Maybe it was time to make the jump.

She spoke to the recruiter and made an appointment to see an open apartment. At the end of the conversation, the young woman asked: "How did you hear about us?"

"I received your brochure in the mail," Ann replied. "It just arrived today."

"That's funny," the sales representative said. "I wasn't aware we were sending anything out right now. I'll have to ask marketing about that so we can be ready for additional calls. Sometimes they forget to tell us."

Ann confirmed her appointment and hung up the phone. She would inspect her potential new home in two days.

After years of delay, the senior apartments in Clayburn had finally been completed. Financing and permitting pushed back the project on multiple occasions, but the facility was finally completed five years after its initial announcement. The owners of the complex had bought the entire one side of the block on Easley Avenue and quite a bit of real estate behind it. They had totally renovated the area, and the beautiful new apartments were surrounded by flower gardens, stone paths, and a grand fountain.

Clayburn itself was experiencing a sort of mini-renaissance, spurred by cheap land, relatively close access to the shale natural gas areas of northern Pennsylvania, and easy access to the interstate highway system that traveled in all four directions. Plenty of remnants of the old town remained, but the developers of the nearby business complexes had carefully obstructed the view of anything unappealing.

Mrs. Paskiel had passed away, done in by too many unhealthy foods and lack of exercise. A massive heart attack killed her before she could even get up from her favorite recliner to call for assistance. Oliver found her when he returned home from work. He called 9-1-1, but there was nothing to be done. Heaven got an earful that day and Clayburn lost its epicenter of local news.

Mrs. Paskiel had left detailed directions for her funeral, which she had paid in full in advance. Indeed, it was a grand celebration of her life. Nearly the entire town – plus a good chunk of the neighboring municipalities – attended her standing room-only funeral at St. Cyril's three days later. The dinner afterward generated enough gossip to satiate the area for the next month. Albert, sadly, was no longer around to provide entertainment with his accordion.

After much consideration, Oliver finally settled into a new routine. The family house was far too big for him to care for, so he eventually moved into a small apartment in the borough of Tamaqua and found a job as a stock boy at a Dollar General within walking distance. He adopted a regimented schedule to control his new-found independence. He purchased a rocking chair, whose rhythmic motion provided comfort and solace. He eventually became more serious about his art, and became an accomplished illustrator in his own right. He achieved a decent level of local fame. Many of his subjects looked suspiciously like Jonah and Katie. Oliver kept possession of Jonah's box of mementos, and added a few of his mother's possessions to the eclectic collection. He went through each piece every day, his sensory needs fulfilled by the various textures in the collection.

Katie had passed away far too early from complications from her MS. Some within the medical community expressed surprise at her sudden death, which came, despite her deteriorating condition, quickly and unexpectedly. Jonah had kept his promise and did not let her linger.

No one was left in town who remembered the true story of what happened in Jonah's house so many years ago. The story had fallen into a list of stories of the town's darker side, with Evelyn's murdered children becoming the lead of the narrative. By now, the tale, twisted and convoluted by countless drunken tellings at local bars and other gatherings, had been made even more gruesome and nearly unrecognizable. Police reports were buried in a dusty file cabinet somewhere in the basement of the headquarters, and even they were inaccurate and incomplete.

Ann arrived a few minutes early to Garden States Retirement Village to take her tour. She checked the furnished apartment and was duly impressed. For a moment, as she walked through the living room, she paused and thought she heard something. But she shook it off as the imaginings of old age.

The guide from the marketing department waxed almost poetically about all the amenities of the facility, the various activities conducted on a regular basis, and the shopping and recreational trips. The price was reasonable. The residents seemed happy. Ann was particularly impressed this was a progressive care facility – if her health worsened, she could transition into one of the assisted living wings of the complex. After only a bit of deliberation, she signed the documents confirming her intentions. She would move into her new home the first of the month.

In the interim, Ann cleaned out her home and packed the few belongings she would need. She gave family heirlooms to her children, donated items to local charities, and arranged to sell both her house and many of her belongings. She gave nearly all of her nursing memorabilia to her daughter.

Time to pass things on to the next generation, she thought. She was content in her decision. It was time to relax a bit and enjoy life.

The day of moving still came as a bit of a shock after so many years in the same home, but Ann overcame her reticence and directed the movers to take the few things remaining. She followed them to the complex in her self-driving car. She made sure they carefully transported her items from the truck to her new apartment, then spent the rest of the day arranging her belongings to create a sense of home. Every so often, she thought she was sure she saw a shadow move along the walls. She shook her head.

New home jitters, she thought. *I guess it will take some adjustment after all thee years.*

When the apartment was in reasonable order, she took a photo of herself in her new home with a big smile and sent it to her children. As night arrived, Ann turned on a few soft lights and relaxed on her sofa. She watched TV. Every so often, she heard an odd noise or a stray bang, but she dismissed them nonchalantly.

Just nervous moving into a new place, she thought. *I have to get used to having neighbors just on the other side of the wall.*

She went to bed by 11 p.m. without further incident. But she was suddenly awakened several hours later by a dreadful cry. She looked at the bedside clock.

3:33 a.m.

Who in the world is up at this hour? she wondered. *This is disturbing.*

Ann thought for an instant that she heard the words, "You should be disturbed" whispered through the night air.

She climbed out of bed to investigate, and noticed that the temperature in the apartment had dropped at least twenty degrees. Ann wrapped a blanket around her.

"What is going on?" she asked aloud.

Then, suddenly, as she walked into the living room, a thought hit her.

Clayburn, she thought, *something terrible happened in Clayburn!*

Ann had long ago forgotten the specific details of the case, but she always remembered Jonah. As the chill became more marked, she felt an ominous oppressive presence fill the room. Suddenly, she remembered what was so important about Clayburn.

Oh my God, she thought, *Evelyn...THAT Evelyn.*

A shadow crossed the room and Ann heard a great disturbance behind her. The sense of foreboding grew unbearable. She whirled around to see what threatened her in her new home. There stood Evelyn, vitriol emanating from every pore.

"You are real," Ann said matter-of-factly.

"Of course I'm real, you medical twit," Evelyn huffed. "I've been waiting for you a very long time. It's taken many years for me to regain my strength once you RUINED EVERYTHING!"

"I did nothing but help my patient," the former nurse said defiantly. "I did my job."

"You destroyed my best laid plans," Evelyn growled. "I almost had him in my grasp. No one believed him. He was a lunatic. But you, you had to meddle, you had to look behind the curtain. What good did that do? He's dead, thanks to you."

"No," Ann said. "You killed him. I saved him from you."

"Bullshit!" Evelyn roared. "You left these bastards go unpunished. Well, I'm back to finish my work. But first, I had to deal with you! It took quite an effort for me to convince some weak-minded fool to send that flyer to you for this place. Then I had to get through your thick skull to come here. But all that work made me stronger. Now I'm back, and I have to go find some other malleable ingrate to continue my undertaking."

Evelyn paused, staring ominously at Ann.

"As for you," Evelyn said, "you're no longer any good to me. I just want to squish you like the insect you are. You've cost me many years of revenge."

Ann backed away and moved into her kitchen. She reached for the knife block on her counter and wrapped her hands around the chef's knife. She pulled the nine-inch blade from its holder and swung it at the demon that threatened her.

"Stay back," Ann said. "I know how to use a knife."

"Evelyn laughed heartily.

"Oh, I haven't laughed that hard in..." Evelyn paused, thinking, "in more than 25 years! Do you think you can really hurt me with that? Come on, come over here and try. I'll give you the first slice. Then it's my turn."

Ann hesitated. She remembered more and more of her conversations with Jonah. If he was right, it would a fruitless, most likely suicidal gesture to attack Evelyn. And there was little reason to doubt Jonah's words anymore.

Evelyn sensed Ann's hesitation.

"Well," Evelyn said, "if you won't come to me, I'll come to you."

The ghost unveiled spike-like nails on the tips of each finger, swinging them wildly as she came closer and closer to her prey. Ann looked for an escape route, but suddenly all the doors throughout the apartment slammed shut and the door locks clamped closed. Lights began to flicker on and then go out one by one. Soon, Ann would be facing Evelyn in darkness.

Then, both Ann and her tormenter heard a male voice in a commanding tone.

"Not so fast, you fat bitch. I'm not done with you yet."

Evelyn stopped and slowly turned around. Ann moved quickly and slipped away from the demon, then stared in the same direction.

There stood Jonah, holding a shimmering sword in his hand.

Beside him, as if she had always been by his side, was Katie, healthy and complete, no sign of the disease that wracked her body. She held a bow-and-arrow that shined with the same unearthly glow as Jonah's sword. Behind them stood six angry children, holding various weaponry and glaring at their murderous mother with nearly a century of built-up outrage seething from their bones. And behind even the children stood nine grown men, cut down in their prime, looking for their own piece of their killer.

"So predictable," Jonah said. "You died on your sofa at 3:33 in the morning, and you use that as the time of your rebirth. I know that gives you the easiest portal back to Earth, but it is a bit overly dramatic, don't you think?"

Evelyn hissed.

"You think you're clever now, boy?" she said angrily. "You weren't smart enough to figure that out when you were still alive."

Jonah didn't flinch.

"With death comes wisdom," he said, "at least for some. Certainly not for you."

Katie now stepped up to face her nemesis.

"We have quite a few debts to settle with you," Katie said. "I think we all want and deserve a piece of your hide."

"You will pay for terrorizing me and my friends," Jonah said. "You want revenge? You haven't seen revenge yet. You were right about one thing. On this site, I did discover my destiny. It's to kick your ass through eternity."

"Oh, son of a bitch," Evelyn muttered. "You want me? Come and get me. I dare you."

Suddenly, there was a flash of light and shuffling among the ranks behind Jonah and Katie.

"Don't you start without me," a robust female voice cried out. "I want my own piece of that devil. She terrorized me for years."

Mrs. Paskiel, complete with majestic wings and a shimmering three-edged angel blade whose cross section formed a three-pointed star, appeared next to her friends.

"Now let's get this spawn of Hades," she proclaimed, even while making the sign of the cross. "She's due for a good helping of God's wrath!"

Jonah, Katie, Mrs. Paskiel and the rest of the brigade advanced forward on their prey. The glow from their weapons became more intense.

"You've disturbed the living for the last time," Jonah proclaimed.

For once, Evelyn looked unsure and even afraid, backing away from her adversaries. Then, she came to a sudden resolve, bared he teeth, and thrust forward.

"In memory of the Molly Maguires," she bellowed.

As Ann watched in horrified wonder, the two sides clashed. From Jonah's direction, she heard Tom Petty's "I Won't Back Down" playing as the battle began.

Well, I won't back down
No, I won't back down
You can stand me up at the gates of hell
But I won't back down
No, I'll stand my ground
Won't be turned around
And I'll keep this world from draggin' me down
Gonna stand my ground

ACKNOWLEDGEMENTS

Writing a book may seem like a solitary exercise, but the support I received along the was invaluable.

Thanks to Reagan Rothe and the team at Black Rose Writing for their continued trust and faith in my ability as an author. The BRW family –both the staff and fellow authors – is a wonderful group that has made me feel welcome since my first book was published in 2015.

My oldest daughter, Chandra Swope, and fellow author James Glass provided valuable insights and encouragement as I worked on turning this book into reality.

Selena Swope offered her knowledge and experiences as both a psychiatric and emergency department nurse in my efforts to accurately depict mental illness and hospital settings.

I have seen various people struggle with mental illness throughout my lifetime. Some of their battles helped me frame this book. My hope is that one day, all who suffer can find peace, solace and contentment.

For those of my friends and family on the autistic spectrum, I love you all and appreciate your unique and wonderful perspective on the world.

A long overdue expression of thanks to all my teachers from grade school through graduate school who encouraged and honed my talents as a writer. Particular thanks to Sister Christa, Jude Schum, Beth Sussman, Sister Rosemary Stets and Jackie Steck. I know not all of you still walk the Earth, but wherever you are, you are still remembered.

My largest debt of gratitude goes to the strong and hearty people of Northeast Pennsylvania, who have faced generations of adversity and have continued to survive and thrive. Ain'a?

ABOUT THE AUTHOR

Joseph J. Swope is an award-winning author, public relations professional, and university adjunct faculty member. He has lived and worked in Pennsylvania his entire career, which spans more than 35 years in both corporate and non-profit settings. *Disturbed* is his third book and first novel.

View other Black Rose Writing titles at www.blackrosewriting.com/books and use promo code **PRINT** to receive a **20% discount** when purchasing.

BLACK ROSE
writing™

CPSIA information can be obtained
at www.ICGtesting.com
Printed in the USA
BVHW03s0012090418
512757BV00001B/2/P